A SIMPLE SOLUTION

John W A Roberts

Published in 2009 by New Generation Publishing

Chapter 1

Dr. Peter Steyn CEO of Steyn Pharmaceuticals looked up from his desk as his PA Samantha Ketteridge came in, "Good Morning Sam, get through the Mad Mob O.K.?"

"Yes, although one ugly bitch broke through the cordon and tried to attack my car. She had something glinting in her hand. I managed to swerve away from her but I swear to God Peter one of these days I'll swing my wheel the other way and knock one of them flying."

"I wouldn't blame you, I've often had the same urge but we can't do it Sam. They'd love to sue us for damages. You can imagine the lies they would tell in court." In a whining nasal accent he pleaded, "I only wanted to hand the lady a leaflet and she deliberately swerved her car into me. I don't know if I'll ever walk again."

Samantha laughed then said "But it's so unfair. If I crashed the car trying to get out of the way of one of them, I'd have no comeback would I? Even if we managed to sue whoever it was that caused me to crash, we'd never get a penny out of them. They'd declare themselves bankrupt."

Peter nodded in agreement "I'm afraid you're right but don't worry. We'll look after you. We've got heavy insurance on all our staff although with all this publicity we're having I wouldn't be surprised if the insurance company refused to renew our policies when the time comes."

"Or else bump up the premiums so high it would become uneconomic to continue with them."

"Whatever, we'll still look after our employees."

"It's the intensity of their hatred that amazes me. They claim to love animals, yet they would have no hesitation in seriously injuring one of us, one of their fellow humans. We're part of the animal kingdom too."

"Very much so"

"They just can't see things long term."

"It suits them to ignore the facts of Nature. All animals use the creatures below them to ensure their own survival. They might as well want to eliminate lions because they prey on Wildebeest."

"That's it Peter. It's not as if we're using our lab. Animals for the beauty business. I often wonder what they'll do in the future if one of them gets Alzheimer's and we've succeeded in developing our drug. Bet they won't refuse to take it."

"No bloody way will they refuse" he said emphatically; his voice reverting to its South African roots. Born into a Boer family he had first

3

come to England to complete his PhD at Cambridge. He had gone back to teach at the University of Witwatersrand for several years before forming his own research company. It was only a calamitous change in his personal life had driven him back here. The past twenty four years had lengthened his vowels and softened the harshness of his accent but it always reappeared when he was angry or excited.

Before Samantha could answer, there was a brief knock on the door and the stick thin Dr. Miles Mallernder, Head of Research came in. At the same moment the phone rang.

Peter picked it up, and after a brief listen, asked loudly," How the Hell did they get up there?"

Looking up at Samantha and Miles he added "It's Jepson, he says some of the nutcases are up on the lab. roof."

Miles walked over to the window saying "They must have cut the fencing somewhere. I thought it was monitored to let us know where it was being tampered with. Why didn't Jepson's men get there in time?"

"That's not how they got in. He says they were hidden in a white Transit that came in a little while ago. Had all the right paperwork for a delivery."

Samantha immediately said "I'm sure it's that bloody temp we had all last month while Maggie was ill. Had her nose into everything. I told you one of the technicians found her trying to get into to the lab. Pretended she'd lost her way."

Peter didn't reply, he was concentrating on what he was telling Jepson on the phone "No. No. In no circumstances are you or your men to follow them up there. That's an order. Ask the police to get reinforcements here pronto. Let them deal with this. I don't want any of these bastards injuring themselves and starting a court case against us. Oh, and Jepson, let me know how soon the police think they'll be here."

As he looked up Samantha said "Should I phone the Chief Constable?"

Peter thought for a minute before he answered. He'd spent a good deal of time in the last few years cultivating Chief Constable Phillip Torrington in his home and on the golf course. "No, better not. Might make him think we've no faith in our local plods. Just make sure this line's kept free for Jepson. Don't let any other calls through."

As Samantha hurried out, he turned to Miles and asked "They can't throw anything down into the lab from up there; can they Miles?"

"No, the louvers automatically close once the alarm goes off. It's all reinforced glass up there, they won't be able to break it"

"What about a gas, some sort of contaminate, spray paint?"

"That would be a problem, the louvers aren't air tight. I'd better get down there and get the animals cages covered or moved just in case they do try something as bloody silly as that"

After he left, Peter sat wondering whether he should stay where he was or make his way down to the lab and see for himself what was happening. His thoughts were interrupted by the phone ringing. After listening to Jepson's message he answered "Two van loads here in about 10 minutes, good, good. Just keep your distance. Don't touch any of them unless they come down and try to run away."

He put the phone down and booted up his computer. He wanted to see if the spread of the virus among the rats was happening in line with the predictions of the programme he'd installed.

The graphs were not what he'd hoped for. It looked… His thoughts were interrupted by the phone ringing.

"Yes Jepson. What's the…What? Say that again slowly. "One of them has just fallen off the roof…leaning over to unfurl a banner. Bloody hell! I'm on my way down. Yes, yes, get our first aiders there as quickly as possible and phone for an ambulance. You've already got someone doing that. Good man. …The police have arrived. Excellent I'm on my way"

He hurried out, pausing only to tell Samantha what had happened and telling her to stay at her desk and make sure no news of the accident was made public

He came out of the office building and rushed round to the laboratory block. As he turned the last corner the first thing he saw was the large banner with blood red letters, BAN ALL EXPERIME…., The rest of the letters were hidden under the cloth where it had folded back on itself. But his gaze was wrenched away from the banner by what was going on underneath it. Two policemen were fighting with one of his security staff. As he ran forward he saw the security man was Jepson.

"What's going on here?" he demanded.

The policemen had managed to get both Jepson's arms behind his back. One of them was saying, "Now pack it in or we'll have to cuff you."

Peter was astounded by his chief of security's behaviour. The man had an impeccable army record and in the seven years he had been with Steyn, Peter had been very impressed with him. He was always firm but courteous even when dealing with outraged interlopers who were refusing to leave the office foyer.

"Jepson, what are you doing?" he demanded.

It was one of the policemen who answered, "He wants to get to them," he said jerking his head upwards to the faces peering over the laboratory roof edge.

"I'll kill...the...bastards..."Jepson gasped, "I will. You can't hold me forever. If I don't get them now, there'll be another day. By Christ there will." He started to struggle again.

Peter waited until the man stopped before he asked as calmly as he could "Jepson, what's the meaning of this?"

The man looked at him wild eyed, "Meaning? I'll tell you what's the fucking meaning is. Look at her "

Peter followed Jepson's gaze to where a group of his security and first aid staff were gathered around a body lying awkwardly on the ground. Coming closer he saw it was a young woman dressed in white jeans and a white peasant type blouse decorated with small red flowers. Her long black hair fell on each side of her face which was innocently young.

"Her neck's broken, sir" whispered a kneeling first aider.

Before Peter could say anything someone shouted "Here's the ambulance."

Peter and the others stood back as the paramedics hurried over to the prone figure. He watched how methodically they worked, talking quietly with each other as they checked for any signs of life. When one slowly shook his head, a loud sob escaped from Jepson and he began cursing and struggling again.

"It's his daughter Desiree "someone whispered.

"Stepdaughter" corrected another.

The paramedics expertly manoeuvred the body unto a stretcher and carried it over to the ambulance.

Peter stayed where he was concentrating on breathing slowly and regularly while he planned what to say to Jepson. Only when he felt he was fully in control of himself did he ask "They're saying this girl is your stepdaughter?"

Jepson, his eyes fixed on the departing ambulance nodded his head.

When he was sure the man was not going to say anything further, he continued, "Jepson, I'm terribly sorry this has happened. But please if these gentlemen release you will you promise not to try to interfere with these intruders?"

"Yeah" Jepson snarled "for now. Must get to the hospital."

He began to walk away. The two policemen moved with him. Peter quickly said "Jepson, phone your wife and tell her briefly what's happened. Does she have a car?"

Jepson shook his head

"Right then. We'll send one of your staff to pick her up and take her to the hospital. Don't argue."

"No need for that sir."

"There's every need. Now don't argue. Get going."

As they walked away Peter noticed one of the policemen kept his hand resting on Jepson's right shoulder. There was a moment of tension when Jepson suddenly stopped and turning back said calmly "Thank you sir."

"No need for thanks at moments like this Jepson,   Please give my deepest sympathy to your family and don't worry about hurrying back."

As Jepson left Peter noticed two lines of police making their way around to the fire escape at the rear of the laboratory. He didn't think there would be any resistance from the intruders now and he was right. They came down quietly and were brought back quite close to where he was standing. As they were being loaded into the police vans, one of them, a tall thin faced elderly woman her eyes red with tears paused and snarled at him "Murderer

CHAPTER 2

Detective Sergeant Bullerton didn't have to attend the inquest into the death of Desiree Mills but he was keen to do so. He had for a long time been following the activities of this group calling itself FAAN (Free All Animals Now). Its protests were becoming increasingly violent. Apart from the graffiti painted on Steyns's workers houses and cars; last week one employee of the firm had had his brakes tampered with and almost crashed into a walking train of primary school children. .

His was highly respected county family, whose ancestors could be traced back at least as far as 16th century. They'd done their own bit of protesting over the years but he couldn't let that interfere with his duties today. He was glad that there were Bullertons in positions of influence in every corner of the county. More than once he had benefited from their local knowledge during his investigations. Apart from his time at Durham University he had never lived anywhere else. As an animal lover, he had a sneaking sympathy with some of the protesters aims even though many of his family were ardent foxhunters. He had ridden to hounds and had been "bloodied" when young but later found other sports, especially Rugby more attractive. Joining Calderford's premier Rugby Club as an eleven year old he had progressed through the junior teams and because of his speed and strength was he was playing for the seniors before he was seventeen. He had played for his University and on returning home and had become one of the regulars for the county as well as an ever present for his club. When fixtures didn't clash he also turned out the local police team.

The courtroom was packed and the press box was full. Reporters from all the National and local papers were in attendance and there were several TV vans outside.

Peter Steyn repeated all that had been said and done in his office from the moment he'd received Jepson's phone call. Miles and Samantha and Jepson corroborated his statement that he had specifically ordered that none of his security staff were to follow the intruders unto the roof of the lab. He hoped that the papers would fully report this. He had already emphasised that to the local press on the evening of Desiree's fall but this had not prevented him getting an avalanche of hate mail blaming him and his firm for her death. One green inked harangue had said "With all the millions you make from your evil trade you could easily afford to have protective railings all around the roof of your buildings. You are as guilty as if you had pushed her over the edge." His wife and colleagues had laughed with him at the absurdity of the letter but nevertheless it worried him. He had three children from this his

8

second marriage, all still of school and he could not stop worrying that people with minds so perverted would try to harm them.

Derek Jepson identified that the deceased was his stepdaughter. Most of his answers were given in a brief monosyllabic monotone but when the he began to say "I would just like to say that I blame my Desiree's death on these mindless…" the coroner interrupted him.

"I am sorry Mr. Jepson. Much as we sympathise with your loss these proceedings are merely to establish the facts of your stepdaughter's death, not to apportion blame. I'm afraid I cannot let you air your personal opinions here."

Jepson's response shocked the courtroom   He turned in the witness box and pointing at the protesters yelled "You can say whatever you bloody well like but these bastards still killed my Desiree."

For a moment it seemed as if he would rush over to them but the coroner's quiet sympathetic tone seemed to quieten him down. He left the witness box with his head held high, glaring at the protestors.

Peter Steyn watched intently as all those who had climbed onto the roof were called. Among them were three elderly women, one of them was the woman who had accused him of being a "murderer." It was a long way up that fire escape. But these women were as fit as they were perky and all gave their testimonies in clear precise English. Janet Carroll, the one who had been nearest to the girl when she fell said in her beautifully modulated Cheltenham Ladies College voice, "All I recall is Desiree moving quickly away from me, saying 'A corner of the banner's snagged' The next thing I was aware of was her tumbling forwards off the roof. I bitterly regret not being close enough to grab her." All the others agreed that Desiree had been out of everyone's reach when she fell.

Dale Overton, the driver of the van that had smuggled the protesters into the Steyn complex refused to say where they had got the false documentation that had allowed them to get past the security guard at the gate. He also denied being the leader of the group. "We are a people's collective, all our decisions are taken democratically" he told the coroner. DS Bullerton knew him well, his thick wavy white hair could always be seen at the forefront of any hunt or animal rights protest.

The coroner cut short all attempts of the protestors to heap blame on Steyn Chemicals because of their experimenting on animals. He told them "You are in the witness box, not a pulpit. I will not have this inquest turned into a propaganda event for any cause, no matter how worthy its adherents may feel it to be." Peter was glad about that and after all the intruders had given their evidence the brief nod he got from Marie Framton the female private investigator he'd hired to surreptitiously photograph each of them helped set his mind at ease. At the coroner's direction the jury returned a unanimous verdict of Accidental death.

DS Bullerton left the court quickly. He was interested in the woman who had sat in the front row of the public seats with her arms folded and her overcoat buttoned up throughout the whole proceedings. It was always a bit draughty in the courtroom but no one else had kept themselves as well wrapped up as she had been. He was sure he had seen her make some sort of a gesture towards Peter Steyn at the end of the inquest. When she came out of the courtroom he watched to see if she made any attempt to speak to the managing director but she walked unhurriedly away down a side street without making any attempted to talk to anyone.

There was a large group of animal rights supporters outside the court. Bullerton recognized the usual local protestors, but he was sure that most of them were not here today because they were in favour of FAAN's extremism. They were mostly kind and considerate animal lovers. Many worked as unpaid volunteers for animal charities and rescue groups. They had been protesting against hunting since he was a boy. He had never known them do anything more violent than throw a placard at the hunt as it set off. The majority of them were middle aged middle class housewives. The three McKinster sisters stood out because of their freckles and red hair. Their father farmed locally and had never allowed the hunt to cross his land. They were standing quietly with a well tanned woman whose abundant jet black hair was held back from her face with a couple of tortoiseshell combs which made him think of exotic Senoritas in the Spanish Holiday posters. He'd no recollection of ever seeing her before at any of the FAAN protests. He must find out more about her.

There were many more than usual young people in the protesting group, most of them he guessed were from the University for the Autumn term had started last week. The little loquacious bald headed Professor Phillip Thompson who knew more about his rights as a citizen than most judges did was there. D. S. Bullerton when a constable had endured several lengthy lectures from him. The professor was with two youths, one an androgynous bespectacled bean pole that the sergeant knew rejoiced in the name of Tristan Wills-Hope. He was crouching to hear what the professor was saying. The other was Jamie Brown, who used to be well known locally as "Bother Brown." When drunk which he was most of the time he had committed so many acts of senseless vandalism that when he was old enough he had been sent to prison. Remarkably he had four older brothers who while not exactly angels had never been in serious trouble with the law. But for the last two years Jamie had stayed out of trouble and was holding down a labouring job in an engineering firm. Word was he had shared a cell with some animal rights protester and had been converted to the cause. Seeing him here on a working day Bullerton hoped he hadn't lost his factory job.

The reporters crowded around Jepson when he emerged from the courthouse but he refused to stop and speak to them. The next day most of the local and national papers reported the inquest under headlines such as "TRAGIC LOSS OF YOUNG LIFE" and laid the blame on the fanaticism and recklessness of the FAAN members. Especially condemnatory was the BRITISH BANNER, a fiercely nationalistic daily that accused the anti-hunt protesters of "trying to overturn centuries of England's traditional rural sport."

In the weeks that followed several FAAN followers were assaulted and vehicles displaying their logo was vandalised. At the next foxhunt when three protesters were cornered and beaten up by "unidentified assailants" there was little sympathy for them from most of the locals.

CHAPTER 3

Next day, Miranda Woolston, the dark haired suntanned woman who had interested DC Bullerton so much was watching a new customer come into the Charity shop where she was a volunteer. She had seen him looking in the shop's window at least three times in the last half hour. Now he was coming in when her last customer had left and she was alone in the shop. He was very smartly dressed, didn't look like a robber. Besides there was nothing of value in the shop that anyone would want to steal. But there was something about him that disturbed her. Just a little too sure of himself perhaps?

"Ah, I've brought a few books."

"Thank you. Just put them down behind the far end of the counter please."she replied

."Sure" he answered. As he crouched to put the bags down where she'd indicated; he tore open one of the bags so that the books tumbled unto the floor.

"Sugar" he said loudly.

She came over to help him gather the books up. She noticed he made sure that the heavy volume on Economics was the last to be lifted up onto the counter. As he laid it down he "accidentally" flipped it open at the flyleaf. "My. My." he said loudly, "Good old Jesus."

> To Stephen.
> Congratulations on your
> Very successful first year
> Your loving mother
> Alice.

She gave him her sincerest smile.

"I hope all your subsequent years were as successful."

He waited until she looked quizzically at him before he replied, "There were no subsequent years. Mother had a stroke a few weeks after she wrote that and I had to go home to look after her."

He nodded hesitantly, giving the impression that it was something he didn't like to talk about. In truth, he didn't. He was very squeamish and didn't like being anywhere near the elderly or incapacitated. In fact, his mother was still alive and enjoying life with her boyfriend in her Walthamstow Council house. Slowly he said "It was quite severe, she needed a lot of attention. It was all down to me being the only child. Dad had disappeared from our lives when I was little. I had to go out to work to pay for all the nursing. When she did pass away my life had changed so much I no longer had the same interest in Economics."

When she nodded he continued, "It's amazing how much something like that takes over your life. Then there was the money."

"The money?"

"Mother had several insurances that fortunately I kept paying. I was amazed how much they came to. Took away any need to work for a year or two."

"So you joined the idle rich. Lived the life of a playboy?"

He gave her his sincerest smile. "Not really, it's just that...well...I got this stupid notion in my head that I could be an author."

"On Economics?"

"Oh no. Mother liked me to read to her. Always murder mysteries and detective stories. I must have read hundreds. .We used to talk for hours about who was the killer. The ways I know to kill people you wouldn't believe

"My goodness. I hope you'll never put any of them into practice."

\"Oh, I'd never do that. But I know they'd make good reading."

"Good luck then."

CHAPTER 4

It had rained all night before Desiree's funeral but in the morning the clouds cleared away to reveal a temperate autumn day. The church was so full they had to open the adjoining assembly room and there was still a considerable crowd outside. D.S.Bullerton was seated at the back of the church with his wife Helene He was glad of her company although initially he had tried to persuade her not to come because he was afraid that if there was going to be any trouble it would be after Desiree was buried. The level of violence both by and upon the protestors had escalated greatly in the last few weeks. But she had argued that since she was the pathologist who had conducted the autopsy on Desiree she was entitled to see her buried.

He had known he had very little chance of dissuading her from coming; she was a strong minded woman. For his youth because of his surname he had, like many other male members of the Bullerton family been nicknamed "Bully" It had never bothered him but ever since they had met she had been waging a campaign to get his close friends to call him by his initials "C.S." instead of "Bully." "It's so inappropriate" she argued, "I've never know anyone less of a Bully than you." All of which was perfectly true for despite his six foot two inch figure and his powerful muscular build he was a quietly spoken level headed man who rarely got angry. His extreme fairness inherited from his Anglos Saxon ancestors and his cornflower blue eyes gave him an appearance of naivety that many villains had sought to exploit to their cost.

But he was far from comfortable with her crusade to have him known by his initials CS. From early boyhood he had done all he could to keep anyone from knowing they stood for "Clarence Sassoon." "Clarence" was an old family name and his mother had fallen in love with Siegfried Sassoon's poetry when she was pregnant with him. He could never decide which was the worst of his forenames and had more than once intended to change them by Deed Poll but had never got around to it. Since his promotion he had quietly let those he met in his professional life know they need only call him "Sarge" if the occasion demanded it. His closest mates (when Helene wasn't present) still called him the old familiar "Bully." Helene, he had long ago decided, for all her intelligence understood very little about Male bonding.

But such thoughts were far from his mind as he listened to the Very Reverend Inworth's sermon. He was dreading something would be said that would become a slogan for one or other of the warring factions. But he need not have worried. The Very Reverend's sermon was a masterpiece of Church of England sophistry; no one could have followed the Apostle Paul's advice to be "all things to all men" more faithfully. He praised Desiree for her love of "all of God's creatures" while regretting that such love had led her" untimely departure from this world." But he also thanked the Lord for giving those who devote their lives to overcoming the many evils that plague mankind the special intelligence to search for cures to overcome them. The congregation were left with a picture of a now eternally happy Desiree reclining peacefully, "where the wolf shall dwell with the lamb and the leopard shall lie down with the kid."

Not as many came to the internment as Bullerton expected but there was still a fair crowd. He managed to find a mound a little way from the grave where he could see most of those assembled. The Spanish looking woman was there again with two of the McKinster sisters. He assumed that the missing sister must be the one who was a veterinary nurse and that the practice was too busy to release her. But his attention was quickly drawn to a group of three men stood in the front row of mourners on the opposite side of the grave to where Jepson and his wife and young son were standing. It was the way they stayed unnaturally close to each other that drew his attention to them but it was only when the service had concluded and the group began moving away that he realised the middle one was handcuffed to the man on each side of him. He moved across the graveyard as fast as decorum and Helene's complaints about her high heels sinking into the damp grass allowed. He managed to come out onto the road where the cars were parked far enough ahead of the threesome so that they had to walk past him to reach their car.

It was immediately evident that the man in the middle must be a bodybuilder or weightlifter. His barrel chest and bulging thighs and arms forced him to walk with that swaying sailor's gait man typical of such muscular men. His head was close shaven but with enough of a dark shadow to indicate he could have had a full head of hair if he wished. His round pink face could have been described as cherubic if it had not been for the deadness of his pale blue eyes. Bullerton tried to acknowledge his stare with a friendly nod but got no response. As soon as they passed he whispered to Helene "What do you think of the man in the middle?

"The prisoner?" she replied quietly "Not someone I'd like as an enemy. Any time I have a body like that on my table it's got at least one bullet in it."

As he was reflecting on how little this woman of his missed he found himself saying, "I wonder who he is?"

"He's Desiree's father of course. Jepson's only her step dad isn't he?

CHAPTER 5

When Stephen returned to the Charity shop the following Tuesday he again waited until she was alone before he entered. He'd had a bad day selling but his spirits lifted when she smiled at him

"Hello, Stephen isn't it? How's the writing going?"

"Quite well" he lied, "I've managed to set up a really good red herring that will send the police, and the reader on completely the wrong trail."

"That sounds interesting. So will your murderer get away with it?"

"I don't think so. Readers like to see justice done. Would you be happy reading a story where the criminal doesn't get caught for some terrible crime?"

"I suppose not but then I'm afraid it's not a genre that I ever read. I enjoyed the Inspector Morse series on the television though."

"They're brilliant. But not every writer's a Colin Dexter. Lots are pretty ordinary. That's what makes me think I could do as well." He paused before adding "Do you think someone could commit the perfect crime."

"I'm afraid I wouldn't know. As a matter of fact when you think about it, if it's not detected then no one will ever know."

"Not unless the killer leaves a confession to be read after he (or she) dies. Everyone wants recognition of their cleverness, don't they?"

"Hmm, I'm not sure that's universally true. Human vanity is very powerful but there must be many grim secrets that have been buried with their owners."

He hoped she was right. He certainly hoped to take his secrets with him to the grave.

"You know, I hadn't thought of that. You've got a good brain. I could do with someone like you to talk over the plots of my stories. You'd soon spot the flaws. Would you care to have dinner with me some evening?"

"Thanks but I'm afraid that wouldn't be possible."

Her answer puzzled him. He'd already checked that she wasn't wearing a wedding ring. He concentrated on arranging his features to convey what he hoped was the right degree of disappointment. He offered her his best bitter-sweet smile.

"I hope you didn't mind me asking? I'm not usually so forward."

"Not at all. I'm sure from your own experience you'll understand when I tell you I can't accept any invitations because I have an elderly father to take care of."

"Ah. It's all down to you, is it? "

"I'm afraid so."

"Doesn't he have any visitors?"

"He has a few but they're all elderly like him. Major Thomas his oldest friend plays cards with him Tuesday afternoons. That's how I'm able to work here. But Major Thomas doesn't like coming out at night. None of Dad's elderly friends do."

He almost turned and walked out of the shop when she told him that. Given a few hours of freedom and she spends them working in a Charity shop! She must be a nutter. It might be best to...No...No. What was the matter with him? If she was such a do-gooder she'd be an easy touch for a sob story. He had to find another easy touch soon. It was seven months now since Sylvia had kicked him out and the commissions he earned from his job were not sufficient for the life he felt entitled to lead.

He said quietly, "You surely must get a break sometimes."

"Mrs Harris next door sits with him Tuesday nights so that I can go to my choir. That's the only evening I get out."

"Have you thought about having someone live in? Someone who'd be willing to help look after your dad?

"Funny you should say that. Dad is always on at me to get some help. Says he feels guilty that he's depriving me of my "youth." He forgets I'm in my middle thirties."

"Never! You certainly don't look it."

"Thanks but I think you're being too kind. Besides age is nothing to be ashamed of."

"Of course not. But (and I hope you won't mind me saying this) A beauty like you would normally have a regular partner by now."

"You like to flatter."

"Tell the truth and shame the devil. That's what Mum used to say."

"Well thank you but I don't regret for a moment the life I lead. It's my choice."

Again he got a feeling he should walk away. A strong minded woman was the last thing he needed. Yet there was something about her that tempted him. He'd been so wrong about Sylvia He'd thought she was just another dizzy blonde but she'd told him to bugger off as soon as he'd mentioned that all he needed was the loan of £1000 to put his business straight. He had to prove to himself that he wasn't losing his touch.

When she looked away he knew it was time to withdraw. He glanced at his watch and said "Duty calls. I hope you haven't been offended by my forwardness."

"Not at all. It's nice to be complimented."

"It was very easy to do, believe me. Look my work brings me here every couple of weeks. Would you mind if I called in to see you occasionally?"

"As you wish but if you really want to see me again you can do so next Saturday." She reached under the counter and handed him a leaflet. "It's a magnificent work but you might find it heavy going if you don't enjoy choral singing."

He studied the words highlighted on the paper. "ST. MATTHEW PASSION by J.S.BACH" The little he knew about classical music came from listening to Classic FM on his car radio. But "Passion," he was all for that. She might be in the mood for it after singing about it. He brought out his wallet and as he gave her the £10 admission fee said. "I'm afraid I don't know much about classical music but anything by Bach is bound to be worth hearing."

She didn't take his money immediately. Instead she said "Look I don't want you coming to this concert under false pretences. I won't be able to come for a drink with you or anything afterwards. I'll have to rush home to Dad; I've promised Mrs. Harris I'll be home for eleven at the latest. So please don't come to the concert if you've anything like that in mind."

"That's a pity. I won't deny I was hoping we could have a drink afterwards. But never mind. I'm a great believer in being open to new experiences. Only fossils never change. So if you don't mind I'd still like to give it a try. I'll sit at the back and sneak out if it becomes unbearable."

She laughed as she took his money and handed him a ticket. "I hope we won't be that bad. If you do manage to last out to the end, find me and let me know if you enjoyed it. I'll have a few minutes to spare "

"Perhaps I could drive you home."

"That's very kind but I'll be taking my own car."

"Well, it was just a thought; I'll be on my way. See you Saturday…"He paused "You know I'm Stephen but I'm afraid I don't know your name."

"Miranda" she replied.

He thanked her and left.

CHAPTER 6

The five people around the table in Miranda's kitchen on Sunday afternoon were the two older McKinster sisters, Alice and Constance, Professor Phillip Thompson, Dale Overton and Tristan Wills-Hope.

They were discussing what was happening to the protestors. Not only were they being attacked when they tried to film "drag hunts" to make sure they complied with the law but outside the factory there now was every day a small group with banners and placards supporting Research and Experiments on animals. Even at Calderford University a Student Pro-Hunting group had sprung up and it had begun picketing the pickets.

Their presence made the animal rights protestors outside Steyn Chemicals increasingly belligerent. The workers cars were being pelted with eggs every day now. The police organized a snatch squad and grabbed three of the egg throwers who were later fined £75 each and banned from going within three miles of the factory.

"We have had enough of the law defending these hunt thugs and animal experimenters. We've got to do something to stop them" said Dale Overton.

Once I'd done that it was comparatively easy to produce an antidote that would guarantee a victim full recovery."

"But isn't there a danger of killing the victim with such a prolonged exposure to the poison" asked Alice.

"No Alice. Curare is toxic only when it enters the blood stream but its molecules are too large to transfer into the stomach lining. That's why the Amazonian natives are able to eat the prey they capture by curare poisoning without any harm to themselves. The poison affects the animal's muscles so that it can no longer cling to a branch and so falls to the ground after being darted. In Brazil I have kept monkeys alive for months after injecting them with my serum and they have been released in good health afterwards."

"I don't know Miranda, what you were doing sounds a bit too much like what laboratories such as Steyns are doing." said Dale.

"That's just what I was thinking" added Constance.

"That was my problem at first and I'm not perfectly at ease with my actions even after all these years but we've never objected to these laboratories paying people to be volunteers for their experiments have we?"

"No, but where are you going to get someone who will let you poison them?" asked Dale.

"Actually, I have found the perfect person on whom to try out the effectiveness of my work. Once I tell you his history you will see that he is an ideal subject." As she progressed her voice and manner became more and more evangelical. It was obvious she had been dreaming and working on this project for years "The thing is" she concluded "Once we can demonstrate that people can both be completely incapacitated and later recover from this poisoning then we can make them agree to stop working in animal research.".

"No. No. Miranda" objected Professor Thompson. "What you're proposing is the very antithesis of all that we stand for. And as for experimenting on this man I could never agree to that."

Before she could answer, Alice said" I don't know Phillip. Look how we treat these people now. Harassing them. Despoiling their property. Telling lies about them everywhere. Aren't we experimenting on them to see how much they can take?"

"That may be so Alice" Phillip replied "But there is a point beyond which we've never gone. We've always known when to stop."

"But as Miranda has said, we've never objected to people volunteering to being paid guinea pigs to try out these drugs" said Tristan.

"No we haven't" Phillip replied" but the recipient of what Miranda is proposing could never in any sense of the word be described as a volunteer"

"That's true" said Constance, "I don't think this is a good idea at all. No matter what sort of person this bloke is, we shouldn't be experimenting on him."

"I don't see why not" said Tristan, "he sounds like a right bastard to me. He deserves everything that happens to him."

"Ah, there's the rub," Phillip answered "Don't you see that by seeking to justify what we'd be doing, we have started dehumanising this person. Surely that is just copying the Nazis? They excused their experiments on the gypsies and Jews and homosexuals on the grounds that these people were subhuman. That's how all totalitarian regimes operate. Once you demonize your opponents as being lower than animals you open up the way for all sorts of mistreatment

"But" Miranda countered "How else could we be sure we don't kill anyone? Believe me I've agonized over this for years. The nights I've been unable to sleep because my mind was flooded with this idea. For a long time I've tried to dismiss it completely but it wouldn't go away. Then when he came along it seemed as if I'd been given a gift from the gods."

"I didn't know you were a believer Miranda" said Constance.

"I'm not." Miranda replied, "Although I've witnessed things in the jungle that do not easily lend themselves to any logical explanation. We cannot continue as we are. Something drastic has to be done. Something that will make the whole world sit up and take notice. We've got to grasp this opportunity .I know what I'm proposing is right. It's such a beautifully simple solution."

"Don't you mean brutally simple" interjected the Professor. He was extremely disturbed by what Miranda was proposing and by the evangelical glow in her eyes as she spoke. He was very fond of her and it grieved him to see her falling into the trap of thinking she had discovered the one simple solution that would lead to the triumph of their cause. It brought back embarrassing memories of his student days in 1968. Those heady times when the triumph of the proletariat had seemed attainable. He remembered being among the crowd chanting anti-imperialist slogans outside the American Embassy and how his girlfriend in those days, a classical music student had spoken of the "fervour in your eyes and the sunlight glinting on the rims of your Schubert glasses."

All that he had learned since had made him fearful of simple solutions and those who advocated them. He was Professor of Russian Literature Studies at Calderford University and he had long since concluded that Tolstoy and Dostoyevsky had exposed the inherent flaws in the psychology of revolutionaries. That is why he never failed to emphasise that the greatest crimes committed against the human race had been perpetrated by those who believed they had discovered "beautifully simple solutions." He had set out his views in the collection of essays that that made his reputation, "The Fatal Flaw."

He was upset to see Miranda falling into the trap that he had described in his book. How she was speaking now was exactly the way he had described many of the advocates of simple solutions.

There was such conviction in her voice as she said. "Well, whatever you say, I cannot prevent myself from believing it would work. If we can avoid permanently harming anyone, wouldn't that be worthwhile?"

"That's a big if" said Alice.

"But if we can obtain living proof that the antidote I've developed works, we're on to a winner. But…before you all say any more, I agree that such an experiment as I propose is contrary to our basic beliefs. However I cannot see any other way of being absolutely sure other than testing this person. He is a most fitting recipient. Anyhow, if you don't agree would any of you volunteer to take his place?"

21

The prolonged silence that followed gave adequate answer to her question,

"You see what I mean? Surely this is better than risking someone's death by using the poison untested?"

"But what if your 'victim'... No, I apologize," said the Professor, "That's too emotive a word. What if your 'subject 'dies? You have no way of knowing that won't happen, have you?"

Miranda spoke very deliberately when she said "Well I agree nothing to do with poison is one hundred per cent foolproof but I'm confident this antidote will prevent any fatalities. I know. I've tried in on myself."

There was a brief shocked silence then everyone started talking at once but it was Dale's question that prevailed, "Then why are you looking for someone else?"

She'd been expecting this and had her answer ready. "The doses I've used have been very weak. I've not been incapacitated for longer than 24 hours and I've been back to normal in another twelve. We need something strong enough to put people out of action for a couple of weeks at least. I don't want to try anything stronger on myself, not because I'm afraid but if anything did go wrong I'm the only one whose got this far with the antidote. If I was out of the picture altogether I couldn't find how to increase the effectiveness of the antidote. It's just that I know I'm on the right lines."

The professor's heart chilled. How often had he heard and read those words before?

"If we could be absolutely sure of that it would I could go along with that." said Alice. "Think of the power we'd have if Miranda's scheme worked. We could close down every animal experimental laboratory in the country."

"Yes "said Tristan, "wouldn't that be worthwhile Phillip?"

The professor shook his head "No. I can't agree. That's the old 'The end justifies the means'" argument."

"It may be old Prof." answered Tristan "but in this case it surely would be worthwhile."

They continued to argue even when they broke for a meal. As always, each of them had brought food to share at these meetings. But the food merely meant that most of them kept arguing between mouthfuls. Eventually Miranda said, "This is getting us nowhere. We're just going round and round in circles. I think we should take a vote. It can be a secret ballot if you wish."

"I don't think there's any need for that" Phillip replied, "I can see that I'm on my own in this matter and I can't see myself changing my mind. But I'd like at least to sleep on it before finally deciding what I'm going to do" This was he knew was merely an evasion on his part but he wanted time to see if he might find some means of dissuading Miranda from her "beautifully simple solution."

"I have to agree with Phillip" said Constance, "I think what your proposing is against all we believe in."

"I know what you and Phillip are saying is true" said Dale" but we've been fighting these animal experimenters for years and not making any real progress. I'm reluctantly willing to give Miranda's scheme a try. It could be the weapon we've been looking for that really will bring a halt to this vile trade."

Miranda's voice seemed unusually loud as she said, "Thank you Dale. As for you, Constance and Phillip, you must follow your consciences but you understand that nothing that has been discussed here is to go any further than the five of us. "

"Of course" everyone chorused.

But Miranda continued "I really do mean only us five. I thought very carefully before inviting each of you here tonight. That's why I have to ask you, Alice and Constance to say nothing about what we've talked about to Patricia. The fewer who know about this the better."

Before Alice could reply the Professor said "My lips are sealed and will remain so no matter what I decide" Then as he rose from his chair he added "If I should resign from this group that will not mean that I'm giving up my fight for the rights of animals. I'll just be continuing doing it in the same ways as we've pursued so far. And of course never for one moment will I ever reveal to anyone what has been said here today."

Despite all their entreaties to stay he rose and walked purposefully out of the room.

Constance also got up and said "I'll wait in the car for you Alice. I think the less I know about all this the better."

When they had gone it was Alice who broke the silence by asking "I take it you are insisting on our silence because if we do agree to your scheme it will be us who will carry out these attacks?"

Miranda nodded, "Well, yes. That's why I thought carefully about who I should invite along to this meeting. That's why I haven't asked Patricia here. I thought she was too young to get involved."

"What about Phillip" Tristan asked

"To be honest" said Miranda" I never expected he would carry out any of these attacks. He's not really a man of action is he? I felt I had to have him here because I half hoped he would he'd come up with some alternative, but he hasn't"

"So it's just us four then?" said Dale

"That's it .We are the vanguard." Miranda replied

CHAPTER 7

On Saturday night Stephen entered the concert hall five minutes before it was due to begin. The choir was already making its way up on to the stage. The number of grey heads among them quickly quelled his hopes of any intense display of passion.

Miranda's deep tan and mass of jet black hair made her easy to spot. It was pinned back with a high tortoiseshell comb that reminded him of imperious women in Spanish tourist posters. He sat at the end of one of the back rows. Although he stared hard at her she gave no indication of seeing him.

He looked at the programme to see her surname. Woolston that must be her for there was only one Miranda in the list. He felt elated that she had such a British name, he never felt completely at ease with foreign women.

He was surprised when another choir made up entirely of children came in and grouped themselves below and to the right of the main choir. He was not a lover of children. They'd caused him nothing but trouble while he was trying to build a trusting relationship with their mothers.

There was not a very large orchestra and the musical introduction they played reinforced his view that whatever "passion" was going to be portrayed it would have little to do with sex. When the choir stood up and sang their voices blended melodiously with the instruments. He couldn't understand what they were saying but the sound was not unpleasant. It took him some while to realise they were not singing in English. Miranda and the women on either side of her sang expressively. He was sure she'd be a real tigress in bed.

After a while he began to tire of the same phrases being sung over and over again and was thankful there were five soloists whose contributions broke the monotony of the choir's repetitions. He planned to leave at the interval but when it came and the choir made its way in two streams to the back of the hall, Miranda gave him an encouraging wink as she passed. He decided she would think better of him if he was still in his seat when she came back.

Wine was being sold in the interval and by visiting different tables he managed to get three glasses of a decent full bodied red before the choir filed back in. He knew he'd done the right thing when she winked at him again as she passed.

The wine made the music more bearable but when the last notes were played he had an overwhelming feeling of relief. He hoped it did not show when she passed him once more.

He left his seat and stood near the door through which choir members were leaving. He was rehearsing what he was going to say to her when she came rushing up, "Sorry, I've got to fly. All that additional applause for the soloists and the children has made me very late. Hope you enjoyed it. Call in at the shop sometime soon" She was gone before he had a chance to speak.

As he stared after her he noticed one of the grey haired choir members looking at him. There was something about her that stirred faint memories. She was no spring chicken and he'd never found one rich enough to be worth bothering about. Nor had he ever tangled with any woman in this town. So he gave her a brief nod in case she was one of his customers and hurried after Miranda.

He was disgusted when he saw her get into a canvas topped Citroen 2CV. Bloody dustbin on wheels. She surely couldn't be that poor, could she? Then he remembered someone on the radio saying "It's only the rich who know how to live cheaply." That probably accounted for her taste for cheap cars. She must be one of these environmentalists, worried about global warming and carbon footprints. He'd have to read more about it if he was to get anywhere with her. He'd buy The Guardian for a week or two and make sure there was always a copy in the car in case he ever gave her a lift.

He was fortunate his BMW was parked facing in the same direction as Miranda's and he had no trouble keeping her in sight. As he expected she obeyed all the speed limits even on the dual carriageway. His spirits lifted when he saw her turn into a wide tree lined Avenue with large detached houses on either side. She gave plenty of warning she was going to turn right into one of the driveways and he was able to stop well before she did so. He didn't want to risk meeting whoever was "daddy sitting" so he stayed in the car for several minutes before he made his way over to the house. Taking his briefcase with him he walked briskly past her driveway. The house was as solid and well appointed as all the others. Only one room downstairs was lit but heavy curtains prevented him from seeing inside. The house next door was "FOR SALE". He took note of the Estate Agents name and address. He'd check them out in the morning; these houses must be worth at least three quarters of a million: the thought banished any doubts he had about pursuing her. It would be a shame to let her waste it all that money on environmental nonsense. He knew of much better uses for it.

The next morning he went to the Estate Agents before he left town and was thrilled to see that the house next door's asking price was £820,000. The information buoyed him up and he had one of his most successful sales days of the year. It would be four weeks before he was due back near Miranda. During that time he often thought of taking half a day off and going to see her but everything seemed to conspire against him. But after three weeks he could wait no longer and finished all his Tuesday appointments by early afternoon and drove the 100 miles in less than two hours to Calderford. As usual he checked the window of the Charity Shop before entering. There was a stout "auntie" type behind the counter but no sign of Miranda. In the next half hour he visited the window three more times without seeing her. When it was obvious the shop was closing he watched from a doorway on the opposite side of the road but only the plump woman came out of the shop. Miranda mustn't work Tuesdays anymore. He thought of driving to the tree lined avenue but decided if she saw him she might not like knowing she'd been followed. He would just have to keep changing his visiting days until he met her again. She might just be off with a cold or something. He'd learned that patience paid when dealing with women.

CHAPTER 8

The following Tuesday Stephen made a special journey to Caldeford and was rewarded by the sight of his suntanned beauty behind the counter as usual. He put on his most charming smile and walked confidently in. One glance told him all was not well. The rigidity of her body and the seriousness of her expression showed she was under a strain.

"Bad news?" he enquired softly.

Her answer puzzled him. "In one way Yes in another No"

Before he could think of a suitable answer she continued "Daddy's dead. I miss him terribly but he'd become so ill and was in so much pain that it's a blessing he doesn't have to suffer any more."

His inclination was to rush over and take her in his arms but he feared she might think him presumptions. Instead he merely reached out and pressed her hand.

"I'm so sorry but I'm sure you're right. It's a comfort to know their suffering is over. I felt the same when Mother died."

"Thank you"

He stood hesitantly, unsure what to say next. When she didn't speak he said "Look, please don't think me presumptuous but I know from my own experience it helps to talk at times like these. Probably you've got lots of friends you've already spoken with and I won't be in the least offended if you refuse but if you'd care to have a drink with me after you close, you'd be more than welcome?"

The directness of her scrutiny unsettled him. The last time he'd felt like this he'd been in court. He was relieved when she smiled slightly and said

"That's very kind. I'll meet you here at five."

"It's a deal" He touched her hand again and slowly left the shop. As soon as he was sure he was out of sight of the shop he couldn't stop himself punching the air and jumping for joy. A passing dachshund yelped as he landed near it, earning him a disapproving glare from its elegantly dressed female owner. His happiness made him offer an exuberant apology "Sorry Sausage dog. I'm most profoundly sorry. Don't go near any butcher's shops." He was shocked when the woman said loudly; "Fuck off."

When he returned at five. Miranda was waiting in the doorway of the shop He suggested that she choose where to eat. She mentioned a pub called The Baker's Arms adding "You can park around the back of the shop; it's only a short walk there." He did as she said, parking beside "The Dustbin on

28

Wheels" and hurried round the side of the shop to meet her. It took all his self-control to prevent himself taking her arm as she set off at a brisk pace.

In the pub she said she usually had a "Five bean stew with rice", so he said he'd have the same. A well done steak, egg and chips were his preferred meal but he could tolerate most vegetarian food. It always made him think of Eleanor, the most scatterbrained woman he'd ever known. She was a vegetarian and sensational in bed. He'd even stayed with her for a couple of months after her money ran out.

Before he could offer she asked him what he wanted to drink and when he told her he liked the local bitter he had to fight hard to keep the surprise out of his face when she said "Good man" and went to the bar to order the meal and drinks. While they were eating he was amazed how randy it made him seeing her drink from a pint glass. If she did everything else as wholeheartedly she'd be another Eleanor in bed. He just had to get into her good books. Thank God he'd been reading The Guardian these past few weeks.

Picking a topic that was being featured prominently in that paper he began to declaim how disgraceful it was that American oil companies wanted to start drilling in the virgin wastes of the Arctic. Her response was a lengthy unbroken flow of predictions on the harm it would do to the local natives and wildlife. It took all his patience and skill to steer their conversation back around to her father's death and what she was going to do with the house.

"I'll sell it of course" she said lightly.

"And do you have any plans for what you'll do with the money? I imagine it will be a considerable sum."

"Over three quarters of a million for the house alone. I'm sure I can find a good use for it."

Her looked her steadfastly in the face and said hesitantly, "I might be able to help you there. Even before I studied Economics at Uni. I'd been fascinated by the workings of the stock market. I read the financial news in the Guardian every day and I still subscribe to The Economist. So if you ever needed any advice on Investments, especially ethical investments, I'd be glad to help."

He had to clench his fists under the table to control his excitement when she answered "Would you? I've got a PhD in Plant Chemistry but I'm rubbish with financial things. I know it sounds silly but I can't get myself to think of them as important. I put everything I can on standing orders and hope I've always got enough in the bank to pay them. Still, it won't be too long before Daddy's estate is settled. He left a very clear and explicit will. I inherit everything apart from what he's left to charities."

He decided it would be prudent to stop any more talk about shares and money for now so he asked her what had made her study Biology at University.

"Daddy was a world authority on Tropical Orchids. He usually spent a few months of every year abroad, usually in South America. His stories about the peoples of the Amazon fascinated me. Actually that's where I did my field work for my degree and later for my doctorate. I intend to go back when everything is settled here. That's why I do Charity work instead of getting a job. I knew Daddy wouldn't last long"

"That's where you got your tan then?"

"O yes, I tan very easily. Friends joke I'm part native"

"You can't really like living in the jungle though."

"Oh but I do. I love the natives; they are so generous and welcoming even though they and their lands have been terribly exploited by prospectors and loggers. I hate anyone that takes advantage of other's goodness. This money of Daddy's will help us combat the illegal activities of these villains."

"Us?"

"I belong to a small group that seeks justice for the Amazonian peoples."

"A small group? Aren't there organizations like Greenpeace that do all that?"

"They do, and we co-operate with them as much as possible. But we don't just gather information, we help the native tribes fight back against the exploiters" She paused, then looking him straight in the eye added, " Not every miner and logger that goes into the jungle comes out again. You should know that logging is an activity where there are an awful lot of accidents."

He didn't like the look on her face as she said that. It made him say, although he smiled as he did so, "You sound like one of these Animal Liberationists."

"I am, don't you approve?"

"Well, yes; up to a point but some of their actions are a bit extreme, don't you think?"

"Maybe but remember animals can't defend themselves. Someone's got to fight for them. If you'd like to follow me home I'll show you some pictures of what's done to them in the name of Science. "

CHAPTER 9

Half an hour later he was seated beside her in the spacious front lounge of her home saying "I hope you don't mind me bringing my briefcase in with me but I've got some very valuable documents inside. Some of those ethical investments I mentioned."

He was telling her the truth for among the literature of several companies who truly were "ethical investors" were several additional pages he'd printed on his computer with his name and smiling photo on them. He was self appointed "Investor of the Year 2005 "on the final page he intended to show her As he rehearsed in his mind the tale he would spin her he was annoyed by an evil looking Siamese cat in the armchair opposite that kept staring at him and meowing loudly while she was fetching the animal pictures.

As she returned with a red box file she said "Don't take any notice of Sisyphus. He's jealous of any other male who comes into the house."

He decided to tell her something that would concentrate her mind if he ever needed to threaten her. "It's perfectly alright; I'm fond of cats. Mind you I once read a story where an extortionist puts this woman's pet cat in a cat box and pours petrol over it. He threatens to set it alight unless she gives him money."

"Oh my God! You'd never do a thing like that, would you?"

"Most certainly not" he lied for that's what he'd in fact done when one of his women had refused to give him the money he knew she had in the house.

She sat down beside him and opened the file. Immediately Sisyphus meowed so loudly that she had to get up and put him out of the room. When she sat back down beside him he was sure she was much closer than before. He had an increasing good feeling she was going to be one of his most profitable victims.

He didn't think the conditions of most of the animals looked too bad but she spoke with such passion about the inhumanity of their treatment that he couldn't stop himself exclaiming, "I wouldn't like to have you as an enemy."

The directness of her reply startled him, "No you wouldn't." He had to concentrate hard on the photographs to hide his discomfort. It seemed a very long time before her voice softened and she said "But we're not going to be enemies are we Stephen?"

"Most certainly not, just the opposite I hope."

She didn't reply but she didn't move away either. After a few more photographs that even he felt were horrible she became so incensed that as she waved one particular photo in front of him the file fell off her lap and its contents spilled onto the carpet. What looked like a roll of plastic bounced away from the scattering photos. There was a broad elastic band holding together whatever was inside the plastic. When he looked closely he was sure it was banknotes.

"Dear old Daddy" she said as she retrieved the package. She put it on an elaborately carved little table to the right of the settee and concentrated on restoring some order to the fallen photos.

"Isn't that money?" he asked.

"Yes" she replied without looking up from the photos.

"Well, aren't you going to count it?"

"No need. It'll be £500. Fifty ten pound notes. That was Daddy's standard stash."

"What do you mean?"

"Daddy got a bit paranoid about money in his last few years. He became obsessed with the idea that his bank was going to collapse and while he was fit enough to get out and about he used to occasionally sneak out to our local branch and draw out 500 quid.. Sometimes he'd do it twice in the one week. Fortunately one of the girls there is a good friend and she always used to tell me when he'd done it."

"Isn't that illegal nowadays?"

"Probably but common sense is more important than any law. Anyway we had this code so no one would know what she was doing. She'd ring me on some pretext and in the conversation would say; 'Your dad was wearing that old tweed hat with the fawn band around the brim when he was in the bank today.' I knew then to search for the money and put it back in Daddy's account. Of course she wasn't always on the tills when he did it. I'm still finding money all over the house. I believe he always meant me to find them for he's hidden them in places where he knew I was sure to go. Now, look at this, how can anyone who calls himself a scientist do that to a poor rabbit?"

He looked at the picture unseeingly. His mind was filled with visions of £500 rolls of cash all over the house. This definitely called for a bit of burglary.

She had so much to say about each photo she showed him that by the time she reached the last one a sly glance at his watch showed him well over an hour had passed since they sat down together. She must have noticed him for she said, "My goodness, I do go on don't I? "

"Don't apologize; I admire you for it. As you say animals can't fight back"

"Indeed. Look I'm still full up after our meal but I've got some Bath Olivers. Would you like some with a glass of Port.? Daddy always had a Port with his Bath Olivers at bedtime and I'm afraid I do too now"

"That would be lovely thank you."

When she stood up, she took the red box file over to the table and put it on the table and dropped the roll of money into it, closing the lid after her. He felt a twinge of apprehension as she did so, didn't she trust him? But when she didn't take the file with her as she left the room he felt reassured. He sat staring at the red box as he listened to her moving around in the kitchen.

He thought of pocketing the roll of notes now but decided it would be stupid. Nevertheless he couldn't take his eyes off the red box. He was two months overdue with his hotel bill. It would…

"Stephen "Her voice made him jump. He hadn't heard her come back. She was waving a bottle at him. "Stephen, would you be a darling and fetch another bottle of port for me? This one's only got a few drops left in it. The bottles are in the cellar. All the port is in the nearest top row, you'll see it immediately."

"Not at all" As he rose and followed her out of the room he saw she was in her stocking feet. She opened a door in the hallway and stepped aside. "The light's to your right just as you go in."

As he stepped into the cellar she was so close behind him he felt uncomfortable. As he reached for the light switch he had a sudden fear that she was going to push him down the stone steps. There was no handrail. As the light came on he stumbled forward scrabbling his hand along the wall for any finger hold he could find.

He heard her voice, unnaturally high, but reassuringly filled with concern, "Stephen! Careful! Are you alright?"

Guiltily he turned to face her as he sensed her come down the steps behind him. "Yes, yes, just missed my footing, that's all."

He smiled at her as he saw her face relax "That top step is so smooth. I was afraid you were going to take a tumble."

"Not me, I was born lucky."

"Well, do take care," she answered as she turned back up the steps. As he stood and watched her he was once again afraid that she was going to shut and lock the cellar door on him but she left it open.

As he descended he wondered why such irrational thoughts were entering his mind. He had always prided himself on his sensitivity; it had served him well in the past. He always seemed to know when his women had had enough and it was time to move on. But he'd only just begun with this one, she couldn't possibly be dangerous. Yet, there was something of the fanatic about her when she'd talked about what she'd like to do to the animal experimenters, and the way she's said "Not every miner or logger comes out of the jungle" was chilling. But she'd smiled as she said it and she'd such a lovely smile. Probably it was all just women's talk, they were so inclined to exaggerate weren't they?

There must have been at least a hundred bottles of wine in the racks facing him. He pulled one out of a top rack, checked it was Port and hurried back up the steps.

They chatted for the next half hour. Then he decided to leave. He liked to be the one to make decisions.

"Do you mind if I use your loo before I leave?" he asked.

"Not at all. There's one downstairs just through the kitchen, we had it installed when Daddy was finding it difficult to get upstairs."

On the way back through the kitchen he undid the latch on the larger of the two windows. It looked directly out into the garden; it would be a doddle to get through if she didn't notice what he'd done. He thanked her when he returned and went directly to the front door. She readily agreed when he suggested that they could do this again when he was back in the town in four weeks and she didn't turn away when he gave her a chaste kiss on the cheek as they parted.

In the car he was so excited he had to sit for a while before driving off. It was all so promising. He wondered when he should return to steal the money. Probably a Thursday for she went to the choir Thursday nights. This Thursday would be too soon, she might remember she'd shown him the money but the longer he waited the more danger there was that she might notice the unlatched window. It would be a risk but if it was true that the £500 stashes were hidden all over the house she surely wouldn't miss a couple. How could she if she didn't even know how many there were? It was a pity it wasn't her mother that had hidden them, he was good at knowing where women hid things. He had to take the risk; he needed the money now. Working mainly on commission mean he only got bare expenses when he had a duff week. He was going to get a lot more than £500 out of her once he got his hands on her shares. That was his forte.

CHAPTER 10

On Saturday night the Caldeford Ex-Servicemen Club (Popularly known as The Retreat) was packed as usual. Ex Master Sergeant Derek Jepson was there with his wife Mary, his long time friend and fellow ex-sergeant, John Rowlands, John's wife Florence and daughter Annabelle and her husband Mick. Derek .drained his glass, placed it carefully on a beer mat and looked around at the others at the table." Right, who's for a refill? My round. Same again?"

John and Mick protested almost simultaneously, "No Derek, I'll get them."

"No you bloody well won't. It's my turn. What the hell got into you? It's a daughter I've lost, not my mind. Do you think I'm so far gone I can't remember when it's my dibs?"

The two men glanced at each other before John replied "Sorry Derek. You're right. I'll come with you to help carry the drinks."

As the two men rose from the table, Derek said once more "Same again?"

Everyone nodded. When the two of them were half way across the room, Mick stood up saying "I think I'll just go and point Percy at the porcelain."

"Michael Hegerty, do you have to be so crude. There are ladies present" reproved his mother in law.

"Sorry Flo." He said with a smile and walked away.

But his apology failed to appease her. Turning to her daughter she said "Really Annabelle that man of yours is completely lacking in manners. I thought when you married a lecturer there might be a bit more decorum in our family. Your father is always rude as that when he's had a drop too much."

"Give over mother" her daughter replied, "You should know by now Mick only does it to get you going. Stop acting like Lady Muck."

"Good for you" thought Mary Jepson. Florence had been a friend from Primary schooldays but ever since she had first discovered the word "pretentious" she had thought it was specially minted for Florry. She had got worse as she got older. When her daughter was born she wouldn't let anyone shorten her name to Ann or Anna. The times the girl had blushed as she'd heard Flo say, "My daughter was christened Annabelle and I'd appreciate it if you would respect that" in a la de da voice. Mary thought shorting names was friendly. She had nearly always had called her girl "Dee." Mick Hegerty had been one of Annabelle's tutors at her Teachers

Training College. She had often told her mum. "He makes us laugh; but he don't half know a lot. And he doesn't mind explaining things over and over again if some of us don't get it first time." Florrie had been over the moon when her daughter had married a lecturer from the Teachers Training College but Mick's earthiness had sadly disillusioned her.

Mary glanced over at the bar before she said "Derek's still very uptight about Desiree. You know he loved her like she was his own but …and I'm telling you this in confidence, things weren't too good between the pair of them. They had the most awful row the night before she died. He'd even yelled at her that he wanted her out of the house. Those were the last words he ever said to her for she stormed out of the room slamming all the doors behind her. He didn't see her at breakfast next morning so he never spoke to her again. He can't get over that. It's eating away at him." She didn't say any more for out of the corner of her eye she saw the two men making their way towards them with trays of drinks.

"Got you some crisps and nuts as well" said Derek as they sat down.

"Got any plans for the Bank Holiday Derek" asked John when they were settled.

"The only plans I've got is to make those animal rights nutcases suffer. I'll waste one or more of them before I go to my grave I'll tell you."

Everyone was shocked into silence except Mary. "Oh Yes" she said angrily "That'll be the day won't it. And when that happens, who do you think will be the first person the police will be round to see? Don't talk such rubbish."

CHAPTER 11

Two Thursday evenings after his visit to Miranda's Stephen was parking his BMW in a nearby road. He had gone to where the choir rehearsed and had checked that her 2CV was sitting outside the hall. He prided himself on never taking anything for granted.

He was dressed in his jogging gear with dark grey running shoes and a woollen hat he could pull down to hide most of his face if necessary.. When he reached her house there were no lights showing in any of the rooms. "Must be a bit of a tightwad not even to leave a hall light on" was his first thought but then he remembered all the "reducing your carbon footprint" stuff he'd been reading in The Guardian. When he shone his little torch on the kitchen window he was thrilled to see it was still unlatched. The window was stiff, it took several hefty pushes to move it but eventually he managed it.

Once in the house he decided to work his way down from the top. He started with the back bedroom furthest along the corridor. He went to the window and even though the houses opposite were lit up downstairs he decided to draw the curtains and turn on the light. The trees in the long back gardens prevented anything being clearly seen from either house. The room was sparsely furnished with only a single iron bed but there were several expensive looking pieces of furniture. He removed every drawer again working from the top down. That was something he'd learned from all his reading of crime novels. He found nothing of value and there was nothing under the mattress either. He made sure he'd turned off the light as he left.

The next bedroom must have been the father's; the wardrobe was full of men's suits but their pockets were empty. Even the leather wallet in one of them was empty. He suddenly wanted to pee and decided to risk using the toilet in the en-suit bathroom. The toilet flushed reassuringly quietly. While he was there he had a look in the medicine cabinet, it was full of all kinds of tablets and plasters but there were no rolls of notes to be seen. He came out and began his search of the furniture. Again none of the drawers yielded anything of value but in a small desk among an assortment of fountain pens and pencils he found a silver pocket watch. It felt heavy enough for it to be very valuable but he decided to leave it; rolls of cash that wouldn't be missed were what he was after tonight.

For the same reason he left all the jewellery untouched when he searched her bedroom. For someone who said she lived simply there were a surprising number of silver and gold necklaces and bangles. But when he examined some of them closely he decided they were so old fashioned they must be her mother's or better still her grandmother's. The older the jewellery the more valuable it was. Stood to reason didn't it?

Once he got his feet under the table he could get such items valued so that he'd know what was worth taking. He lifted the edges of the carpets to see if anything was hidden underneath. But it was a fruitless and disappointing task. None of her underwear was in any way exotic or sexy so he couldn't even get a thrill from handling it. He was alarmed when he noticed that he had already been searching for three quarters of an hour.

When he open the door of the last bedroom he almost closed it immediately again. It wasn't a bedroom, it was a laboratory. When he looked closely he saw many of the phials had various coloured liquids in them with numbered labels attached. The metal drawers and sink made the room feel sterile and uninviting. He decided it wasn't worth the risk of searching.

Downstairs he switched on the light in the room where he'd sat with Miranda. He searched it thoroughly, again turning up corners of the carpets and looking behind the pictures and down the back of the settee but found nothing. He left the light on and went into the kitchen. Lots of his women had hidden their cash and jewels there. He went first to the fridge and looked in every container. Nothing! There was nothing in any of the canisters on the kitchen shelves and the drawers had only cutlery in them. The pots and pans proved equally empty and the cupboard under the sink contained only cleaning materials.

Despairingly, he leaned back against the sink and looked around. The glass doors at the end lead to a conservatory. There was a key in the lock. When he opened it he was immediately aware of the heat. He had to fumble about for a while before he found the light switch and when he did the lights were so blindingly bright he almost switched them off again. When his eyes adjusted to the brightness he saw that three sides of the room there were shelves of plants that he guessed were orchids but on the fourth side were three extra large glass tanks. When he looked in them they were full of tropical vegetation. He didn't go too near in case they contained snakes; he was afraid of snakes. They gave him the willies. He looked at the tanks but didn't see any snakes. There were a few small brightly coloured frogs that he first thought were there as food for the snakes but when no snakes appeared he concluded the frogs must be pets. Frogs! Bloody stupid things to keep as pets! He remembered reading somewhere that the more colourful the frog the more poisonous it was. Nobody would be so stupid to keep cash in their tanks would they? Nevertheless he studied each tank carefully but there were no boxes or envelopes visible in any of them. What if some money was buried is the soil of the orchid pots. He could poke around with one of the bamboos holding up the orchids. Naw. What if one of the frogs jumped out! His watch showed it was almost ten o'clock. It was too risky to bother with the orchid pots now.

It was as he came out of the conservatory that he saw the red box file on a top shelf in the kitchen. He hurried over took it down. He lifted the lid and there right on top was the, £500. He searched through the rest of the file being careful not to disturb the sequence of the papers but there was no more cash. He put the money in his jacket and looked around the room to see if there were any other places where another bundle might be hidden. Failing to think of any he switched off the lights, came out of the kitchen, closed the window he had come in by and left by the front door.

CHAPTER 12

Two weeks later it was Stephen's time to visit the town again. He'd decided it would look too suspicious if he didn't go to the Charity shop as usual. He paused at the door to compose himself and walked confidently in. She was serving a youth so ill dressed he had to be a student. His left ear and both eyebrows were pierced with an array of silver rings which with his pale wispy beard made him look even more repulsive in Stephen's eyes.

While she was handing this creature his purchase she looked up at Stephen and smiled at him. He congratulated himself on his acumen in coming here today. He must be in the clear. Her total lack of suspicion was proof he would that he would do well out of her. He was just going over to her when three women entered the shop. One of them seemed to know Miranda well for she immediately went up and started to talk to her. Even when one of the other woman came over to pay for some trinket she'd picked up the first woman merely stood aside and immediately resumed their conversation when the transaction was finished. He was going through the titles of the books for the fourth time when he sensed her behind him.

"Hallo Stephen. Nice to see you again."

As he turned to answer her he saw that the woman was still at the counter.

"And you Miranda, would you like to go to The Baker's Arms again?"

"I would but it would only be for a quick drink. I'm afraid I can't stop for a meal I've got another appointment tonight."

Although he was disappointed to hear that he decided to concentrate on the positive and arranged to meet her as he had done previously. She evidently knew nothing about missing £500. He left the shop with visions of the wonderful future he would have with her.

When he came back he had to wait while she locked up. He felt good when she took his arm as they walked to the pub. They got their usual pints and at her urging he ordered the five bean stew again. She said she'd be eating later with the friends. He was glad it was "friends" rather than "a friend." When they'd settled themselves at a corner table she took a good drink of beer before she said, "By the way, you know I plan to sell the house and go back to the Amazon. Well, it seems as if I won't be able to do that as quickly as I hoped. Something has come up that will keep me here for a while."

He didn't answer or ask her anything, he was too eager to hear what she had to say. "Well, the thing is Stephen it seems silly for me to be living in that big house all by myself. There are three bedrooms going to waste and I am thinking I might as well rent them out. There are already washbasins in two of them and I could put in a small cooker as well although people would be able to use the kitchen and the cooker there when they wanted. Do you think that's a good idea?"

His certainly did. It was just the chance he wanted. He'd been travelling light for years. He bitterly regretted not investing in property when he had the money. Once he'd got over £20,000 out of a silly woman called Sally. What a gullible fool she'd been. Practically asking to be robbed she was. He'd blown the money on a world cruise hoping to pick up a wealthy heiress on board. But Esterbelle the American woman he'd set his sights on turned out to be a bigger crook than he was. He was still haunted by her mocking laughter when everything had unravelled. He's sworn some other woman would pay for his humiliation.

In the house he would be in a better position to influence her. It would be better if there was only the two of them; it might be a while before she found other tenants. In the meantime he'd be able to search the house more thoroughly when she was out. He'd soon have her eating out of his hand. No woman had ever been able to resist his charms for long.

As he put his glass down he said," You know Miranda, You must be psychic. All this last month I've been looking for somewhere else to live. I foolishly sold my flat when I took a job in the States four years ago that didn't work out and I've been staying in hotels and flats since I came back. A bed sitter would suit me fine."

"Really? That sounds good to me. But I should warn you it would only be for a year or maybe two at the most. I am determined to get back to the Amazon by then at the latest.

He was desperately searching for a convincing reason why he should move on such a temporary basis when he suddenly remembered something he'd read in The Guardian this morning. Some woman had won a big literary prize with her first novel. She'd only just completed a "Creative Writing Course" at the University of East Anglia.

He looked down at the table and said hesitantly "Well the thing is Miranda. I've told you about my ambition to be a writer, haven't I?" Now I know I've not really had any success so far but I can't give the idea up. Something just compels me to keep on trying."

When he stopped to take another sip of his drink he saw she was looking at him sympathetically.

He looked down at the table top again before continuing "The thing is, I've been thinking for some time of going back to University to do a "Creative Writing" course. I've heard very good reports about the course they run at East Anglia. Anyway, the thing is, these courses cost a lot of money. So I want to save as much as I can. I'm paying over £350 a week where I am. If I found somewhere cheaper I would help me considerably to accumulate the money I need quickly. And if you're only going to let these rooms for a short while before you return to the good work you do in the Amazon, it would seem a good deal for us both."

Her eyes were shining when he looked up at her.

"That's wonderful Stephen. I think you're right to follow your dreams and I'd be glad to help. I was thinking of charging about £80 a week for the rooms. That would be for everything. No extras for heating or lighting. Would that be fair?"

"I certainly think so. I'd soon be able to save my uni. fees at that rate."

"Well, you'd be more than welcome. You could have one of the big bedrooms. It's got an on-suite bathroom. You could have as many showers as you want."

He was just going to say he referred baths but remembered in time that she would think showering would be helping the planet much more than taking a bath. What a load of cobblers it all was. The thought emboldened him to add "Of course, I've been taking showers for long time now but I must admit I do have the occasional long soak in the bath."

"I know what you mean; I too have the occasional wallow with lots of scented candles around. But I do feel guilty afterwards."

He decided to take a risk and said laughingly said "It would be more environmentally friendly to share such a bath, would it not?"

"It would, as long as you could get someone to want to join you."

"Do you think there is any possibility of that?"

"You never know your luck Stephen. You'd just have to wait and see."

Many of the other women he had known would have said that coyly but she spoke frankly and openly. She certainly wasn't a tease, he was sure of that.

"I'm a patient man, Miranda, very patient" he lied.

"So you will think about it? You don't have to decide straight away."

"No I accept. I'll have to give a full months notice where I am. You don't mind having to wait that long, do you? I'll pay a month in advance if you like."

"No, I wouldn't think of it."

He got out his diary "Let me see, its Tuesday now. If I give notice from this Friday it would be the 22nd. I could move in four Saturdays from then."

"That would be fine. Let's drink to that." They touched glasses and laughed like guilty children as his meal arrived...

"Now I've really got to dash Stephen. Here's my phone number, you can either phone or call in the shop to let me know when you're coming. I'm there full time now so you can easily get in touch"

"It's a deal then."

He held out his hand to her and she took it readily. As she picked up her empty glass she said "Tell you what, the night you come, I'll cook you a meal to celebrate. That won't be the case every night but I see no reason why we shouldn't occasionally eat together. Now I've really got to go."

He rose with her and kissed her lightly on the cheek. He was thrilled when she did not pull away.

As he ate he began to plan his campaign to get his hands on her money and her body. He'd have to have all his financial proposals well prepared and convincing. She wouldn't be easy to fool. He'd have to sell her a couple of genuine investments first before he moved in with his own "goldmines" If he played his cards right he might be able to talk her out of this nonsense of going back to the jungle. This was going to be a long campaign and he'd have to proceed with the utmost caution.

But first he had to get out of his rented flat. But why leave it? He could sublet it; there was a big demand for flats where he lived because so many East European immigrants had arrived in the area. His lease forbade subletting but to hell with that. He'd get away with it as long as he could. If he charged at least £100 more than he was paying now it would build up a nice little nest egg for him to fall back on if things didn't work out with Miranda. Immigrants could easily afford that because they would crowd some of their mates in with them. Everybody knew that was what they did.

He advertised the flat next day and had several enquiries straight away. By the end of the week he had arranged to let the flat let for £120 more than he was paying and he got a £200 deposit. He'd make sure they never got that back. .Everything about this move seemed to be going right for him. He'd have liked to move in with her straightaway but he didn't want to appear too eager. He was sure he had her trust. He had a good feeling about how this was going to work out.

CHAPTER 13

"Siggy, any chance you'll be shunted off onto one of these Public Awareness courses the police are so keen on at the moment on a Thursday night?"

"What's she up to now?" DS Bullerton wondered. They were lying side by side in bed after a bout of extended lovemaking. They hadn't switched the light off; he was wondering if it would be wise to pick up the Joyce Carol Oats novel from his bedside table.

"Why do you ask? It's Tuesday now. Getting tired of me are you? Looking for another stud to satisfy your insatiable sexual appetite?"

She hit him across the chest with the back of her hand. "I should be so lucky." Then she added," You know Hester that blonde paramedic?"

"The one with the sexy voice and a peach of a bottom plus a 38 inch bust? No, I can't say I've ever noticed her."

She laughed as she hit him again.

"Anyway, what about her?"

"Well, I was talking to her for quite a while lunch time and we got around to discussing choral music. The Calderford Chorale is putting on a Christmas performance of Elijah and they had a piece in the Gazette asking for new singers. It turns out Hester already sings for them. She's says it's good fun and she's asked me if I'd join?"

"What? You want to join the Cowgirls?"

"The Cowgirls? How rude! What on earth do you call them that for?"

"They're in a corral, aren't they? And a lot of them are from the farms, milk a lot of cows they do."

"Rubbish."

"All the men in my family have always called them "The Cowgirls." Aunties Sarah and Margarita are members. I think Grandma Bullerton was one of their founder members. She now a patron or something; gets a free seat at all their concerts."

"Jeezus, Siggy. Is there nowhere in this bloody county that the tentacles of your family don't reach? You're worse than the Mafia. "

"That's what D.I. Morison says. Still, all these connections have come in useful more than once. Want me to have a word with my aunts. See how big a bribe you've have to slip them to ignore your voice and let you sing on compassionate grounds."

"Listen Mr. Clarence Siegfried Bullerton, I'll have you know all the years I was at University I was a member of a Choir. And it was a bloody good one, full of choral scholars and suchlike. We twice sang in the Albert Hall. Anyway, the paper said you don't have to audition and Hester says that's right."

Siggy smiled to himself. Secretly he thought Helene had a deep sexy voice.

"Well, you could give it a go. I think they're short of baritones."

He received a sharp dig in the ribs for that. "Alto. I'm an alto, a bloody good one even if I say so myself."

He turned and squeezed her left breast as he sang in his best Willard White baritone "Honk! Honk!"

"Ha, ha. Want me to squeeze your balls to see how high a note you can reach."

"You dare. But, joking apart, I think you'd do well with the Cowgirls. I quite like your voice. "

"Thank you, kind sir. But please don't keep calling them Cowgirls. If I join I'm sure to remember you saying it at some totally inappropriate moment and they'll chuck me out for laughing."

"They wouldn't, not after they'd heard you sing. You could be on the threshold of an entirely new career."

"Keep talking like that and I'll sing you to sleep."

"Don't threaten me when I'm being so nice. I've got a busy day tomorrow. But you know it's funny you should mention aunties' choir. They put on Bach's St. Matthew Passion a while back. I was thinking about going but something came up."

"When does it not in our work! It's most inconsiderate of villains not keeping office hours isn't it?"

"I suppose that's one of the things that make them villains."

CHAPTER 14

He arrived with his belongings just over four weeks after she'd invited him to stay. When she opened the door to him on that Saturday evening he'd never seen her looking more beautiful. Her jet black hair was swept down and back, caressing her bare shoulders and her low cut dress revealed more of her cleavage than he'd ever seen before. He intended to kiss her only on the cheek but she moved her head so that their lips met. She didn't pull away. Everything about her offered promise of a sexually exciting night ahead.

He'd spent £20 on what the wine merchant assured him was a bargain Merlot and after he'd put his suitcases in his room he brought it down.

"What a lovely wine. I'm afraid I've already put out Beaujolais to breath. Do you mind if we have that first?"

"No not at all" he replied, his mind flooding with images of what they could get up to after two good bottles of wine.

The vegetarian curry she served up was as hot and spicy as any he had ever tasted. He was thankful that the large wine glasses enabled him to take copious draughts to alleviate the fire in his stomach. The thick dark chocolate cake she served as a sweet clung to his mouth and he drank eagerly from the strong black coffee that accompanied it. When the meal was over she led him to the large red settee in the lounge and just as she was going to sit down beside him she hesitated and said "Oh, there's something I want to show you. Excuse me a minute."

As soon as she left the room he took the opportunity to loosen the top button on his trousers he felt so full. After a few minutes he started to wonder why it was taking her so long but he felt so comfortable that he couldn't prevent himself lying back and relaxing. Suddenly a sharp pain at the back of his neck jerked him forward as a loudly meowing ginger shape flew past his right shoulder.

"Sisyphus, you wicked animal "said Miranda's voice from immediately behind him."I'm sorry if he's scratched you Stephen. It's my fault, he was creeping along the back of the settee and I grabbed for him. I think that was what made him lash out."

When Stephen reached behind his head he was surprised how little blood he could feel. It had felt like a deep scratch.

"Stay still Stephen while I get something to bathe this" Miranda said reassuringly. "I won't be a minute."

He tried to sit forward and reach the back of his neck with his hankie but his right arm and head felt ridiculously heavy. He was relieved when he heard Miranda hurrying back.

He expected her to start bathing his neck but instead she came around in front of him and levered him further back onto the settee.

"You'll be feeling a bit weak now Stephen but don't worry. You'll stay fully conscious for a while. You can go up to your room soon but I want you to see this first."

She crossed the room and opened the doors of what he'd assumed was a drinks cabinet to reveal a television screen. He tried to sit forward but failed. What was the matter with him? He could hardly keep his eyes open.

Even when the shock of what appeared on the screen registered with him he still had to fight to stay awake. It was a picture of a woman and a man and young girl and boy all in swimming costumes sitting under a green sunshade. He'd certainly seen it before. He was the man in the photo and the woman was Sally, whom he had loved and left what was it, four or five years ago? He had always taken great care to stay out of photographs but this had been sneakily taken by that little bastard Mark, Sally's eleven year old who'd just got a camera for his birthday and had set up the timer so as to get himself in the picture. He'd tried to turn away but the camera had caught him in full profile. There was no mistaking him.

"Recognize yourself Stephen?"

Fighting his drowsiness he mumbled "Er…it could be me…but …but I don't remember it being taken." He was trying hard to think of some plausible reason for being in that photo but his thoughts were all jumbled. How…how could Miranda have got hold of this? She couldn't possibly know about Sally, she'd lived over 100 miles away. Poor old Sally. Sad old Sally. Always living on her nerves. She hadn't been easy to live with. Still, he'd done well out of her, very well… well…; he didn't feel so well…what was wrong?

"Remember that woman?"

What was Miranda up to? This was none of her business. He tried to make his voice sound as plausible as possible but the words were coming unnaturally slowly.

"I …think…it might be…one of my clients. It…it…was one of her children's birthdays… a boy…yes. That was it. I was visiting …the boy had just got a camera…. wanted to take a photograph, yes… that was it. A photograph…just visiting…yes…nice family."

"They were until you robbed them out of over twenty thousand pounds. The woman, Sally, had a nervous breakdown after that. She's only just getting her life back together again now."

"Me? No. No...All nonsense. Who told you ....rubbish?"

"Gwen Frazer. Sally's mother. She sings in our choir. She recognized you at the concert."

He wanted to protest further but just now he felt he couldn't be bothered. He wanted to sleep…this was all a bad dream…he would…he…felt himself being roughly shaken. "Stay awake Stephen, there's something else for you to see."

The television flickered, a room appeared, so brightly lit it was difficult to make out details. There were shelves with pots on them and someone was…Christ … it was him … him in the conservatory….he watched in horror as he saw himself take the money from the red file…how…?"

"Don't think we need see any more of that Stephen. You take a good photo. "

He tried to protest but the words wouldn't come. Nothing mattered except sleep…lovely sleep.

He became aware of others in the room. He'd no idea who they were but he found he had no will to resist when they pulled him up and dragged him from the room.

CHAPTER 15

DS Bullerton had just started on his second slice of toast when the phone rang. He picked it up reluctantly. Bound to be bad news at this time of day. He was right; it was very bad news indeed. After he finished listening he asked "And he been positively identified?" He found himself repeating the answer "Wallet in pocket. No doubt at all."

He put the receiver down and met Helene's enquiring look. "One of the Steyn Protesters was killed last night. The man who drove that van into the factory grounds. Dale Overton. Hit and run."

"What makes them think it was a hit and run?"

"There are witnesses. Young couple having a snog in a shop doorway. Heard and saw it all. Jepson's been a bit quick off the mark, hasn't he?"

"You're sure it's Jepson. Might it not be just some drunken yob that's lost his licence?"

"Perhaps," he replied, but privately he didn't think so. In spite of all his police training about never prejudging a case, he had a bad feeling about this one.

"But, surely Jepson wouldn't be so stupid to do something like this so soon after everybody's heard him make those threats in court?"

"You wouldn't think so. But what if by some terrible coincidence he just happened to be driving along and suddenly sees Overton in his headlights and loses it?"

"That's stretching it a bit, don't you think? I'm not a great believer in coincidences. It could just as well be anybody as Jepson"

He shook his head. "Won't make any difference, that crowd outside the factory won't see it any other way than an attack on them. They'll need no convincing it was a deliberate act of revenge. They'll want to retaliate."

Helene knew he was right. "Better have some more breakfast then, God knows how long you'll be working on this today."

His inclination was to get down to the station immediately. But, he didn't want to argue with her. "I'll make another couple of slices of toast" he said rising from the table.

"And I'll put a couple of Jordan's bars in your pocket. No sneaking into Salim's for a Donner kebab when you eventually realise you're hungry. We're not breaking our diet no matter."

She'd gone on a diet immediately they returned from their Greek island holiday. He was one of those fortunate people whose metabolism enabled him to eat in abundance without any thickening of his waist or hips but in a moment of weakness he'd promised he'd join her in dieting. She was always so disconsolate when diets that started so successfully developed some fatal flaw that led to their abandonment. He didn't like to see his wife unhappy and he was giving her some moral support by sharing this latest diet with her. Encouragingly it seemed to have more stamina than previous ones. Now she was talking about "a whole change of lifestyle." The only good thing about it was far as he could see was that it insisted that breakfast was the most important meal of the day.

"I might get the P.M. "she mused; "Claude's been at some conference in Oxford. He's usually a bit delicate when he comes back from there." Helen's boss, Professor Claude Rettendon, was a great believe in keeping abreast of the latest developments in Forensic Pathology especially if it involved staying away from home for a night or two. Word was his wife being a devout Roman Catholic wouldn't give him a divorce. But, as Helene said "At least he lets me attend any of the one day conferences in London. Gives me a chance to do a bit of fashion shopping done."

She suddenly said "Of course, we're talking as if this is a deliberate killing. If Overton's alcohol levels turn out to be high it might be just an accident that's all his own fault."

"That would put a better complexion on things from our point of view. But then why didn't the car driver stop?"

"Could be a banned driver."

"Or somebody who is concerned about his standing in the community who knew he was well over the limit."

"Maybe he'll turn out to be a local solicitor."

"Naughty, Naughty, Siggy." She knew how much he hated solicitors, even though he had several cousins in the profession.

The phone rang again. He picked it up, listened to his superior's instructions and said nothing except "I'm on my way" as he put it down.

"I've got to interview Jepson" he told Helene. "They've already dropped off Union Jack outside his house." DC Jack Paislee, a six foot Ulsterman who, although he denied any family ties with his Reverend Northern Irish Phonetic Namesake made no secret of his admiration for the man and his Unionist views.

She smiled guiltily as she always did at the D Cs nickname. The woman's group she attended didn't approve of nicknames. They'd have expressed even more displeasure at her next remark when she said "Good job you drive a Volvo. There'll be plenty of room for you both in the front." She must have realised her "sizeist" mistake for she quickly added "Isn't Jepson back at work then?"

"Not as far as we know, I'd better be on my way."

He kissed her goodbye but as he went to leave she grabbed hold of his sleeve and led him into the kitchen where she took some wholemeal bars from a tin and stuffed them in his pocket. "I've put a couple extra in "she said "You know what…she paused… a good appetite Jack has."

"Good girl. Very tactful of you." he said with mock approval "I'll tell him you no longer think he's a vulture."

She waved a hand dismissively and said "You do and it's lettuce leaves for dinner" But she still came up and kissed him goodbye.

DC Jack Paislee was standing on the pavement right opposite Jepson's house. "Discreet surveillance is it Union?" Bullerton asked as he drew alongside."

"No Bully, just the opposite" the big Ulsterman replied "I was ordered to let him know I was watching. They want to rattle him I suppose."

"Give him time to think up an alibi more like" Bullerton thought.

Together they walked up the narrow concrete path to Jepson's door. Before they reached it, Mary, his wife opened it. She was wearing a light fawn overcoat and had her handbag with her.

"If it's Derek you want you've too late. He's gone to work."

Bullerton nodded and said "Pity that. Still, it must be a relief to you that he feels well enough to resume working. How long has he been back?"

"Today's the first" she responded," But what do you want? I've got to get going myself."

"We won't keep you then" he replied, "It's Derek we wanted a word with."

"What about?"

Bullerton decided not to tell her about Overton's death. "Just some general enquiries we're making. Was he with you all yesterday evening?"

"Yes, he was. Why? What's happened?"

"I'm sorry I can't tell you any more at the moment. Derek will no doubt tell you all about it when you see him."

She hesitated, then stepped purposefully forward saying "Have it your own way. ". Bullerton moved aside to let her pass but she turned left and went around the front of the house. Surmising she was going to the garage, he turned and said to Paislee," Get over to the far side of the drive. Have a good look at her car as she leaves. I'll check my side."

For a big man Paislee moved remarkably quickly. He was there and turning around to face the garage before Bullerton began ambling down to the gate. He hoped his relaxed pace would make Mary drive slowly so he could get a good look at her car. Suddenly he was aware of a big smile lightening Union Jack's melancholy face. He looked behind just in time to avoid being run over by Mary on a shocking pink mountain bike.

"Leave the gate open" she commanded as she passed, followed by a prolonged ringing of her cycle bell. He wasn't sure what message she intended to convey. .

CHAPTER 16

When Stephen awoke he found he was stretched out on a bed. His breathing was laboured. He was without energy and everything was happening very slowly. His head ached and his tongue seemed too big for his mouth. Eventually he realise he was under a duvet and naked except for his boxer shorts.

What the Hell was going on? Miranda, the bitch, had trapped him. What was she up to? She must be mad. She couldn't keep him like this for long. Maybe...maybe... the thought excited him...Maybe ... she was some sort of sexual pervert. She'd been wearing that low cut dress hadn't she? Perhaps, they'd... No. No. He'd never forget a thing like that. No way did he feel like he usually did the morning after a good nights screwing. If she wanted it rough by Christ rough was what she would get.

He must have fallen asleep again for he was conscious of awaking as he heard the room door open. The sudden glare from the light being switched on hurt his eyes "Good afternoon enjoyed your beauty sleep, have you?"

It took him a while to remember where he'd seen the speaker before; those silver rings and wispy light blonde beard …it was the student in the charity shop. "Time to sit up" he said.

The student lifted Steve's arm up high; when he let go it flopped limply back down on the bed. Steve ignored him and tried to sit up but found he hadn't the strength to do so. Christ that wine must have been strong. The beringed student said kindly "You won't be able to walk yet"

Stephen nodded; he would humour him.

"Steve"

He looked up expectantly.

"Steve we've some important things to tell you. Can you hear me?"

Stephen nodded and smiled.

"O.K. You're going to be spending some time in here so there are some things you have to understand. Most of the time you're going to feel rather weak but it will pass. But if you try anything silly when you think you're stronger we can easily make you a weakling again."

Before he could answer the student said "I've brought you some water. Don't think you'll be able to keep any solid food down for a while yet but do drink; best you don't get dehydrated." Stephen looked at the litre bottle on his bedside table. No label. Probably just tap water, He drank only the best bottled water.

Stephen felt the anger rising within him. Who the Hell did these wankers think they were? He'd had enough of this crap. He'd always taken good care of himself. Lifted weights twice a week at the gym. He'd cripple this wimpy student with a good kick in the balls. He forced himself up.

"Fuck you. I've had enough of this nonsense."

He lunged forward, intent on giving himself enough room to deliver a good kick.

To his surprise he crumpled forward on to his knees, his legs felt as if they were made of elastic. He hadn't time to turn his head aside before hitting the floor. A sharp pain shot through his forehead as it banged on the wood.

"Over thirty hours and it's still affecting you, that's good" the student said.

The student lifted him up with surprising ease and laid him down on the bed.

"Best to rest, Stevie boy."

He heard footsteps moving away from him. Then, a far away voice said "There's an en-suit bathroom in the corner. If you get desperate and feel you can't hold on, crawl over to it."

As soon as he heard the door close he levered himself up again. The effort made him sweat. Why was he so weak? What had they done to him? Even as he asked himself the question he knew the answer. A drug. Some sort of knock out pill .Like that stuff he'd put in that busty bird's drink at The Trocadero bar some years ago. He couldn't think of her name…Didn't matter…it had bloody well worked…she been putty in his hands… But the sex had been bloody useless. That's what he was now…putty. Limp as a piece of string. It was….out of nowhere came more memories of that woman in The Trocadero. "Joe" she'd called herself, said it was short for Joelene. Great body but…no response. He could do what he liked with her but she'd been a zombie…living dead. Christ …was that what was in store for him? What were they going to do to him? What? "O my God, O my God" he found himself mumbling…Neither the student not Amanda had covered their faces. They didn't care that he had seen them. That meant only one thing. They were never going to let him leave here alive.

He lay back on the bed and curled him up into a ball the way he'd always done when he was in trouble. Memories of one of his mother's "Fellas" coming into his bedroom and beating him with a leather belt because he'd stolen some money from her purse came into his mind. Christ, he'd take a beating like that any day instead of what was going to happen to him here.

He tried to make himself not think about his predicament. Curl up nice and tight, sleep, if only he could sleep but his stomach was churning so much. He had to have a piss. He'd never get to sleep if he messed up the bed. Gingerly he uncurled himself and got both feet down on the floor. Somehow he slid down onto his hands and knees. His neck and throat felt unnaturally tight and his chest heavy. He wanted to take another drink but he had to get to the bathroom first. He inched painfully on his bottom across the room to the bathroom and after several attempts managed to pull himself up onto the toilet. He only just made it. He sat there until the cold made him move.

He was able to stand upright by holding on to the washbasin but when he bent over to pull up his boxer shorts he fell forward. This time he was able to break his fall by holding unto the washbasin. He didn't try to stand again but shuffled on his bare bottom like a baby across the room to his bed. On the way back he recognized the big wardrobe, he must be in her father's room. But it had been moved to a side wall. He thought there had been a little window there. What was that in the corner, a treadmill? There was some other sort of machine there as well. They hadn't been in the room last time. What the hell were they doing here now? The curtains were drawn across the three bays of the main window but they didn't fully meet. A ray of sunshine shone between them. He looked at his fake Rolex, ten minutes to four. Whatever they'd given him must be hellish powerful. That bird Jolene had been wide awake and yelling her head off before six o'clock the next morning. It had taken all his powers of persuasion and £50 for her taxi to calm her down.

Once he had hauled himself back into bed and pulled the duvet tightly around him he intended to concentrate on planning how he could escape but in a few minutes he was unconscious again.

CHAPTER17

Peter Steyn picked up the internal phone wondering what cock up was happening now.

"Mr. Jepson would like to see you Sir"

"Send him in Sam" Jepson had been away a fortnight, perhaps he wanted to get back to work. It would be good for everyone's morale if they saw him back at his job. These protesters were a bloody nuisance. The sooner the government did something serious about them the better. He got up from his desk and came around it to shake Jepson's hand as he entered the room.

"Good to see you Jepson. How are you?"

"I've surviving Sir. I've brought you this." He handed Peter a white envelope. It wasn't sealed. Before he could open it, Jepson said "It's my resignation."

"Your resignation? What on earth for?"

"If you open it you'll see why sir."

Peter took out the three sheets of paper inside. The top one was Jepson's typed resignation which he only glanced at before putting it underneath the other two. They were a neatly typed list of firms who supplied materials and services to his firm. Beside each entry were details of each when each delivery was expected and to where it was to be taken in the firm.

"I don't know why you've brought me this list Jepson but as far as your resignation is concerned I have no intention of accepting it unless you re intending to move away from Candleford and before you say anything if that is the case I hope you'll forgive me if I say I don't think that would be a advisable."

Jepson shook his head, "No, it's nothing like that Sir. It's the list her mother found it in Desiree's bedroom when she was tidying it up. She had no business with that list sir. It a copy of the one I kept in my briefcase. Desiree must have somehow got hold of it even though I've got combination locks on the case."

Peter immediately saw what Jepson had concluded. "So because your daughter had this list you're blaming yourself for the vanload of protesters being able to get into our premises."

"Stands to reason, doesn't it sir. It's entirely my fault. I should never have taken stuff like that home."

"Perhaps not, but your daughter, Desiree, did you know she was one of this protest... group (he had to stop himself saying "mob).

"Not really sir. We did argue it's true about what she thought went on here but I'm sure she was never among those ones screaming outside. All my men know all about me and my family, one of them was bound to have recognized her if she'd been there. I just thought it was a young girl's love of furry animals. You know how sentimental they are at that age."

"Indeed. Perfectly natural assumption. My oldest girl's much the same. I don't see how you can hold yourself to blame."

"But it must be my fault sir. I was employed to keep this firm secure. Yet it was through my carelessness that they got in. There's no getting away from that. As the Yanks say, 'the buck stops here.'"

"True but I think in this case you're taking too much of the blame on yourself. You've been with us, since we came here six years ago and this is the only breach of our security that's happened in all that time, isn't it?"

"Yes…but it couldn't be much more serious."

Peter went back around his desk and sat down gesturing for Jepson to do sit in opposite him. "Listen Jepson, what I'm telling you now I'd appreciate it if you told no one else, not even your wife if you can avoid it. Seventeen years ago I lost my wife and three year old son in a car crash. My wife was a mad driver. She was a scientist like me, with a brilliant mind but she was a thrill seeker, always after an adrenaline rush. As soon as she saw a long straight road ahead she would try to push the acceleration through the floor. The police said a tyre must have burst when she slewed off the road and smashed into some rocks. They reckoned they would have been killed instantly. The wreckage was all over the place. This was in South Africa. But…"he paused "but that's all in the past. The reason I'm telling you this Jepson is that if you are thinking of moving away because of your daughter's death, I can tell you from my own experience it doesn't work. Distance doesn't lessen the pain. I came here less than a year after the accident but it still stayed in my mind just as much as if I'd never left Natal. It's a cliché when they call Time the Great Healer but it's the only thing that's helped me. You need time, lots of it. Now I'm happily remarried with as you know three healthy kids."

Jepson waited for him to continue but when Steyn remained silent he said "Very sorry to hear about that sir. It must have been terrible for you. I'll not say anything to anybody. But we're not thinking of moving. I just that I feel let you down and that's that."

Steyn remained silent. Eventually he said, "Look here Jepson, obviously I can't make you stay if you are determined to leave but I wish you'd give it a bit more thought. What does your wife think?"

Jepson looked down at the floor "She doesn't know…yet"

"Well, man don't you think it might be wise to talk to her before you finally decide what you're doing. Shall we just forget about his letter in the meantime?"

"It's good of you sir but I don't know" Jepson replied hesitantly "I've was always told the greater the authority the greater the responsibility, that's what my old brigadier used to say every time he gave me another stripe."

"An admirable sentiment, wish to hell some of our present political masters believed that. But in your own case it wasn't an act of negligence that got these protesters into our premises. You're assuming your daughter must have worked out the combination of the locks on your briefcase."

"She didn't have to sir. It was her birthday. That's why I know it's all my fault."

"Well, I still think it would be a pity if you left us. Bit of a victory for the protestors don't you think? You've kept us secure for a long time until this happened. The thing is, not only are you a local man, you're well respected by all the staff here. I've never had any reports of any of them slacking or moaning they've been unfairly treated during all the time you've been in charge."

"I've always made sure of that sir."

"Indeed you have. Also I know you often come back here when you're supposed to be off duty. You do a very good job Jepson and I would take it as a personal favour if you would reconsider."

Jepson didn't immediately reply but stood up before he said "When you put it like that I'd be stupid not to give it some more thought. I'll talk to the wife first, like you said sir, if that's all right with you?"

Steyn waved the papers in front of him "Good man. We'll bin these eh?"

Jepson shook his head "Shred them or better still burn them sir. We don't want the suppliers' names getting into any more wrong hands."

Steyn smiled to himself, he knew he'd been right trying to get Jepson to stay. As the song said "A Good Man is Hard to Find." He was just rising to say goodbye to the man when his internal phone rang.

Reluctantly he picked it up, "Yes Sam."

"There's two policemen here sir. They want to speak to Mr. Jepson."

"Did they say what about?"

"No just that they want to see him."

"How do they know he's here?"

"I think reception must have told them."

"Right, just stall them for a minute or two."

Resting the receiver on his desk he turned to Jepson and said, "Apparently there's a couple of police here who want to talk to you. Any idea what it's about?"

"Haven't a clue sir."

"Do you want to see them?"

"I suppose I'd better."

Picking up the receiver he told his PA, "Right Sam. Let them in."

They entered without bothering to knock. Both physically impressive men, each well over six feet. He recognized the fair haired one immediately as one of the county Bullertons. It wasn't possible to do business in this county without meeting one of them. He also knew this one from the rugby club. Very fit for his age. The more lugubrious one he'd never seen before.

After Bullerton had introduced himself and DC Paislee he asked "We'd like to have a word in private with Mr. Jepson, if you don't mind sir."

Steyn decided not to offer them the use of his office. Whatever they wanted he'd reckoned that the more time he gave Jepson to collect his thoughts the better

"That's all right. Mr. Jepson is just leaving. I'm afraid I've got some urgent calls to make. Mr. Jepson would you like to take these gentlemen to your office? It'll be more private that the reception area outside."

Jepson nodded his assent and lead the duo out to the lifts. When they reached the ground floor, Bullerton said, "There's no need for us to go to your office Derek. It's just a brief inquiry."

"I'm not going to the office; I'm on my way home"

"We'll accompany you to your car then" said Paislee.

They had received all the details of Jepson's Vauxhall Astra from the police computer but had been unable to find it in any of the firm's car parks.

"So what's this all about then?" Jepson asked as soon as they were outside.

"Patience, Derek, patience," said Paislee.

He led them around past the smaller of the firm's car parks and on into a tall building with large double doors which Bullerton though were opening automatically until he saw the device in Jepson's hand.

Immediately inside were two large unmarked white vans parked alongside a loading platform. Bullerton assumed they were Steyn's attempts to keep their property as anonymous as possible. Jepson went up the steps onto the platform and along to the end where there was a dark blue Vauxhall Astra parked at right angles to the loading bay.

"I keep the car in here in case any of those nutters cut the fence and go ape in the car parks with a can of paint." Jepson explained.

When they reached the car Bullerton and Paislee walked along it on opposite sides.

"So you were at home all last night Derek?" asked Bullerton.

"Yes" Jepson replied "so where was the accident?"

"Who said anything about an accident?" asked Paislee.

"Don't treat me like a fucking fool" replied Jepson "It's obvious you're more interested in the car than me. Somebody knocked down were they?"

"Somebody killed" said Bullerton softly "Somebody you know. Dale Overton."

"The bastard who drove the van! What happened?"

"A hit and run."

"Oh well, that settles it then. I mean my motor's exactly what you're looking for, isn't it?"

"Nobody's making any accusations Derek" replied Bullerton, "examining you car can just as easily puts you in the clear."

"Well, bloody well examine it then, you won't find as much as a scratch on it. I keep my car same as I kept my uniform. Spotless."

"Then you've nothing to worry about have you?" said Paislee coming around the front of the Astra. Bullerton could see from his body language that there were no signs of any impact marks on the front of the car.

"You were at home all last evening? "asked Bullerton

"Yes and Mary will tell you the same if you ask her."

"You didn't just go for a little drive then Derek."

"No. I…" he paused "I did go for a Chinese. It's only a couple of streets away but it was pissing down wasn't it? I wasn't out more than ten minutes; we'd ordered what we fancied over the phone beforehand. You can check with Lee Yu, knows me well he does."

"We will" said Bullerton before adding "You didn't go out afterwards in a mate's car by any chance?"

"What a bloody stupid question. I've told you, except for that ten minutes I was at home all evening."

"And Mary was with you the entire time; she didn't go out?"

"Bloody hell, now you want to mark her down as a hit and run driver. You must be getting bloody desperate."

"No need to get upset Derek," Intervened Paislee, "After the threats you made at the Inquest, we'd be failing in our duty if we didn't interview you, don't you think?"

"What I think is that I've got better things to do than stay here talking to you. I'm saying no more. So unless you're going to arrest me, sod off."

He jumped down off the platform and got into the Astra. The detective thought he was going to drive off but instead he rolled down his driver's window and said "I don't think Mr.Steyn would appreciate you being in here all night. So shift your arses before I leave. The doors lock automatically and you've no chance of opening them." He put the car in gear and drove out through the large doors, stopping just outside

Paislee started to hurry after him but Bullerton checked him, "He won't lock us in, you heard what he said about Steyn. Take your time."

As they strolled to the door Jepson revved his engine and the doors began to close but Bullerton and Paislee kept to their leisurely pace. There was more engine revving from Jepson but the just before they reached the doors they stopped moving, leaving just enough of a gap for them to squeeze through sideways. As soon as they were out they closed behind them and Jepson drove off.

"He's not exactly leaving in a hurry, is he Sir" noted Paislee.

"And what does that tell us about him, Dr. Watson?" responded Bullerton.

Paislee took his time before replying, "He's no hothead that's for sure."

"Exactly, a man in control of his emotions"

"Bit of a change from when he was in court"

"True, but he's had time to do a lot of thinking since then. There's no way he would have used his own car to run Overton down, he's either got another vehicle somewhere or he got someone else to do it."

"You think it was that deliberate? It wasn't that he just suddenly saw Overton in his headlights and went for him?"

"No. I don't think so. It must have annoyed him that we took so long exiting that shed but he didn't lose his cool. This man thinks before he acts. When we investigate Overton's movements I think there's a good chance we'll find that he was knocked down on one of his regular jaunts."

"Then whoever killed him must have been stalking him for some time to find out his habits. We'll have to do some legwork around the crash scene to see if anyone saw anything suspicious. "

"You will indeed Jack, I'll see if the super will let you have some uniforms to help. I'll interview Overton's family to see if he mentioned anything to them about being followed."

"That'll be a bundle of laughs. How do you think we ought to frame our enquiries? Something like, "Excuse me, have you seen a car which may or may not be a Vauxhall Astra parked around here the last few Sunday nights?"

"That'll do as a starter for ten. "

CHAPTER 18

Dale Overton's funeral was a fitting climax to a life of protest. Every cause he had espoused was represented. There were Trade Union Banners recalling his days as a shop steward in the Ford Motor Assembly Plant at Dagenham, the inverted black crosses of CND. Amnesty International placards. At the head of the procession was the banner of FAAN with the crimson stream of blood flowing from a cage of imprisoned animals.

In keeping with his beliefs his family had chosen a Humanist service and a Woodland burial. His wickerwork coffin was decorated with wild flowers woven into it top and sides. It was carried into the large marquee by two of his sons and two men from FANN. The Humanist speaker after giving a brief resume of his life as an activist spent the rest of the service introducing friends from the many protest groups that he had worked for who all gave glowing tributes to his dedication and his organizational skills. Several speakers referred to his death as "needless "and "symptomatic of our sick society" but it was Tom Etterick a weather-beaten man from FAAN who received the biggest ovation when he declared that "The animal murderers who are, no doubt at this very moment rejoicing that they have rid themselves of one of the most persistent thorns in their flesh had better think again. For every Dale that they kill a hundred more will rise up in his place. We will remember him not only here today but in every blow we strike against these callous criminals. Let us continue his fight with renewed vigour and purpose until we achieve what would be his most fitting tribute of all, the total closure of the Steyn Chemicals torture factory." The service ended with entire congregation singing "The Ballad of Joe Hill with its memorable chorus of "I never died, said he."

His flower bedecked wicker coffin was led to its grave by a solitary piper. Afterwards in an orderly procession they marched back into Calderford on a route that took them past Steyn Chemicals where their chants were interspersed with prolonged booing and fist shaking at the building and at the long row of police who had been stationed there. But apart from this verbal abuse the marchers respected the words of the last speaker at the service, Dale's wife Constance who had concluded her moving tribute to him by saying "Let us honour Dale's memory today by our dignified behaviour. Let us not give the pigs any opportunity to disrupt or interfere with our march with the hackneyed excuse of 'maintaining public order.'"

These were the only police the marchers saw that day. The county's Chief Constable had ordered that none of the local force should attend the funeral. He knew there was no need for them to be there because he had been informed that the Special Branch members who had over the years infiltrated many of these protest movements would attend and that a detailed report with the names of all the speakers and what they said would be on his desk the following day. Dale Overton's activities had for many years been of interest to those in power.

Despite his budget restraints he gave orders for the police numbers to be increased outside the factory for the next three days. Even so the police were not able to prevent a dangerous escalation of the protestors' attacks. Some of them had got their hands on Paintball guns and the impact of their shots totally obscured the vision of the two car drivers they hit. Both crashed their cars, one just avoiding careering into the last group of protestors. Once the guns had been fired others crowded around the marksmen so that they were able to affect their escape without the police being able to grab them.

Next morning the police were there in greater numbers to push the protester away from the pavement to keep them further away from the Steyn workers during the last half mile of their journey on the dual carriageway. But it could not prevent similar paintball attacks on their cars as they left their homes or while they were on earlier parts of their journey The FANN protestors had long since identified where most of the Steyn staff lived and the routes by which they travelled to work. The tactic was only overcome when the company hired coaches to pick up their staff at assigned points within walking distance of their homes. The higher coaches meant that their windscreens could not be so easily obscured with paint

Meanwhile DS Bullerton's visit to Dale Overton's family proved fruitless. They refused to let him enter their house and he had to interview Dale's wife, Constance, the only member of the family who would talk to him on the doorstep. While she was grudgingly willing to concede that Jepson might be the one who had killed her husband; she was much more inclined to believe that "The hired thugs of the Establishment" had finally decided to silence Dale. "I hate all that you stand for Mr. Bullerton. You may think you are serving the interests of your so called justice system but really you are just a paid lackey duped into working for the interests of your capitalist masters. All Dale ever wanted was to make the world a better place for humans and animals." She said he was well used to being spied upon but had not said anything to her about any persons or vehicles shadowing him in the weeks preceding his death.

When he met Paislee back at the station he found that his deputy had been much more successful. On the only side road that gave a clear view of the spot where the "hit and run" occurred there was a Retirement Home and Jack had interviewed an 81 year old resident who spent most of his time looking out of the window of his upstairs flat. Daniel Freestock was an ex-motor mechanic who was still was interested in the cars that were on the road today. "Can tell them all, even the newest ones" he'd told Paislee while waving a copy of Motoring under his nose. He hadn't seen the "accident" as it was well past his bedtime when it happened but there had been a white Mark 2 Ford Cortina parked in the side road for "At least a couple of hours before yon fellow was killed. There had been a newer car, a Mercedes in the same spot the week before with two blokes in it. But there was only one in the Cortina the night of that hit and run. Not many Cortinas about nowadays. You can pick them up for a few hundred quid. Good engine. Roads used to be full of them. The hours I've spent under their bonnets. He hadn't seen the driver clearly but "he was wearing one of them baseball hats." The only thing he could tell about the registration was that the plate was "plenty dirty, but even if it had been spotlessly clean he couldn't have read it because as he said "I'm still good with shapes but I don't read numbers no good any more at that distance."

"Well done Union" Bullerton told him. "As the old boy says there's 'not many of them about nowadays', so if it's local it shouldn't be too hard to trace."

"We'll probably find it dumped and burnt out somewhere" was the response.

"Ever the optimist. I though now your namesake has adopted some of the IRA as his best mates, you'd have a much more cheerful outlook on Life."

"One miracle in my lifetime is enough for me, Sarge."

"So you don't think it was Jepson, then?"

"No, I'm not saying that. But he's seen enough of the world to know how to plan a crime. But he wouldn't be so stupid to use his own car to kill somebody but he might have thought a few hundred quid was well spent just to get his revenge, mightn't he?"

"True. True. If we do find the car burnt out, if the engine number's still readable we should be able to trace it from that. "

"You're thinking if we find the seller we might be able to find the buyer?"

"Or get a good description of him."

Paislee was detailed to fill out all the necessary forms for the County's Police Intelligence Unit requesting details of all Cortina Mk.2's locally and for a request to be sent to all the car scrap yards within a 50 mile radius to report on any recent dealings they had involving that model

CHAPTER 19

When Stephen awoke his chest still felt heavy and his neck tight. Breathing was still difficult. But his main feeling was one of hunger. He'd no idea when he'd last had something to eat. Looking around he saw a bottle on his bedside table. There was a card propped against it which said in heavy black print SAFE TO DRINK. He shook his head, what kind of fool did they take him for? With difficulty he turned his head away from it and began to think of how he could escape. He was getting out of here. He would get fully dressed and stay under the blankets, then jump whoever came into the room if they were on their own. They'd never know what hit them.

It was only when he tried to sit up in bed that both he and his scheme collapsed. It took him several attempts to pull himself upright; he hadn't the strength of a baby. What the Hell had they done to him? He stayed where he was for a while, telling himself he was gathering his strength for his assault on his captors but when he put his feet on the floor and went to stand he collapsed back on the bed. He lay there cursing and thinking of all the pain he would inflict on these animal loving bastards when he got his strength back. But when he'd exhausted all his planned vengeances he still wasn't able to sit upright.

He found he couldn't take his eyes off the bottle. It contained some sort of white liquid. Perhaps it wasn't poison. He began to think they must want him alive otherwise they could have killed him by now. He pulled himself over to it, but when he tried to pick it up, it was too heavy for him to lift.

The sudden realisation that he needed the toilet ended his attempts to get a drink from it. He'd try again when he got back from the loo. Once more he let himself slide to the floor and snake his way across the room on his hands and knees. This time his bladder emptied as he hauled himself up onto the toilet. As he kicked away his soaking pants he swore he'd make them pay for humiliating him like this. He stayed where he was until cold and cramp made him wriggle his way back leaving his wet pants where they were. Before he got into bed he pulled himself up alongside the bedside cabinet and grabbed hold of the bottle with both hands. Holding it tight in one hand and grabbing hold of the iron frame of the bedstead he inched himself up until he could throw he bottle on the bed and use both hands to get far enough up to collapse onto the mattress. He pulled the duvet over his legs and kept himself sitting up in bed by pressing his back against the headboard. The drink was within easy reach and very sweet when he tasted it. He dank it very slowly, alert for any more drug effects but nothing deleterious happened. When he finished he threw the bottle across the room to the door hoping whoever came into the room would step on it and at least twist their ankle. As he lay back he kept telling himself that while he wouldn't have the strength to escape today, the time must surely come when he would have enough strength to do so. The important thing would be never to let his captors know when he got his strength back. Until then he would, "play possum"? He'd always thought that was some sort of sex game until he'd picked up a copy of The Readers Digest in his dentist's waiting room that had an article on "American Idioms" He snuggled into his pillows and comforted himself with planning the vengeance that he would one day wreck on his captors. When he could no longer think of any more injuries and reprisals to inflict he decided not to think any more about the future. However pleasing it was to contemplate revenge there wasn't much chance of achieving any of it for a while.

He started to concentrate on his surroundings. They had changed this room a lot since his first visit. That bitch Miranda must have been planning this all along. But how had she sussed him? He certainly hadn't had to cover up any slips of the tongue with her. No, it was just sheer bad luck with that cow in the choir. Who'd have thought of Sally's mother living here? He couldn't ever remember her mentioning it. That was the trouble with women; they talked so much that you couldn't take in half of what they said.

That running machine in the corner; what the sodding Hell did they want that for? Surely they didn't want him to get stronger? And that other machine with all the wires sticking out. He was in serious shit. A sudden shaft of sunlight made him look at the bay window; he curtains weren't very thick, he could …

His thoughts were interrupted by the door opening. The tall skinny student came in on his own carrying a tray. He saw the bottle and kicked it aside.

"Morning Steve brought you some breakfast. Don't know how you like your coffee but there's sugar and milk separate if you want it." He leaned close and laid the tray across his knees. "There's porridge with raisins and molasses and another bottle of glucose. It's easier if you don't try to eat solids for a while." Without another word or even looking closely at him he turned abruptly and left the room taking the empty bottle with him. Steve was annoyed he hadn't been given a chance to ask even one of the many questions that were flooding his mind.

"Fuck you" was all he had time to call out before the door closed.

Steve looked down at the tray, it looked like baby food but by closing his eyes he got it all inside him. He slid the tray over unto the small table on his right and lay back thinking that he would conserve what little strength he had by sleeping. But his mind was too active to let him rest. When he thought over what had happened that first evening he realised that the drug must have been injected when Miranda had blamed Sisyphus for scratching him. How could he not have seen what a cunning conniving cow she was? Pretending to love a bunch of bare arsed banana eaters in the jungle and then doing this to him. But they couldn't keep him as weak as this forever. What purpose would it serve? What the Hell were they doing anyway? He'd nicked a few hundred quid of her dad's money but that wasn't sufficient reason to treat him like this. He wasn't rich and if she had any ideas of turning him into her sexual plaything she was certainly going the wrong way about it. He could hardly lift his little finger never mind anything else. It didn't make sense.

Unless, unless…Jeezus Christ No! No. If she knew about Sally, she might know about some of his other women. Was this her idea of revenge? Did she want to cut his balls off? Naw, that was preposterous. There were at least two blokes with her. They wouldn't let anything like that happened to another bloke, they wouldn't. But what?

An even more horrifying thought crossed his mind. Suppose he was left like this, growing weaker and weaker until all his bodily functions stopped working? Then they could leave him on some street or at the side of the road where when he was found people would think he'd collapsed from some disease. What if there was no cure for this drug or poison or whatever it was? Were she and her mates experimenting on him in the very same way that they objected to scientists experimenting on animals? That was ridiculous. They couldn't be such hypocrites, they just couldn't.

But what if it was a complete cock up and he died? What would they do then? He shook his head; he was being stupid. They couldn't let anything terrible happen to him. They'd be murderers. Murdering people was against their beliefs wasn't it? But, but, what was it she had said? "Not all who go into the jungle come out of it again." He remembered her face as she spoke. She looked as if she'd just had an orgasm. Jeeszus H. Christ! He could be the first British victim of a bunch of homicidal nutters.

He refused to let himself think any further. It was all getting too ridiculous. They were bound to let him go once they'd finished with him. Bound to. It stood to reason didn't it?

CHAPTER 20

When Helene Bullerton got home just after 7 o'clock there was a message on the answer phone saying that "Come Hell or High Water "her husband would be home by eight o'clock. She immediately called his mobile and suggested that they eat at their favourite Curry House. He would have to pass it on his way home and he was more than glad to accept her suggestion.

Nevertheless it was only by a self induced bout of deafness as he left the station that he escaped and got to The Star of Bengal only some six minutes after his wife. They had got into the habit of choosing certain dishes on certain nights and their "Tuesday Night Specials" were quickly brought to their table.

Helene had already ordered their drinks and as soon as he had settled himself and taken a good swallow of his Lager she asked "What's up?" They had long since broken their resolution not to "talk shop" after work.

"Something and nothing," he replied, "It may only be a coincidence but Janet Carroll was burgled last night" When he saw that the name did not immediately register with her he added "the woman who was on the roof alongside Desiree when she fell."

"You think it might be another revenge attack?"

"Could be, it's a strange affair. There's no sign of a break in yet much of her property has been vandalised. Yet, none of her jewellery was taken from her bedroom although she has what she claims are several very valuable pieces. It was all lying out on view on her dressing room table. As I've said, it's mainly that the place was trashed. It was more destruction than robbery. All the oil paintings of her rescue animals were slashed."

"Oil paintings?"

"By Frank Hastings. He's local and he's very good. Ma likes him. Those two foals gambolling in a field in our drawing room that you like are by him."

"O Yes. He's expensive isn't he? "

"I suppose so. He's an R.A. But I don't think Janet's short of a bob or two but it's the fact that the paintings are irreplaceable that's really upset her They're slashed beyond repair."

"How awful; such deliberate nastiness."

"Yes. There were lots of family photos in silver frames in the house but apart from a few being smashed most were left untouched and none of the silver frames were taken."

"Are you bringing in Jepson for questioning?"

"Not yet. If it's him he's sure to have fixed up an alibi. We're making a few discreet inquiries first. We haven't the manpower to watch him full time but as both these attacks took place on a Saturday, we're going to see if we can set up some sort of surveillance on him at weekends."

"The FAAN people must be getting very worried. Have you given them any warnings?"

"Not directly. They don't seem to have any central hierarchy. We did suggest to Janet Carroll that it might be a good idea if she spread the word around her group what had happened to her. But do you know what she said? Her actual words were 'I'll tell them of course. but if you spent less time protecting those animal torturers you'd have more time to protect the public from burglaries."

"Surely they'll be sensible enough to take precautions. These FAAN people may be weird, but they're not stupid"

. "Far from it. I'll try a have a word with Tom Etteridge, he's a decent bloke. Lectures in IT. He runs their website. Trouble is, both these events needn't be related. They may not even be revenge attacks at all."

"But you think they are?"

"Personally, I do. But whether they are or not the problem will be what my bosses decide. If we do nothing and there's another attack on a group member they'll be complaining that we're not protecting them because we're the side of the vivisectionists."

"Be a bit ironic wouldn't it? That lot protesting you're not protecting them when they cause you so much hassle."

"Indeed. Of course they'd argue that it's the Steyn people that they're hassling, not the police."

"So you shouldn't stop them persecuting the animal experimenters but you should protect them?"

"The righteous can do no wrong. That's what we have to live with."

"Has it ever been any different? "

"Not really. I suppose it's all so much out in the open now."

"So much for the Age of Reason. It's fashionable to be a fanatic, isn't it?"

"That's what many of them are but there's no chance of them seeing it like that. And as far as this FAAN lot are concerned, they've not killed anybody."

"Not yet, you mean. Look how close that walking train of kids came to being harmed."

"I wonder what would have happened if they had harmed those kids. They'd certainly have lost a lot of public sympathy."

"Instead they're the ones benefiting from that poor girl's death. They're really milking it. Have you seen those leaflets they're handing out in the Cornmarket? "

"We have. Matter of fact some kind souls have posted some of them to us just in case we missed them on the streets."

"Nice of them to think about you. Anyway, still having Lychees for a sweet?"

"You know me, Lychees it is."

"Stolid and unimaginative I would say. I think I might see if this Frank Hastings would do your portrait. He does paint donkeys doesn't he?"

"Hee Haw. Hee Haw."

At the same time as the above conversation was taking place, the same subject was being discussed at Miranda's

There were four of the original five there because professor Thompson had come along He had returned not because he had changed his mind but because he was the first one that Janet Carroll had approached.

"Janet's convinced that we're all being targeted because of Desiree" he was telling them.

"Do you mean all of us who are members of FAAN or just those of us who were on the roof that day?" asked Tristan.

"I'm not certain but I think it would be prudent to assume that every member is in danger" he replied.

"I agree" said Alice "We must all be on the lookout."

Miranda agreed even though she didn't think she was in any danger. What had happened to Dale and Janet had made her all the more convinced that what she was doing was right. But she was certain she wasn't in any danger. She hadn't been on the roof protest. Ever since she had thought of using an incapacitating poison she had been keeping herself well in the background.

"It certainly would seem too much of a co-incidence that it should be Dale and Janet who have been attacked," interjected Alice.

"You think Dale was murdered then?" asked Tristan.

"Not at first I didn't" she replied "but after what's happened to Janet I do now. It's clear from what she's told us that robbery wasn't the main motive for whoever broke into her place."

"So what do we do about it? There's little point in going to the police." said the Professor"

Everyone agreed that would be pointless.

"We must quickly get out a warning on our website" said Miranda.

"Indeed, but we've still got to look out for each other" said Alice,

"Or strike back quickly" Miranda said softly.

As she expected the Professor was the first to respond. "I take it you mean by that, we should carry out one of your poison attacks as soon as possible. You know I'll never agree to that."

"Yes Phillip, that's why I so appreciate you coming here today. There is no need for you" she paused "or anyone here taking part in something they don't agree with. As a matter of fact when I first thought of this I fully intended to do it all on my own. It was only when I realised all that would be involved that I decided to reveal my plans to you. But that doesn't mean that I expected anyone to take an active part in what I've proposed they want to."

Phillip coughed apologetically before interrupting "What will you do Miranda if your scheme works here but then you find that they have just transferred their activities abroad?"

Miranda nodded as she said, "I've no easy answer to that. It's probably what some of the bigger companies will do."

"But there are activists like us everywhere" said Tristan.

"Maybe" said Phillip" But in some third world countries those in control can make it very difficult for organizations like ours to operate."

"They could hide their factories well out of the way" said Tristan.

"But, they can't hide their relatives and families. Well, not all the time. We'd always be able to get to them, wouldn't we" said Alice.

Miranda quickly interrupted "Look, I don't think we should overly concern ourselves with the international consequences of this until we have got a positive result here. If we can stop these vivisectionists here I'm sure it will prove equally effective in stopping them anywhere in the world. So if you don't mind I suggest we concentrate on the here and now".

No one raised any objections.

It was Alice who broke the silence. "So, what about the antidote?"

Miranda looked around at them all before relying; "Well, I've got, or I should say I'll know for sure I've got it if Stephen continues to recover quickly."

"But the doses of poison are very weak aren't they?"

Yes, I've managed to create a dose that is not life threatening."

"What if someone works out an antidote themselves?" asked Tristan.

"Or what if they find your formula?" said Alice.

"Even if they search here they'll never find it. I have a friend who is willing to keep the formula on his computer. He's set up an e-mail address and will forward it to three of you if anything happens to me."

CHAPTER 21

Stephen was dreaming. Dreaming about wild horses. They were wild but they weren't free. They had been corralled and he was standing on the stout fence that enclosed them, a rope in his hands. He was trying to lasso one of them. Despite the melee of their thundering feet and their wild eyed tossing of their heads as they rushed past he was calm and controlled. He was swinging the loop of a rope in easy languid circles waiting for the right moment to cast it over the head of his chosen prey. It was a .roan and it was coming nearer and nearer. In a few seconds it would be alongside and it would be his. Once he got his noose over its head there was no chance of its escaping for the other end of his rope was securely fastened to the stout wooden post beside him. Here it came, now right on the outside of the herd, no other animal between it and him. With an accomplished flick of his wrist he launched his rope…and missed. As it thundered past he felt the fence shaking, and shaking. The shaking continued although it was now far away. He…he…he was being shaken

"Stephen, wake up…let me help you sit up."

He resisted until he was sure of the words. Slowly he opened his eyes and found himself gazing into Miranda's deep brown ones…She was leaning over him; her left arm was around his shoulders. He thought if he could get a head lock on her neck he could force her to let him go free but his arms wouldn't obey him, they hung uselessly by his sides. He let himself be lifted up, his head burrowing into her breasts, so deliciously soft and….

"That's a good man" she said as they eased tantalisingly away from him.

"Here drink this."

He shrunk back immediately, shaking his head. "No…no way. He would have dashed the plastic beaker from her hand if he had the strength. He compressed his lips and sunk his head down unto his chest, tightening his throat muscles, readying himself to spit out whatever it was she had, he wasn't…

"Relax. Take some, please. It will help you breath. Honestly, it will."

He kept his head down, what sort of an idiot did she take him for? She was trying to kill him, finish him off.

He felt her drawing back from him, lowering the plastic beaker in her right hand.

"Alright Steve. I won't force you although I could. I have already injected you with an antidote; this is just to help you get your strength back

75

more quickly. Believe me; we want you to get better. When you're fully fit again we can let you go free. Honestly, we will."

He stayed tense, not lifting his head even though he saw her put the beaker down on the bedside locker. She wasn't going to fool him. She sat down on the edge of the bed over an arm's length away.

"Steve, listen and I'll explain what's happened to you. Four days ago I injected you with a South American Indian poison. It, as you now known only too well, is a muscle relaxant, depriving you of the ability to move easily around. In its extreme form, a high dose can kill but I have been working for some time to produce a mixture which, while it totally incapacitates, isn't fatal. People and animals can recover naturally from this poison over a period of time. Normally the muscles of your diaphragm would by now be so weak that you would have to be on a respirator to help you breath. But the dose you have received is very weak. I won't bore you with the details but I am fairly certain that you could be kept alive in this weakened relaxed state for several weeks at least.

"Thanks a bundle" he snarled.

"Hmm. The thing is that it is now more important to us that you recover quickly. If you take this antidote I believe you will regain your natural strength in a few more days; a week at the most."

He shook his head. Lifting it slightly he whispered "Do you think I'm stupid? Let me free will you? Free to go straight to the police and tell them what you've done."

It was Miranda's turn to shake her head, "But I don't think you'd do that Steve."

"Why not?"

"The video. You know, the one of you stealing £500 here."

Although he knew what she would say he couldn't stop himself asking, "What about it?"

"Don't waste my time Steve. I've got too much to do. Would you like the police to see it?"

He stayed silent.

"You will also I'm sure not be too pleased to know that the police are looking for you in connection with the £20,000 you stole from Sally Foulds. You may have thought she was an easy touch because she was such a highly strung woman. Unfortunately for you her nervousness made her take extreme care of any documents she considered important. You thought you were being clever when you left you took with you all the fake share certificates you'd given her. But, because she was scared of losing them

Sally had already scanned them into her computer. The police were very interested when she showed them the copies. "Quite a convincing forgery" is what one of them told her. But they didn't hold out much hope of finding you. Then when Gwen, Sally's mother saw you at our concert, she told Sally who wasted no time in going to the police. They've already been to the shop asking about you. I told them what little I could but that was when I decided I must get to get to know you better."

"Trap me you mean."

"Rather crudely put but yes. You've no idea how long I'd been looking for someone like you. I'm a scientist Steve and I shouldn't believe in fate. But for a long time I'd been racking my brains to find a way to test this serum on someone. Then you come along, a thief and conman. The ideal subject. Someone in the habit of disappearing. It's almost as if you were sent to me."

"Don't kid yourself; you're nothing but a scheming bitch. You should be ashamed."

"Listen who's talking. The thing is with the video and what Sally given them I'm sure the cops could put you away for a few years. Long enough to put a spoke in your career prospects as a gigolo, Eh?"

He didn't want to listen to her. All he could think of was that she was a bitch. He'd get even with her no matter how long it took. The big thing was to get away from her as soon as possible. But he had to make sure what she was offering.

"O.K. So if I take this stuff you'll let me go?"

"As soon as we are sure you are fit and well you'll be free. We'll have to keep you under observation for a few weeks just to make sure you don't suffer any after-effects. We don't want to harm you."

Her answer seemed so stupid to him that if he could have laughed he would have done so. Slowly he raised his right arm, "Gimme"

She ignored his raised arm. "It's best I give this to you. Can't risk you spilling any. The amount is carefully measured. I need to know exactly what will work and how fast. Don't try to gulp it all down at once. Take sips."

Once more she helped him sit up but her breasts were not as close. Had she noticed his reaction last time? The beaker was at his lips. He took small sips as instructed. It was slightly astringent but not unpleasant; it reminded him of his first taste of beer. As she eased him back onto the pillow he closed his eyes and tried to relax and feel the strength returning to his limbs. But after a few minutes when nothing had happened he opened his eyes and tried to struggle up

She put out a hand and pushed him gently back down. "Relax Steve. Nothing will happen for a few hours. Try to get some sleep. You'll feel better when you wake up."

He tried to resist her but he was every bit as weak as before. She was walking slowly away. She suddenly turned and took a few steps back to him.

"By the way, Steve, I almost forgot. You may be having your 15 minutes of fame soon. Sally's mother's told me last night she's got plans for you. She's a very clever woman. Not long retired as headmistress of our Grammar School. Turns out she's quite a whiz at websites. She said she was thinking of setting up one called "Frauds Reunited." It would ask viewers to post photos and any information they have on anyone who had disappeared owning them money. And guess what? You are going to be the first person featured on it. What do you think of that?"

He decided to ignore her and turned his face away.

"Don't be shy Steve you take a good photo. I'm sure some of the other women you've defrauded will quickly recognize you." With a little laugh she turned and left the room.

"Women" he thought He'd been right about them all along. Scheming conniving bitches. They could never be trusted. He's find a way to pay them back. Especially this one."

CHAPTER 22

"You did what?"

"Ripped all her fucking animal pictures to shreds. Lizzie said that they were what she valued most."

Derek Jepson couldn't believe what he was hearing. His wife Mary confessing to having burgled Janet Carroll's house. How could this woman who chided him for exceeding the 30 mile limit when he was driving in town have done such a thing?

"You don't seem too pleased."

He listened carefully to her words; there was no slurring or exaggerated emphasis on some syllables. She wasn't drunk, he'd been with her all night in The Retreat and she'd had nothing more than her usual two pints and a Blue Ice. Yet when they'd gone to bed as he'd reached over to give her a goodnight kiss, she'd stopped him and blurted out this amazing confession. He didn't know what to say.

"You don't believe me, do you?"

He found his tongue at last, "How did you get in?"

She gave him a look that reminded him of his mate John's supercilious wife, Flo. "Through the front door, we had the house key."

"Where did that come from?"

"Janet's house you silly bugger. Listen I'll tell you what happened. But first you've got to promise not to interrupt. Keep your mouth shut until I finish. I've been bursting to tell you ever since I done it. I don't want to forget anything."

"Right" he said "Want the light on or off?"

She was tempted to say "Off" but resisted the idea "Keep it on, and then you can watch my face and see I'm not telling porkies. You…"

"Wait" he interrupted her, "Let me shift my pillows so I can get a better look at you." He wriggled about for a few minutes and then said "Shoot, pardner." He was a great fan of Westerns.

"Well, you don't know Sadie Karden. She was at Desiree's funeral but I don't think you'll have noticed her. Then you might, she's got a great pair of knockers on her, implants, mind…"

He waved his hand across her face and shook his head to interrupt her. He'd promised not to speak, that was all. It would be after midnight before she even got into the house if he let her meander on at this rate.

"Sorry. I get carried away sometimes. Well, as your cowboys on the telly are fond of saying 'I'll 'cut to the chase.' Sadie and I have been friends for years but I don't see her as often as I used to. She lives out in Burrden; you know where I used to live when I was married to Frank. Anyway, a couple of weeks ago I bumped into her in the Cornmarket and we went for a coffee. It was Sadie who first mentioned Janet Carroll. She'd got a right hump with her. Sadie I mean, not Janet. Janet has never met Sadie. Stop looking at me like that. What I'm trying to tell you is that it turns out that Sadie's eldest girl, Bethany, used to clean for this Janet. I say 'used to 'because she left. Over a month ago a silver ring, some sort of family heirloom went missing and Janet kept asking Bethany if she knew anything about it. Kept on and on, Sadie said. Not directly accusing her you understand but every time she went to the house she was getting the third degree about this ring. Well, Bethany eventually has had enough of it and tells Janet where she can stick her ring when it turns up. She must really have had the hump because she had just split up with that wanker of a husband of hers, Miguel. He was a waiter in their Hotel in Marbella some four years back, and he followed her over here like a bloodhound and in no time at all they were shacked up together. Then after a while he tells her that they've got to get married because his mother is such a good catholic it would break her heart if she found out he was living in sin. Load of codswallop, it was, all he wanted was to get the right to stay here, I said so at the time. Both Sadie and I were against the wedding right from the start. We warned Bethany no good would come of it but of course she wouldn't listen. But we were right. Soon this Miguel starts knocking her about. But her dad and some of his mates, including Frank gave Miguel a good seeing to. That helped him realise the error of his ways. But it's not 'happy ever after' Oh No. This wanker starts putting it about a bit, tries to tell Bethany she's imagining it all but she keeps fining thing like knickers that weren't hers under the passenger seat of their car."

Derek was just about to break his promise not to interrupt but Mary forestalled him "Alright, alright, lean back, you're putting me off my stroke. The thing is, Bethany dumps this Spaniard and moves in with Sadie, temporarily like. But naturally she's at bit short of the readies; won't sponge of Sadie though. One night she's emptying out her purse to see if she's got enough for the bus to get to a job she's seen in the paper, never one to hang about, is our Bethany. Always worked hard she has. Any rate, as I was saying she's emptying out her purse and out falls this key. Turns out it's the key that Janet gave her so she could come in when she's away and feed her three cats. Bethany was fond of them cats; there was a beautiful grey one…"

"Mary!"

"Alright, alright. Anyway Bethany just leaves the key on the mantelpiece saying she'll take it back sometime and goes off. Now, Sadie swears she didn't mean to do it but something made her pick up that key and stick it in her purse. She had it on her when we met. She takes it out and shows it to me and without thinking I just happen to say, 'Wonder what the old cow's place is like.'

Sadie says, "Let's put the key back and we can have a look while we're there. We only had to get one bus, the 97 you …

"You went there?"

"Yes, yes. Don't rush me."

"Sorry. But you was going in to wreck the place?"

"No. Honestly, we wasn't. We was …well…if you want me to put it politely, just being nosey. It wasn't even that at the start. Sadie and I half intended to just put the key through the letterbox. But then when we get there we knock and no one comes. We keep on knocking like and then we looked at one another and without a word Sadie sticks the key in the lock and in we go"

"So why did you trash the place?"

This time Mary didn't rebuke him for interrupting. He thought she might look away but instead leaned slightly forward as she said, "It was me who did it. Me, not Sadie; well, not at first, she just mucked a few thing about afterwards. I still don't know what came over me. It was just all those pretty pictures of animals, I don't know how to describe it, it was somehow as if they were mocking me. They all looked so smug and well fed, so…fucking happy. They made me think of Debbie when she was young, she … she had such a lovely smile but now she was gone. I'd lost her and this old cow that might have saved her had all these happy pictures. She'd not lost anything. The rage just boiled up inside me. It was like I was in a trance. I got my nail file out of my purse and I began slashing this poncy Yorkshire terrier picture with its hair all decked out in red ribbons. I only meant to do one, honest, I did, but somehow once I'd started I couldn't stop. The funny thing was that after a while I sort of could see myself doing all the slashing. It was like as if it wasn't me, as if I was watching someone else doing it …I wanted her to know, I don't know what… something like…why shouldn't she suffer too."

When she suddenly stopped, Derek didn't know what to say. He knew his Mary was a feisty woman; that was one of things that had first attracted him to her. It was not that she ever looked for trouble nor got into many arguments. But there was something about her that made people take care not to upset her. He did too especially since she'd told him what she'd done to Frank, her first husband. Tough guy that he was, with his weightlifting and everything, he had a reputation of being a cold calculating bastard, always boasting how much he was in control of himself. He was well into some Japanese fighting system that was big on never losing your rag. But very occasionally, if he drank too much, he would go all morose and at the slightest provocation would lash out at whoever was nearest. One night he'd come home in a rage and started on her. She'd run out to the shed, grabbed a claw hammer from his toolbox and attacked him. Being so strong he was soon able to subdue her but not before she'd bashed him about the head a few times.

That had amazed him but what had been more astounding was what she said had happened afterwards. She'd told him, "I thought when he got the hammer off me that he'd kill me, but he just threw it away and held me tight until I stopped kicking and swearing. Then he throws me down on the settee and stands staring at me like he's never seen me before. I think it was as if he couldn't believe anyone, especially a woman would hit him back. He made me swear I'd never tell anyone what had happened but somehow word got around that I could be a bit of a devil when roused. I mean, I don't know how. I never said a word to anyone, except I might have mentioned it in passing to Flo and you know how prim and proper she is. I can't imagine her telling anyone."

She paused for so long that he thought she'd finished but just as he was about to speak she added "I must have infected Sadie in some way or other for she suddenly starts throwing things around and smashing up some photos, them in silver frames and all. I think I was the noise of the glass breaking that stopped me. You have been amazed if you could have seen us. We were stood there looking at each other like a couple of naughty kids. How long we were like that I don't know but without a word we just upped and left, walked down her path cool as cucumbers. We could have got a bus back to the Cornmarket from right outside her door but we walked on for three or four stops before we caught one"

"But won't the police think it was either Bethany or Sadie, when Janet tells them about the key. There'll be no sign of a break in, will there?"

"No. but we thought of that. Before we left we wiped our fingerprints off the key and dropped it down the back of her telephone table in the hall. All her keys hang in a rack above it. Sadie will make sure that Bethany swears she gave the old cow the key back. They're bound to find it sometime; they'll think it just dropped down there. We'll be well in the clear, won't we?"

82

When she looked at him expectantly he still didn't know what to say. Before he could speak she added, "And do you know what, I'm not sorry I done it. I know I should be but I'm not. I feel I done something for Desiree. Do you know what I mean?"

He did. He most certainly did. He understood only too well.

CHAPTER 23

When Steve awoke he immediately remembered Miranda's visit. To his delight he was able to sit up much more easily than before and when he swung his feet out on to the floor he was able to stand up straightaway. But when he tried to move forward everything became woozy and he had to sit back down on the bed.

He sat there until he felt confident enough to try again. This time by holding on to the metal frame of the bed head he managed to inch his way over to the wall. By keeping one hand there he was able to shuffle along to the bathroom although he had to stop three times on the way. After using the toilet he grabbed the edge of the wash hand basin and swung himself around to look in the mirror. He was not as dishevelled as he thought he would be but he was unearthly pale; almost as if all the blood had drained away from his face. His eyes were sunken and he had the makings of a beard. He'd had one on a few occasions when he thought it would be a good disguise but… Suddenly he felt light headed…he had to concentrating hard to manoeuvre himself back down onto the toilet seat. He stayed there until his head cleared. By using the wall again as a support he made his way back to bed.

Just before he pulled the duvet back over him he looked across at the spy hole in the door. He couldn't see anything that indicated he was being watched. He hoped he hadn't been seen for he didn't want his captors to know how well he had recovered. He still reckoned that his best hope of escape was a surprise attack. He knew now he'd have to be really strong before he attempted something like that, there was no use just running out of the room and down stairs. He'd have to find some way to incapacitate whoever it was who came in. Miranda often came on her own. If he could fake weakness sufficiently well enough maybe he could grab her. He'd give her something she'd never forget, by Christ he would.

He quickly closed his eyes as he heard the door opening. It was Miranda and the silver studded student. He intended to pretend they'd awakened him but then thought they might have heard the toilet flushing. No way did he want them to ever think he was acting. So as they approached he struggled up.

"Strength coming back Steve?" Miranda asked.

"A bit"

"But you can walk now?"

"Only if I use the wall to support me."

84

"Still, you're recovering well. Of course you're a pretty fit bloke. I knew the dose I gave you would certainly knock you out but what I didn't know is how long it would take you to recover. I had to allow for your relatively small frame when I was working out how strong a potion you should receive. I certainly thought it would take you longer to recover. If you can walk unaided in the next two days it will have all worked out almost exactly as I estimated."

"How long have I been here then?"

"This is your twenty-ninth day."

"Can I go then?"

She shook her head, "Afraid not. We need to keep you a while longer make sure there's no deleterious after-effects. Don't want you dying on us."

Her words inflamed him. The cheek of the bitch. Treating him like he was some fucking rabbit. "That would never do, would it?" he muttered sarcastically.

"No it wouldn't" said silver studs "We're not murderers."

"Then let me go. You know this fucking stuff works. Why can't you leave it at that? I've got work to do. I won't tell anybody. I won't"

"I hope you won't. That would be extremely foolish of you. You'd lose a lot more than you'd ever hope to gain if you did."

"So when am I going to be freed? My firm will be wondering where the hell I am."

She shook her head. "Afraid not, you've resigned."

He tried to lunge forward and grab her but she stepped back so quickly his hands merely flailed the air. He almost fell out of bed head first. The student seized him roughly by the shoulders and thrust him back onto his pillow

"What the fuck are you playing at? "

"If you stay where you are and don't try any more nonsense I'll tell you." She waited until he'd nodded his head before she continued. "You'll be out of circulation for at least two months, maybe longer. That's why you had to resign; we couldn't have anyone looking for you." She paused before adding "I might as well tell you we've sold your car. You're a very tidy man Steve; you keep everything very neatly filed and quickly accessible. I suppose you're so good at that because you've left so many of the women you've duped in a hurry. Quite an expert escape artist, weren't you? And before you ask, your car was sold to recover the £500 you stole and help pay for your keep here. Don't worry, we won't send you out penniless, no matter how much you deserve it. But, you will be wise to keep in mind that how much you'll get will depend on how you behave here. Is that clear?"

He turned his head away. He was almost incandescent with rage. If only he had chosen to have a company car instead of having an allowance for using his own. But all they offered was a bloody Ford Mondaeo, that was no car for a man in his position to be seen driving. What a fool he'd been.

"Suit yourself" she said," Your breakfast's here and there's some fruit and water to see you through the day. We'll be back tonight."

CHAPTER 24

Three were meeting in DI Janet Morison's room. She turned to DS Bullerton and asked "What's the latest then Bully?"

"Not much progress" .he replied. "It definitely looks as if Overton's death was preplanned. He took a Thai Chi class regularly at the High School Friday nights and walked the half mile back home along the same route each week. Union's witness from the care home says the car that killed him had two men in it observing him the week before."

"Am I right in thinking there hasn't been any progress in finding the Cortina?" she said.

"Nothing yet" said Paislee," I don't think we're going to find it now. Probably been crushed and is well on its way to China now as scrap."

"So what can we assume in the absence of hard evidence?" she asked, then added "What about motive? Had Overton any other enemies apart from Jepson?"

Paislee was the first to speak. "He was a well known agitator but wasn't known to have any personal enemies. Of course there's Steyn Chemicals. He was a long time thorn in their side. He was among the very first to protest against them. I'm been told that at the beginning he used to be all on his own with a placard outside their factory ".

"A voice crying in the wilderness" she said. DI Morison was a daughter of the Manse and fond of Biblical allusions. She continued "What have we found out about the boss of this company, Peter Steyn. South African isn't he? A Boer. Any record of him being involved in politics or shady dealings against the anti-apartheid movement Bully"

"I know him slightly from the rugby club. Seems a decent enough bloke. Doesn't lose it when he's had a few. I've also checked with the South African Special Branch like you suggested and they give him a clean sheet but then considering their own past that doesn't count for much.. During his student days at Witwatersrand University there is no record of him being involved in any political activities. Keen student and very keen rugby player. Played for his province but not international standard."

"Just like you then Bully."

"Indeed, a man after my own heart you might say. Any rate after graduation he married a fellow student, another Boer Kathryn De Klerk, both their families very well to do so there was no financial problems with their both pursuing PhDs here in England. They were at Cambridge for three years. As soon as they got their doctorates they returned to South Africa where they married and a year later their son was born. Three years later she and the boy were killed in a road accident in Zulu Natal. No other driver known to be involved. The following year he came back to England. Worked for Smith Kline for three years before setting up his own company?"

"Was he involved in animal experiments right from the start?"

"Yes, right away but there are no detailed records of what they were doing except that their prospectus mentioned they were seeking a cure for Alzheimer's. Only five people in addition to him were involved at the start but they grew rapidly. All five are still with him and they own 49 percent of the shares. He has the rest and the company finances seem sound. As far as I can ascertain, these protests haven't hinder their work to any great extent. There's been extra expenditure of course with increased security measures and in getting their staff to and from work safely. Staff that have been interviewed discreetly all speak well of him as a boss. Expects them to work hard but pays top rates. None that I can find have left due to FAAN's activities"

"And we've nothing more on Jepson?"

"Nothing to his detriment" replied Union. "Exemplary army career. Went to work for Steyn immediately after leaving the Army. Met Mary there."

"She was married to Frank Mills then wasn't she?" asked DI Morison. "He's banged up on a manslaughter charge, isn't he?"

"Yes" replied Paislee "and before that he had a couple of convictions for GBH, when acting as strong-arm man for the Gomer brothers. It's the death of one of their debtors that's got him banged up."

"Hard to imagine him taking his wife's leaving him and taking their daughter with her without him doing something about it."

"Mary had left him a couple of years before he was convicted." said Paislee"

"Was he beating her up?"

It was Bully who answered "There were one or two accounts of fights between them. I heard Mary could give as well as she got."

"So why did she leave?"

"Dolly birds." Bully replied "Frank developed a taste for them. Seems they're one of a doorman's perks. If he lets them in the club free they'll let him into their knickers."

"Really Bully, what would Helene say if she heard you talk like that?"

"Not much. That's mild compared with some of the stuff she comes out with. Dirty jokes are part of all pathologists' defence mechanisms."

"Be that as it may, let's get back to Mills and Jepson. There's no record of any fights between the two of them?"

"None"

"Reckon he was he afraid of Jepson then?"

"Hard to say. Mills was on probation for GBH when Mary and Jepson got together. Personally I think the fact that Calderford's an army town might have something to do with Mills not hassling Jepson."

"Mills was never in the Army was he?" asked Union.

"No, but Jepson's still very much involved with it. He's on some servicemen's' welfare committee and he's also on the committee that runs The Retreat."

"Are you saying Mills was afraid if he did anything to Jepson, his army pals would come after him?" Morison asked.

"Could be but I think it more likely that the Gomez brothers might have warned him off. They get a lot of money from the squaddies here with their nightclubs and pubs. They wouldn't want any hassle between them and one of their employees."

"If Jepson's got as many good military friends as you imply, could he have got one of them to kill Overton?"

"That would be stretching friendship a bit far" injected Union.

"Nevertheless it's not impossible" replied Bully, "With Jepson and his wife being at The Retreat at least a couple of nights a week, they'd have plenty of chances of meeting a sympathetic hit man wouldn't they?"

"It would cost them, though wouldn't it? But there's no record of any big withdrawals from either of their bank accounts."

"No. Their banks were unhelpful at first but this anti-terrorist legislation has given us a lot more leverage with them than before. Their accounts show nothing out of the ordinary, no large withdrawals." replied Union".

"Is there any record of Jepson ever saving any soldier's life or anything like that? Something that would make that person willing to help him get his revenge on Overton without being paid for it?"

"We did look for that" said Union "But Jepson's got no medals for bravery, just the usual campaign ones."

"What about Mills then? Desiree was his daughter. "asked Janet.

"He got a ten stretch and he's due to come up for parole in a couple of months" said Bully"

"So unless we get lucky with something like the Cortina turning up we're stymied" she said.

Union suddenly sat up a bit straighter and said "There's the vandalism at Janet Carroll's, we might get something out of that."

"Yes, it must be related to Desiree's death. It was certainly a revenge attack seeing nothing was stolen. The SOC people have turned up several sets of prints, we might get something out of those." agreed Bully.

"The thing that puzzles me most about that is that there was absolutely no sign of a break in." added Janet.

"That" replied Bully" might just be our lucky break."

CHAPTER 25

For the past three mornings Stephen had been able to get easily out of bed and walk to the bathroom without any feeling of weakness. His restored physical strength made him restless and he had explored every part of the room looking for a way to escape and checking to see if there was a surveillance camera in the room. He discovered that the wardrobe that was over the side window was screwed to the floor and had metal plates fitted at the back. Since nothing was ever said about his searches he concluded there weren't any watching cameras. That meant his original idea that he could escape by overpowering one of his captors was certainly possible.

He told himself that he was planning to escape in case they didn't keep their promise to release him. On balance he believed that they would but he didn't fully trust them. He had survived several tricky situations in the past only because he had relied on his own wits and always had a plan B in hand in case of any unforeseen snags cropping up.

It was the question of how much money he would be given on his release by these nutcases that made him willing to wait. His car was just over two years old; he hadn't finished paying the H.P. on it. If these nutcases had any business sense at all they should have got at least £20,000 for it. He'd demand at least that.

He could start a new life couldn't he?

That evening it was Miranda alone who brought his food, another curry "Christ" he complained "Can't I have a decent bit of steak for a change?"

"No chance of that" she replied" this is a vegan household."

"But I'm not one. I'm a red blooded male"

"Dream on Steve. But tell you what; we'll get you some Linda McCartney vegetarian sausages tomorrow."

His first impulse was to tell her exactly where she could put them but then he decided it prudent to keep quiet. She seemed much friendlier tonight. While he was eating she went over to the running machine and switched it on and started to run. He couldn't stop himself admiring her. She ran as smoothly as she walked. There was something of the wilderness about her. After a few minutes she switched it off and came over to him.

"You ought to make use of the treadmill. It'll help restore your fitness."

"I'll try it tomorrow."

"Good. Remember to set the incline at one percent so you get nearly the same conditions as if you were running on a flat road."

"Jesus, what was she? A fitness instructor?"

"I'll remember. What's this other machine with all the wires sticking out?" he answered.

"That's your safety device. It's a ventilator. It's in case you get too weak to breathe unaided. We haven't had to use it yet but it's here just in case "She came over and poured out his coffee from a café tier. "This is a special treat tonight Steve. Fresh beans straight from Brazil."

The coffee tasted unusually strong, but he wasn't going to let her know that. He was a man.

"By the way, Janet's got your website up and running. You look good in it. We used a photo we found among your files. People will have no trouble recognizing you."

He wanted to throw what was left of the coffee in her smirking face but controlled himself. Feeling as good as he did he must surely be out of here soon. He stopped himself from asking her when he might be released because he didn't want to appear too anxious. Instead he decided to try and find out more about her. The more he knew the more he could tell the police if he ever needed to.

"Do you think your father would have approved of you treating me like this?" he asked.

Her answer came quicker than expected. "Probably not, but then he lived for his plants not people. I don't want to give you the impression he was uncaring or that he ever neglected me or my brother but there was never any doubt that his orchids were what came first in his life."

He thought that explained a lot about her. "Don't you think you're the same?" he asked.

She didn't answer straight away and when she did it was with another question. "What do you mean?"

"Look what you're doing to me. Treating me as if I was some laboratory rat. Aren't you supposed to be against things like that?"

She nodded slowly. "You're certainly not stupid Steve. You'll never know the years of heartache its cost me thinking of this experiment. It goes against everything I believe. But I've convinced myself I'm doing it for the greater good. If everything works out exactly as I've planned you'll be famous but not I'm afraid until after you and I are long dead."

That startled him, "What the fuck does that mean?"

"Don't fret yourself, it doesn't mean you'll come to any harm. You'll live your normal life span, unless some woman takes a knife to you. All I mean is that I will leave a very comprehensive account of what has happened here which will not be revealed until after my death. If I die much before you of course, you may be able to bask in some of the reflected glory. But then you might prefer to remain anonymous. I'm writing all this up in such a way that you'll not be easily identified unless you want to be".

If she thought that made him any happier she was out of her tiny mind. She was a strange cow. His instincts had been right about her right from the moment he saw her. He'd been a fool to ignore them.

Her next question startled him, "What about your parents? They live in Walthamstow, don't they?"

He blurted out before he could stop himself "My mother does."

She nodded knowingly, "And your father left when you were young?"

He nodded in reply although he couldn't understand how she knew that.

It was her next words that really shook him "And I suppose your mothers had quite a few boyfriends since then?"

"Mind your own fucking business."

"Strictly speaking, I am enquiring about your mother's fucking business but let's not quibble. Sorry to be so nosey, but I'm right, aren't I?"

"If you say so."

She was silent for a while, then said quietly "That explains a lot about your attitude to women."

What the Hell was she on about? Did she think she was some trick cyclist of something? He wanted to challenge her but he couldn't be bothered. He felt tired.

She leaned over and picked up his tray. "You've been through a lot lately. You probably feel quite tired. I'll leave you in peace; you'll need all the rest you can get in the days ahead."

CHAPTER 26

It was the fact that the investigation into Dale Overton's death was getting nowhere that made DS Bullerton decide to visit Frank Mills. The jail was in the middle of town and only an half a mile from the Police Headquarter. He took Union Jack Paislee with him.

The prison car park had recently been computerised and caused them a needless delay. It was only after Union's threatening to leave the car parked and locked across the exit that the metallic voice at the barrier condescended to allow them to enter, with the proviso that "You must report immediately to the gatehouse after parking your car correctly in the assigned visitors' slots." Union Jack was not in the best of moods as he approached the booth and the frowning official in a badly creased white shirt had only time to say "You are supposed…" before he was halted by Union shoving a blue form under his would be supercilious nose and saying in a voice that his more famous namesake would have been proud of "Gatekeeper. I assume you are able to read but in case I am overestimating your intellectual capacities I will point out that this document not only gives the day and time of Her Majesty's police force's visit here but also contains the registration number of the car they will have arrived in. I will also point out that this document is the copy of one that was sent to you three days ago and which you should have had in your possession long enough to be able to recognized the registration as the one I quoted to you on our arrival."

With only the briefest of glances at the form, the gatekeeper replied "We haven't had one of those in here mate. Not today. You…"

Union interrupted "In that case we won't waste any more time talking to you but be assured it will be the first thing I shall take up with your governor Marion McKenzie when we speak to her. Good day" Grabbing the form back he marched off with Bully following but not quickly enough to prevent him hearing the gatekeeper's muttered "Suit yourself mate.".

The prison entrance was unlocked by an officer who was a fellow Ulsterman and knew Union well. He seemed to be expecting them and after a few friendly words of banter with Union told them "I'm afraid you won't see Mss McKenzie today. She off on some management course or other but Bill Featherstone would like to have a word with you before you leave." He then handed them over another officer who escorted them to the room where they would interview Mills. Bully had never experienced any difficulties with the ambitious Marion McKenzie but he was glad it would be Bill

94

Featherstone he would be talking to instead of her. Bill was married to one of Bully's cousins.

The escorting officer had warned them that they might have to wait a while before Mills was brought to them. "We're so short staffed," he added by way of apology. It was over fifteen minutes before Mills was brought in. Both officers had already come across Frank on several previous occasions but Bully wasn't in any hurry to get to the pointed of the visit.

"Thanks for seeing us Frank."

"No problem Mr.Bullerton, anything to get out of the cell for a bit."

"Still, we appreciate you seeing us. How long is it till you get out?"

"I've got a parole hearing in six weeks. If it goes well I should be out in another three months at the most."

"Looking forward to your freedom?"

As soon as he saw the scowl start to spread across Mills face Bully realised it was a badly phrased question. "Why shouldn't I be? I'll have done my time won't I?"

"Of course, Frank. I wasn't implying there was anything wrong about your release. What I meant is do you have any plans about you will do. Where you will stay and so on?"

"No need for me to worry about things like that. I've got very good employers."

"Really? You don't think that working for them is one of the reasons why you're in here?"

"I was stitched up. There's lots of other club owners who would like to see the Gomez brothers put out of business, but they couldn't get to them so they paid some scummy shop owners to lie about me All I was doing was collecting the rent."

"And you always said 'Please'" interrupted Union

"Naturally. Mr. Paislee. My mother brought me up proper like"

Before Union could reply Bully said quickly, "Still, don't you think your chances of staying out of places like this would be better if you found some other line of work?"

"I'm going to have my own gym someday. Do you both a good deal on membership, when I do."

"Thanks, hope it happens soon."

Mills suddenly sat up straight and said "Right. Enough of this buggering about. You've come to see me about Overton, haven't you?"

"What about Overton?"

"Don't mess me about. He was run over, wasn't he?"

"How did you know that Frank?"

"I can read, that's how. I may look thick but I'm no retard. I've not been wasting my time in here. I've got three GCSE O Levels and I'm well into this English A level stuff. Have you read Crime and Punishment? It's by a Russian bloke Dostoyevsky?"

"Years ago" Bully answered, "but if you don't mind we won't talk about Raskolnikov and his misdeeds at the moment. Let's get back to Overton. How did you know he was killed by a car?

"It was in the papers."

"How did you feel when you read about him?"

Mills took his time before replying "Nothing really. Didn't know the bloke, never met him? I was neither sad nor glad"

"You don't blame him in any way for your daughter's death?"

"It's alright, you can mention her name. Desiree. It was me that called her that you know. Mary wanted to call her Debbie after Debbie Harris but I wasn't having that."

"She must have been special to you then" said Union quietly.

"She was. There are a couple of other kids that some tarts say are mine but there's only their word for it. But Debbie was my girl alright."

"Her death must have been quite a shock to you then."

Mills nodded before saying "I don't dwell on it. Nothing can bring her back. So let's get to the point of all this. You're here because you think I might have had something to do with Overton's death. Well I haven't. They don't let us out at nights here. Do you think they did?"

"No Frank. But a man is dead. Murdered. All the indications are it was a preplanned hit. So we've got to interview everybody who might have had a grudge against him and you had more than most."

"What makes you say that? There's no proof that Overton led her into this Animal Rights mob. Desiree was always a strong willed girl; she had a mind of her own. You might as well say I've got it in for the woman who was right next to her before she fell. Maybe I think she could have saved her."

"Janet Carroll. Her house was burgled last week."

"Christ, I'm on your list for that as well am I…?"

"Relax Frank. Nobody's accusing you of anything."

"You just want to get the facts, that's all is it? Well, the facts are that I've been banged up here for the past four and three-quarter years and I've kept my nose clean all that time. I've got a good chance of parole soon and I don't want you lot coming along and buggering it up. Understand."

96

Bully pushed back his chair and rising slowly said "Alright Frank. I'm sure our visit won't adversely affect your parole application. We won't detain you any longer."

Mills stood up and turned away without replying. The warder outside the door must have been watching for he immediately came into the room.

After Mills left, Union asked "What do you make of that sarge?"

"I'm not sure. Mills always had a reputation for being quick tempered. On the two previous occasions I've interviewed him he was much more aggressive. He was much too calm this time for my liking."

"I agree Sarge. It was not just that it seemed as if he was expecting us. After reading about how Overton died he had every reason to think we would visit him. It was more as if he had all his answers and reactions rehearsed. Sometimes he sounded like a ham actor."

"That's very perceptive of you Union. Didn't know your talents extended to being a drama critic. Go to the theatre much?"

"My wife and her mother have parts in a lot of the Caldeford Players productions. I've seen a fair few ham actors in my time."

"I take it you've never told your wife or your mother in law that."

"Never. I might have mentioned that they're wasted on the amateur stage, that's all."

Bully was still chuckling to himself as they reached the Deputy Governor's door. The warder who had accompanied them knocked, announced them and retreated rapidly; giving the impression that he wanted to disappear before he was given any other task.

Bill Featherstone was a small dapper man with an unusually deep voice for such a slight frame. He was a well respected local baritone who regularly sang with the choir where Bully's aunts had been long time members. He came around his desk to meet them and extended his hand, giving them both a firm handshake. "Nice to see you Bully and you too Mr.Paislee. How did you get on with Mills? I don't suppose you got much change out of him?"

"No, he was expecting us. Had all the answers. Just like bloke who married his wife, Jepson. He's the security chief at Steyn."

"Funny you should mention him. Mills doesn't get many visitors. This Jepson you mention was the last one to see him before you. Saw him twice as a matter of fact."

Bully and Union looked at each other both thinking the same thing. If only they had known that before they interviewed Mills.

"You've got a record of the dates of Jepson's visits, of course?"

"Of course, Bully. Day, date and time. I can get you a copy if you like "

"We most certainly would"

Bill Featherstone picked up a telephone and instructed someone to look for the records of every visitor that Frank Mills had had this year, make a copy and bring it to his office asp

During their long wait Bill told them more about Frank. "He's only gone off the rails once since he's been here. He beat up another inmate who was mocking him for always having his head in a book. Got solitary for that but had the cheek to tell me that it was a good thing because it meant he could study in peace."

When the information about the visits arrived it showed Jepson had visited Mills the twice Bill Featherstone had remembered. The first was six weeks before Overton's death and the second a fortnight before.

Bully explained to the deputy why the dates might be significant. When he finished Union added "It's a shame the law doesn't let you record their conversations. But then of course any information you obtained would never be allowed in court, would it?"

"Sadly not. Of course they know the prison phone is recorded but apart from preventing them threatening anyone or harassing their women, it's a waste of time. Many of them have their own mobiles anyway. The things are so dammed small they're easy to smuggle in and a devil to find."

They decided against bringing Mills back for a further interview but Bill said he would try to let them know if Jepson asked for a future visit. "Can't promise you'll get the information in time though Bully. It the old days I'd have got the staff to tell me and then phoned you Bully but now everything has to go into a computer and God only knows what part of the universe it goes to after that. I'll tell the staff to inform me immediately if there's a request from Jepson but again I can't promise they'll manage it. But if by some miracle they do I'll phone you."

Bully thanked him, and they chatted about the oratorio that would be "the cowgirls" next performance while they waited to be escorted out. On the drive back he and Union discussed the merits of informing Jepson of what they'd learned. Union agreed with Bully, it would be best to not let Jepson know. After a brief silence the big Ulsterman added "Mind you, Mills will probably warn him we've been. He'll have a mobile phone stashed somewhere. Probably will have told him already."

"Thank you Union. It's such a comfort knowing I can always rely on you to look on the bright side."

"Say what you like Sir but I don't suffer from so many disappointments as others do"

"You sail through life on a sea of tranquillity Eh?"
"If only" Union replied "If only."

CHAPTER 27

Bully sat at his desk, staring unseeingly at the report in front of him. He was thinking what a pity it was that they had no way of knowing what Jepson and Mill's talked about.

The telephone interrupted his reverie. He picked it up hoping it was good news. It was one of the civilian staff, Annie from the control room. "Sir, there's a message for you. It says "We may have found the Cortina. I assume you know what it's about"

"I think so Annie. Who's the we?"

"The we? Oh yes sir, Sorry I didn't say straight away" Annie was new to the job and very keen to please. "It's from a constable out at Bournham…I think."

"What's his name Annie?"

"Yes sir. It's Smith. But I don't think he's still there sir. But he left this number."

Bully checked the number twice with her before he ended the conversation. He dialled and was answered immediately.

The voice conveyed the same eagerness as Annie's, "DS Bullerton I presume?"

"Indeed it is. Yes Constable Smith. How did you know?"

"It's a headquarters' number, sir."

Bully was pleased the constable didn't offer any further explanation. This young man sounded promising. Before he could speak Smith continued, "I know you've been looking for a Ford Cortina. Well there's one on my patch. Burnt out I'm afraid. It was reported by the farmer whose field it was fired in. He said it was done three weeks ago today. He passes that field every day and that was when he first saw it."

"Three weeks? And it's not been collected."

"I'm afraid the local council out here aren't top of the league for speedy action. At least Peterson's the scrap people they employ aren't."

"Have you seen it?"

"Yes sir. Went out there as soon as I was told about it. Pity the farmer didn't tell us at once instead of the council. It's a Cortina alright. No number plates left. Whoever torched it knew what they were doing. But the engine block's still got its number on it. It should be easy to trace through that sir."

"Yes, but I hope you haven't been clambering all over the wreck?"

"No sir. Not at all. Not when it might have been used in that hit and run killing."

100

"What makes you think that?"

"Bit of a coincidence it being torched the same night as the hit and run wouldn't you say, sir?"

"Very shrewd Smith. So you were careful around the wreck."

"Yes sir. Had a good look around for fag ends and any scraps of paper. Didn't see any I'm afraid. Only bits I've touched are the bonnet and the side of the engine block. I kept my gloves on all the time sir."

"Very good Smith" He thought about going out to see the wreck but decided against it. It would be more important to get the forensics people out to it. He told the constable what he intended to do and asked if he could make sure no sightseers blundered around the wreck."

"I'll drive out there now sir and wait until forensics arrive. If they can't get here today I'll tape the site off and put a notice up to keep people off.

"Excellent, Smith and can you let me have a full report of all that you did regarding the car. Don't leave anything out no matter how insignificant it may seem. You'll have plenty of time to compose it while you're sitting watching the grass grow And stay away from the wreckage or forensics will chew your balls off"

"Of course, sir. You'll have it by e-mail in the morning at the latest." Constable Smith put the phone down.

Bully was amazed. When he was a constable he'd never have ended a conversation with a superior officer first. He'd have a look at this Constable Smith's record. Bourham was the furthest station away from Headquarters. He was either a bumptious fool or he was too good to be left out in the sticks.

CHAPTER 28

As soon as Stephen awoke he knew something was wrong. The room was filled with sunlight that was too strong for it to be early morning. How come he had slept so long? His head ached and there was a metallic taste in his mouth. He went to ease himself up but failed miserably. All his strength had disappeared again. They must have poisoned him again. He lay back on the pillow, trying to ignore the pains in his head and cursing Miranda and the rest of the Animal Liberation morons with every swear word he could think of.

He tried to sit up but couldn't manage it. He became aware the he was wet; a wet cloth was clinging to the top of his legs. Christ, was he incontinent! Had they fucked up his innards? He began to panic, thinking that this was the end. They'd found out all the needed about the effects of the poison and its antidote and he was of no further use to them. His whole body was shaking with fear. The pains in his head were getting worse. He always had had a low pain threshold and the thought that he would die in pain terrified him. He thought of turning over and burying his face deep in the pillow so that he would suffocate but his cowardice stopped him. In desperation he began to chant some of the positive thinking slogans he'd so consciously learned by heart from his Self Help books. "You have nothing to fear but fear itself. You have nothing to fear…" That was it. He mustn't let these bastards win. He wouldn't let them, he couldn't let them. The sun would rise tomorrow and he would rise with it. He…he heard footsteps approaching. His first thought was to turn over to see who it was but he decided against it.

"Stephen" The voice was Miranda's but it was strangely muffled.

"Stephen, turn over."

He made them wait; turning laboriously and moaning to make sure they understood how much pain he was in. He kept his eyes shut until he was on his back. When he opened them, he couldn't prevent himself letting out a squeal of protest. Miranda and the student were masked. This was it. They'd come to finish him off. He…

"Stephen. Don't panic. We're masked because there is a lot of flu about. Understand?"

It was the concern in her voice rather than what she said that reassured him. He allowed himself to think he could see genuine concern in her eyes. Not that he would ever trust her. He wasn't that big a fool.

"We can't risk you catching anything the weak state you're in. Your resistance to infection at this moment must be practically nil. We're going to give you a solution that will help build you up. "

As she spoke he saw a tall metal frame with a bottle with tubes and wires hang down from it. She must have seen the fear in his eyes as she spoke for she added hurriedly, "There's nothing to fear Stephen, it's mostly glucose, really. Look." She reached up and unhooked the bottle from the metal frame. The student handed her a cup. "We thought you might be frightened about what we're going to give you, but it's safe .Really it is. Watch." She held the tube from the bottle over the cup and let him see the liquid flow into it. As she handed the tube back to the student she raised the cup to her lips and drank, turning the cup upside down to prove that it was empty when she'd finished.

"Now we can stay here for a while to let you see there are no adverse after affects if you want but it will only be a waste of time for there won't be. There's nothing is this bottle except what I've told you. It will help you recover quickly. Do you believe me?"

He amazed himself by shaking his head affirmatively.

She held out a little blue plastic shape towards him and said, "Good man. Now listen carefully, this solution will do you the most good if it enters your body at a controlled rate. We can only make sure that it does that if we drip feed it into you. To do so we need to put this little plastic stent into your arm. Afterwards you'll need to lie still until you can see that the bottle's empty. When you're sure it is you can pull the tube out if you want but make sure you keep your arm with this stent facing upwards. OK?"

Again he nodded his approval but he had to fight to control the panic arising within him when he saw the hypodermic needle in her hand. "It's only for the stent" he told himself, "It's only for the stent." It wasn't until she moved away from him that he let himself relax.

"We're going to leave you now to get some rest but we'll come and renew your glucose regularly. But before we go I think we owe it to you to explain what has happened to you.

"You poisoned me again." He grunted.

"Yes, I'm afraid we did. The first time you only had a rather weak dose but this time you got what I worked out is the maximum your body can take without making it impossible for you to recover. You've been immobile for thirty seven days in all with the two doses but we were regularly monitoring you. Every check we made showed although all your bodily functions had slowed they had not done so irreparably. Recovery was always possible. We know we could have kept you in this state much longer but we decided about five weeks were long enough and we've been feeding you the antidote for the last two. You were never..."

"Why?" he interrupted, "Why are you doing this to me?"

She didn't answer immediately. She sat down on the edge of the bed and leaning towards him said earnestly, "It would take too long to give you all the reasons just now but we had to know what dose we could use to give those who torture animals sufficient cause to take us seriously. That's the whole point of this noble experiment. We could keep you unconscious for as long as we liked. They've got to believe that if they don't do as we say then they are sentencing those among them that we select to a living death. We will only offer the antidote if they do as we say. It's thanks to you Steve we can prove that we have the means to effect a full recovery. So as you lie there you can think to yourself that at last you have done some good in this world. That's quite a change for you isn't it?"

He refused to dignify her question with an answer.

CHAPTER 29

Sam Ketteridge braced herself as she opened the door of her house. Luna the twenty month old rescue Lurcher she had brought home eight weeks ago was fleet of foot but slow of brain. Her canine life had changed so much for the better that she just couldn't see the point of commands like "sit" and "stay" when there were so many more important things to do like leap for joy at her mistress's return

. Sam braced herself as the moon coloured bitch thundered down the hall towards her. "Down" she commanded in what she hoped was a convincing reproduction of the voice of Judy who ran the Saturday morning dog training class she and Luna attended. Luna skidded to a halt and lifted her front paws up unto Sam's shoulders and tried to lick her to death. "Down" Sam repeated, reinforcing her command with a two handed push on the bitch's shoulders. Luna allowed herself to be pushed down but instead of sitting tried to bury her head in Sam's skirt. . "Good Girl, good girl" she repeated patting the large head as she closed the door behind her by collapsing against it. She always felt better when the door was closed for Luna seized every chance she got to escape outdoors.

Sam came home lunch times to give Luna some companionship and a brief walk. The big dog was proving to be more effective than any diet she had ever tried in reducing her weight. Sam took her out three times every day. She could tell from the way Luna was looking up at her now that she was wondering why Sam had to waste time footling around in the kitchen instead of opening the front door and getting out in the fresh air

Sam had recently split from her partner Mark, because she could no longer tolerate his lying and thieving. Marijuana which had once been only an occasional recreational indulgence for them in the company of friends had become for Mark the most important thing in his life and he would do anything to get it. He was never violent but all his money (and as she had discovered) much of hers was spent on obtaining it. The final straw had been her accidental discovery of the letters threatening eviction because of the unpaid mortgage bills. Bills which Mark had sworn he had been paying as usual. No way was Sam ever going to lose this house in which she had invested so much of her savings.

The house had seemed so empty after Mark left that she had followed friends advice and "got a dog for company." She had envisaged an older more placid companion but Luna had looked at her so longingly when she was walking by the holding pens at the rescue kennels that Sam had lost her heart to big Lurcher before she could take another step.

As they stepped outside Luna's evident pleasure filled Sam's heart with joy. She felt a surge of pleasure as after only a few minutes pulling Luna began walking to heel. This was her one big success as a dog trainer and she constantly reinforced it with an abundant supply of treats. Everything was so good for her now. She had this wonderful dog and a wonderful job. Travelling to work each day through the rows of jeering protestors wasn't agreeable but she'd been doing it for so long now that she accepted it as an unpleasant fact of life. Besides her life in the office more than made up for what she had to endure to get there.

The activities of the protesters had generated a sense of camaraderie among the Steyn workers. When she'd started there as an office junior she'd never though that one day she'd be Dr. Steyn's P.A. She liked Peter Steyn, one time she'd though she was in love with him but now she liked to tell herself that it had only been a girlish infatuation. He'd never made any advances to her anyway. She was a practical woman, never one to keep pursuing lost causes. She'd proved that to herself the way she'd got rid of Mark.

Although she enjoyed working for Peter Steyn and was fiercely loyal to him she found he had within him a steely determination that at times was frightening. He was a considerate boss who worked himself hard and expected all his employees to do the same. While he was willing to overlook occasional failure he wouldn't hesitate to instantly get rid of anyone he thought was not pulling their weight. Every worker including the most senior staff had signed a contract that allowed them only two weeks' notice of dismissal. He cared little for people's paper qualifications, what mattered to him was the ability to do the work expected of them. Sam herself had benefited greatly from this attitude. She had started working for the firm at 18 as a very minor office junior but in 5 years she had been continually promoted until she was his P.A. "You're reliable and you get thing done as and when I want" he'd told her when he'd offered her the job. Now their private joke was that she kept the job because "You know how to keep timewaster's out of my hair."

Steyn Chemicals although only a small company with just employees had developed several successful drugs over the years. It was one of these drugs, a contraceptive pill that provided the bulk of the Company's income. It had always paid well above the top rates for its staff and had a much higher ratio of PhD's among its researchers than many larger firms. But there were no room for "head in the clouds day dreamers" among them, they were all practical hands-on researchers with a "can do" attitude that the Firm fostered. Sam had soon realised that it was because of this philosophy that there were so few English graduates among them.

Peter made no secret of the fact that his big passion was to find a cure for Parkinson's disease. He had a poster of Mohammed Ali lighting the torch at the 1996 Atlanta Olympics prominently displayed in his office. The firm's research into this illness had been the area where they had had the most disappointments in recent years. Several trials that had seemed to offer hope of producing a drug that would conquer this affliction had all eventually had to be abandoned. Peter refused to let anyone he employed speak of these abandoned trials as "failures." His oft repeated mantra was that "We've learned something from these trials, even if it is only another avenue not to pursue." He'd never told Sam why this illness obsessed him; she thought that there must be a history of this disease in his family back in South Africa.

Peter kept a strict division between his private and his business life. Sam knew a lot about his wife Esme and his children Adam, Carla and Jacob as far as their birthdays and their likes and dislikes were concerned but generally she only met them once a year at the Annual Barbeque Peter gave for the firm's senior executives. If Esme came into the office to see Peter she always stopped to gossip with Sam. For years there had been talk of her restarting to work for the firm as a researcher but she didn't seem in any hurry. "I'm enjoying the children too much to rush back to work" she had told Sam, swearing her to secrecy as she did so.

Luna's tug on her lead as they reached the entrance to the cricket pitch brought Sam's thoughts back to the here and now. She made sure she was first through the gate as Judy had instructed her. "The pack leader always goes first- always." was her daily mantra. She couldn't risk letting Luna off the lead during these lunch time walks. Luna got her freedom in the evenings and weekends. After completing a couple of circuits of the cricket pitch Sam headed home. As she was leaving the pitch she began to look for the two women who she had started to meet regularly at this spot for the past five days. She thought of them as the "Jackie Kennedys" because of the large sunglasses that they both wore. But there was no sign of them today. Because of the attacks on Steyn workers homes she was always suspicious of any strangers near her home but these two seemed harmless enough.

She hurried back home and as she neared her house she was surprised to see them coming towards her. They were obviously behind their regular schedule today. She gave them a brief nod of acknowledgement as they paused to let her open her gate and received two friendly smiles in return. As she opened her purse to take out her door key that she sensed there was someone close behind her. Before she could turn around she felt a sharp pain in the back of her neck. She only had time to wonder what insect it was that had bitten her before she lost consciousness.

She did not fall to the ground because the women were alongside to support her. One took her key and opened the door while the other held onto Luna's lead as they hurried indoors.

"Nobody saw us, did they?" asked Miranda as they dragged Sam into the living room and laid her gently on the couch.

"No, I checked" answered Alice.

Luna bewildered by what happening was decided it was time to do something and started barking loudly. But she immediately stopped when Alice offered her a tripe stick. Holding the treat just out of her reach Alice lured the dog into the kitchen and after checking that there was water in the dog's drinking bowl threw the treat along the floor and closed the door.

When she returned to the living room Miranda was holding Sam's mobile "She's got both Peter Steyn's home and work numbers keyed in" she told Alice,

Miranda gave her the thumbs up sign as she spoke, "Hallo Mr.Steyn, I'm ringing to tell you that your secretary Samantha Ketteridge, won't be coming back to work this afternoon. Never mind who this is…listen carefully, there is no time to waste. At present Samantha is lying unconscious in her front room. She has been poisoned…Listen…listen will you…the more you interrupt me the worse it will be for Samantha. No, her life is not in immediate danger. Samantha is in the front room of her own home, you must know where she lives. She has had enough poison to render her unconscious but she will need hospital treatment to help her survive as all her major organs will soon be greatly weakened. Now …stop interrupting…listen… just listen.

She will soon have to be put on a respirator to help her breath so you had better arrange that straight away. No. No. This is not a windup. I'm standing looking down at an unconscious Samantha right now. Her life is not in immediate danger. She will need intravenous feeding with glucose and nutrients. That's important. Do not, I repeat, do not let the hospital give her any drugs. She will revive when we send you the antidote. We do not wish her any harm. When will she recover? When you listen to the demands of FAAN. This is from some of their friends. We want your evil experiments on animals to cease. No. No. I'm not telling you any more at present. Just get that ambulance here as soon as possible and do not tell the police. That would be fatal for Samantha." She stopped as she saw Alice pointing frantically to the kitchen. "Oh, and there's her dog, it's in the kitchen, you'll have to make some arrangements about it. That's it; we'll be in touch again in the next 24 hours."

As she slipped the phone into her pocket she turned towards the door, "Let's get out of here; I think her was trying to keep me talking so he could send some of his security thugs round."

CHAPTER 30

Much to Union's surprise both the police and the DVLA computer systems worked in harmony and two hours after the forensic team had given Calderford police the Cortina's engine number they had an owner's name and address to match it. But as the car had been reported stolen the night before the hit and run, Bully and Union did not have high hopes of finding much out from the owner as they drove up the block of flats where he lived.

They had informed the local East End police station why they were coming on to their manor. Bully from his Rugby playing and previous co-operative occasions knew one of the local detectives DS Ray Loomis and as they drove up he called them on the radio to confirm that the Cortina had indeed been reported stolen the morning after the hit and run and that the owner was not known to the police to have any criminal connections. He invited them to call in to East Ham station for a chat afterwards.

The flats were in London's East End, just off the A12 in Canning Town. It was a School holiday with lots of kids playing around the flats so Union stayed in the car while Bully went to flat. It was on the ground floor and the inhabitants must have seen him coming because the door was opened before he knocked.

"Have you found me motor?" The speaker was a slim man of medium height with short grizzled grey hair. He waved a small black brier pipe in his right hand that gave off a slightly scented rather pleasant smell. Bully wished his father would smoke a mixture like this rather than his foul concoction that not only made you gasp whenever you were assailed by it but clung as if glued to your clothes for hours afterwards.

"Yes we have Mr. Edwards "Bully answered" At least what's left of it. I'm afraid it has been torched."

"I knew it, after all this time I knew that's what would happen. That fucking Danny O'Halloran, he's an evil bastard if ever there was one. He wants putting away again he does"

While Bully was wondering how best to respond to this unexpected news the man beckoned him in. "Go through to the living room "he said pointing to a doorway on the right

The first thing Bully noticed as he entered the room was how spotless and tidy everything was. But it wasn't "a don't you dare "disturb kind of tidiness, there was a comfortable warmth permeating room that made you feel welcome. Prominently above the gleaming gas fire fireplace was a portrait of a young soldier in an officer's dress uniform. "That's my boy

Tom, he's named after me .Call me Tom, would you, I don't like all this Mr. Edwards stuff in my own home. Tom's in the Royal Artillery. That's him passing out at Sandhurst. They took him from the ranks and made him an officer. He was always a smart lad, great at Maths he is. Gets his brains from his mother, not me. She's out shopping just now. Don't let the fancy dress uniform fool you, he's as hard as nails. A few years back he really sorted that cunt O'Halloran out, put him in hospital for a few weeks."

"You're sure he's the one who stole your car, Tom?"

"Too bloody right I am, but of course I can't prove it. At least not in any way that you lot would accept. But I could tell from the smirk on his face when he saw me next day that he was the one who did it."

During the next ten minutes Tom told Bully how long he'd had the Cortina, how he'd cared for it. He had won many certificates with it at Vintage Car Rallies and how despite the both the car and the garage door being locked it had been stolen from his garage.

"But you've no actual proof that O'Halloran stole it." Bully said.

"Not until my lad gets back from Iraq where that fucking poodle Blair sent him and his mates just to please that cowboy Bush. Tom will get the truth out of O'Halloran, he's a black belt you know."

"I understand your feelings Tom but I don't think it would do your son's army career any good for him to be involved in a brawl when he was home on leave, do you.".

"Perhaps not" Tom said after a longish pause "but I'll find some way to pay that bastard back. I was a Stevedore in the docks for thirty years. We had our own ways of dealing with scum like him."

"Well, you'd better not tell me any of them Tom" said Bully "I'd hate to have to give evidence against you."

Tom laughed and offered Bully "a cup of tea or something stronger if he was allowed" but Bully said he had to get back to Union. He was giving Edwards details about how to retrieve the remains of the Cortina and the local council involved when he saw on the sideboard a photo of a green and white Cortina.

"Tom, is that your Cortina that was stolen?"

"Certainly is" Tom replied going over and bringing the photo over for Bully to examine.

"It's very distinctive. If you let us have a couple of photos we'll get them copied and widely circulated. Someone's bound to have seen it around the town."

Tom left the room and came back with two foolscap envelopes full of photographs of the car. Bully chose three giving an overall view of the gleaming car. "These will be a great help I'm sure Tom."

."You're welcome. Perhaps I'll bring it back and rebuild it" Tom said as they parted, "Bored stiff I am with nothing to do."

Bully wished him good luck and he and Union drove to East Ham police station. When they told DI Ray Loomis about what Edwards had said he told them Danny O'Halloran was well know as a local villain "He was a bit of a Stock Car Racer. Won a few trophies. We know him mainly as a get-away driver. He's done time for a series of smash and grabs five years ago."

"Who was he working for?" asked Union.

Loomis's answer was the best they could have hoped for "You know them. The Gomez brothers."

When they told him about Mills and his connection with Jepson he said "I think we'd better have Danny boy in for a chat. You want to be here when we interview him? We might be lucky and get him in the next hour or so. If you want while we're waiting I haven't had any lunch yet. The Madras Curry shop just round the corner does an excellent mid-day spread. Care to join me?"

The curries were as appetising as Loomis had said; Bully had plenty of Nan bread in the hope of disguising his indulgence from Helene. During the meal Loomis told them more about Danny. "When he came out of the Nick the Gomez's had other drivers working for them and didn't need him. He's been sniffing around doing all he can to get back in with them."

"Do you think he would knock down and kill a man to get back in their favour?"

Loomis didn't answer directly. After a good long draught of his lager he said "On balance I think he would. He a cocky bugger. Thinks of nobody but himself. Tries to give the impression that he's always up for a laugh and a joke but there's a nasty streak in him. He's got two sisters who hate the sight of him. They wouldn't testify against him in open court but they'd no hesitation in telling me things that helped put him away when he was driving for the Gomezes"

Their conservatism was interrupted by Loomis's phone ringing. Watching his face Bully got the feeling that O'Halleran had been picked up. Loomis nodded as he slid the phone back in his pocket, "He's on his way in." They finished their drinks and walked back to the station. They decided to let O'Halloran stew for a while in the interview room while they discussed their tactics. Loomis was obviously the best one to lead the interview so they went over once more all that they knew about Overton's killing.

When they went into the interview room Loomis introduced Bully and Union without saying where they were from. O'Halloran was casually dressed in a light blue Nike tracksuit and bottoms. Both so spotlessly clean that it was obvious no physical exertion had ever taken place in them. He was lounging back in his chair looking if at any minute he was going to put white his Nike trainers up on the table. When he spoke it was as if he was auditioning for the part of a stage Irishman in a comedy.

"I'll be hoping you gentlemen will not be detaining my good self here overlong. 'Tis important business I have to do this afternoon, sure it is. It is."

"Cut the stage Irish crap Danny" Loomis said, "the only times you've been in Ireland is when you run away to your grannies like a skulking schoolboy you were. Now sit up straight and listen. This isn't one of your escapades about you driving about with lead in your boots. This is about something that will put you away for a long time if you're in any way involved."

"I'll be needing a solicitor then will I soor?" replied Danny with a smirk.

"You will, if we charge you. This is just a few friendly questions. You've no need for one just now unless you want to confess and save us all a lot of time. You can decide what to do while I set up the tape and video recorders."

After Loomis had identified everyone present and noted the time and place of the recording he asked "Now Danny, I want you to think back a few weeks. To a Friday night, June 9th it was. Can you remember where you where on that date?"

Danny didn't even pretend to think about his answer. He immediately shook his head and said, "Depends what time of the night you're talking about. I get around a lot on Friday nights. Lots of birds wanting to see me Friday nights."

"You'll have no trouble getting one or two of them to confirm your whereabouts then on that night then?"

"None at all. What's all this about then?"

"Patience Danny, Patience."

"No soor. Don't know any birds named Patience."

Loomis ignored his attempted humour. Lowering his voice he asked "Working now are you Danny?"

"Self employed soor. You should know that soor."

"So what was your last job then?"

"Can't quite remember. Things have been a bit slack lately."

"So not much money coming in?"

"Only what Her Majesty's lets me have. You know job seekers allowance and all that."

"Really? Those Nike Air Max trainers you're wearing cost over £120. And the rest of your gear looks brand new. Had a win on the horses then, have you?"

Danny shook his head, "No soor, no big wins lately. Although I've got a great tip for the Derby. I'd tell you only I know you'd tell all your mates at the station here. I don't want to shorten the odds now, do I? You understand don't you soor."

"I understand what a useless tosssser you are Danny boy. And I'd advise you to learn to say 'sir' instead of your cod Irish 'soor.' The warders don't like it. They've ways of improving your English inside as I'm sure you well remember."

Danny reacted to the detective's words as if he'd had an electric shock. His smirk disappeared as he shouted "Fuck you Loomis. Keep your fucking lies to yourself. Nothing happened in the nick, nothing. I'm telling you."

"You seem to be getting very upset over nothing, Danny." Turning to Bully and Union he added "It's seems Danny boy here found out inside that he was DC as well as AC. I'm told he really enjoyed it."

Bully and Union started forward as Danny pushed his chair back and stood up with his fists clenched but Loomis leaned further forward into Danny's face. Bully realised that Loomis wanted Danny to hit him. Danny must have also realised what was happening for he stepped back as he said "You're a cunt Loomis. You're not going to catch me like that. Trying to get me nicked for assaulting a policeman. No chance. I wouldn't touch shit like you with a bargepole. At least not in here I wouldn't. But some dark night, you wait," He picked up his chair and sat down a foot away from the table "You wait."

Loomis said to Bully and Union" You heard that threat gentlemen. Real hard man is what we've got here. Gets a hard on every time he sees a man he fancies, don't you Danny boy?"

Danny gripped the sides of his chair and looked down at the floor. "So" added Loomis "All this flash gear you've got, where did the cash come from?"

"Mind your own business. What I wear 's got nothing to do with you."

"I'm not interested in your sartorial tastes Danny. It where you got the cash from that I'm interested in."

"Saved up, didn't I" Danny muttered.

"Very commendable, take you long"

"I'm saying no more until I have a solicitor"

Loomis paused then looked enquiringly at Bully to see if he wanted to ask anything. Bully mouthed "car."

"Very well Danny. Just one other thing though. You know a Ford Cortina was nicked from the garages behind you."

Danny's smirk returned as he looked up "Yeah, that old git Taylor's. Really cut up about it he is."

"And I suppose you know nothing about it?" Danny shook his head as Loomis continued "The thing is Danny, we believe this car was used in a hit and run incident. Know anything about that?"

Danny shook his head again.

Loomis again looked at Bully who hesitated then asked," Get out into the country much Danny?"

Danny looked at him as if he was stupid, "Never, unless I'm going to see West Ham playing away. See enough of it then."

"Ever out Caldeford way?"

"What for? There's only piss pot teams out there in the sticks. Only time I've been that way is when one of them flukes it into a Cup tie."

"So if anyone identifies you as being in Caldeford recently you'd deny it."

"Too bloody right, I would. Couldn't happen. Nobody knows me out there."

"But what if someone has seen you there? They could pick you out of an identify parade."

A triumphant grin spread across Danny's face. "No way. I was always in...he quickly checked himself before adding "Canning Town, that's the only place I've been these last few months. You can put me in as many deadbeats cat walks as you like."

None of the detectives had any more questions. Loomis eventually broke the silence saying "OK Danny. That's all for now. You can go."

"Where's me motor then? Same couple of plods driving me back?"

"Sorry Danny, all the cars are out on calls. You know how much villainy there is around here. You'll have to make your own way back I'm afraid."

"Like fuck you are. I'm going to see a solicitor about this. Persecution that's what this is."

115

"Clear off Danny" Loomis paused before adding "And Danny…don't speak to any strange men on your way home."

"Fuck you" he replied, throwing the chair to the floor as he got up and made for the door.

When he'd gone, Loomis said "Near thing Bully. You think he was going to say 'in the car all the time'?"

"Yes Ray. That's just what I think."

Loomis told them he didn't have the manpower to mount a surveillance operation on Danny but he would get out a request for all staff to report when and where they saw him in the following weeks. "I'll ask them to get their snouts to keep an eye on him as well. I've got one grass who lives quite near him. He'll go out of his way to get me any info I ask for because he's a really avaricious bastard but he's never lied to me yet. We'll let everyone know we're especially interested in any contact Danny has with the Gomez's mob."

CHAPTER 31

Professor Collins, the consultant who had been called to treat Sam Ketteridge when she was brought into the hospital yesterday ushered Peter Steyn into his office. When they were both seated he said "Well Mr. Steyn, it seems as if the information these assailants gave you is correct. .She has been under constant observation since she arrived and all her organs are continuing to function but she would be dead without the ventilator. It's enabling her lungs to continue to do their job. The glucose solution she is receiving is lower than we would normally infuse but it view of what you insist you were told on the phone we are obeying your instructions to the letter. She is showing no adverse reactions so far but if there are any signs of trauma we must be allowed to increase the intravenous glucose mixture as we see fit. As a medical man yourself I'm sure you will understand."

Peter who was normally so decisive didn't know how to respond. He normally wouldn't tolerate any outsider telling him what to do. Where had these FAAN people got their knowledge of such a poison from? Probably, the internet. The world was a fruitcake's paradise nowadays. Hesitantly he said "Yes, of course. Samantha has only put an aunt who lives in Northampton as the next of kin on her application form. We've been in touch. She she's too busy to come down here in the school holidays. Got six kids and another one due to pop out in a few weeks. But I don't think Samantha is in any danger. These fanatics seem to know what their doing."

"How do you think they've done so? Not by trying this poison out first on other mammals, that's for sure."

"No, but it is possible that they may have experimented on themselves. They are fanatics aren't they? Don't forget, they claim it isn't a fatal toxicant. They must have some proof of their claims."

"I hope you're right in your assumptions. But as I've said, I must reserve the right to do what we think best."

Steyn nodded "If you think her condition is becoming critical, of course. But if there is no deterioration you'll hold to the dosage they've insisted."

It was Collins' turn to nod. "Bloody fanatics. You're not giving in to them are you? I mean, they're not going to let Miss Ketteridge die. That would really put the kibosh on them wouldn't it?"

"That's exactly what I think. They couldn't let that happen." Although he spoke confidently, Peter was far from sure he was right. All his years of dealing with anti-animal protesters made him think there was nothing they would stop at to achieve their aim. If Sam died there was nothing to prevent them claiming it was the wrong medical treatment she'd received in hospital that was the cause. That was why he'd been so insistent on telling the doctor's exactly what FAAN had prescribed when Sam was admitted. He didn't like this Professor Collins. As a student he'd met more than one consultant with a "god-complex" and Collins gave every sign of being in full possession of one.

Almost as if he could read Peter's mind, the professor said in a more reflective tone, "Of course if we identify the poison it may be possible for us to manufacture our own antidote."

"It's amazing what medical mischief is being developed and of course the police keep their own watch. I've recently been to a symposium where the amount of information the police possessed on poisoning amazed me. Have you contacted them about Miss Ketteridge?"

"No," Peter replied "That doesn't mean I'm not going to do so but I've got to go the long way round in case any of these FAAN people find out."

"Very wise" said Collins. When he remained silent Peter took it that the interview was at an end.

Peter's inclination was to return to his business but he went straight home instead. He justified his action on the presumption that the FAAN people might have some way of listening to his work phone calls. After sidestepping Luna's exuberant welcome and taking five minutes to calm her down he reassured his wife Esme that Samantha was, if not OK at least there was no evidence of her condition was deteriorating.

He had no idea where Bully or his parents lived and he didn't want to contact Bully at the police station, in case it was somehow leaked to the poisoners. He was wondering how he was going to get surreptitiously in touch with him when Esme came into the study.

"What are you looking so worried for?" she asked, "Is the news about Samantha worse than what you told me?"

"No not at all, I'm trying to get hold of a chap at the Rugby club who's also a policeman. But there are so many bloody people with his surnames in the book I don't know where to start."

"Phone John Topless, he'll have a list of Club members. If he's not at home he'll be on the golf course. We've got his mobile number as well haven't we?"

He reached out and grabbed her and pulled her onto his knee; "How do you do it sweetheart? The times I've spent hours puzzling over something and you come up with the answer immediately"

"Just because I'm a housewife doesn't mean my brain's died," she said as she pinched his cheek.

"I think" he replied," the sooner we get you back in the lab. the better"

"We'll see. Make that call."

Rugby Club secretary, John Topless was at home and three minutes later Peter had Bully's home and work phone numbers. John was proud of his computer skills and kept Peter talking for another ten minutes while he enthused about the new membership programme he'd installed that "was an absolute whiz" at bring up all their details "at the press of a couple of keys."

Now that he had Bully's work and department extension numbers Peter decided to risk phoning the police station after all. He had no trouble contacting Bully. After some preliminary chat about Rugby Peter briefly explained why he was calling and told him of FAAN's prohibition on informing the police. When Bully assured him that his phone extension was secure Peter told him all that had happened to Samantha and how she was being treated. As soon as they'd finished Bully got up and went to see his boss DI Janet Morison.

CHAPTER 32

"You think it's time we got rid of Stephen?" asked Tristan Wills-Hope.

"Don't say it like that Tris "said Alice "You make us sound like gangsters."

"You know what I mean Alice."

"We'll have to let him go sometime." replied Alice "The question is how we can be sure he'll keep his mouth shut?"

"Well, we've got the video of him stealing and most certainly the police will want him for those fake share certificates" said Tristan.

"You think that will be enough to keep him quiet? What if he informs on us anonymously?" asked Alice.

"I've thought of that" said Miranda, "Above everything else, well, apart from himself, Stephen loves money. So I'm going to pay him to keep quiet."

"You can't do that" said Alice.

"I can, easily" replied Miranda, "This house which Daddy bought for peanuts forty years ago is now worth almost £900,000. Also Daddy had amazing insurances that I knew nothing about. I've had over £70,000 from them. My brother in Australia gets half of course but it still leaves me with almost half a million. So I can easily afford to pay him off."

"So what do you propose to do?" asked Tristan.

"I'm going to offer him £10,000 a year for 3 years, paid in quarterly instalments through an Australian bank. He'll have to live there. I've found that I can arrange for the money to go only from one Australian account to another. I'm starting his deposit account off with £3,000 pounds."

"My goodness," said Alice" but what happens when the three years are up?"

"By then, we'll either have succeeded or we all will be in jail" said Miranda calmly. "So let's concentrate on the present, we've not had anything but threats from Steyn concerning Samantha."

"No" said Alice, "So how long can we keep her unconscious? We can't let her die."

"Hang on, hang on. I think we're getting a long way ahead of ourselves folks" said Miranda. "It's only been thirteen days since we hit her. Even without the antidote I'm sure she'll not be in any danger for another week. We've got to put as much pressure on Steyn as possible before then."

"Should we have a go at another one of them then?" asked Tristan.

"I've been wondering if that might not be a good idea" said Miranda.

"Who've you have in mind?" said Alice.

"Well, as you know we agreed we'd target first those who live on their own because there are no partners to make a hoo-ha .immediately they go missing. Unfortunately there's not so many of them as you might think. The most likely one is someone whose loss would really hit them hard; for example their head of research Dr. Miles Millinder. He's on his own. His wife left him three years ago went off with a younger bloke who was doing his PhD at the firm, Lives in Cambridge now. As far as I know he hasn't met anyone else yet. The electoral roll shows only him living at his address."

"How'll we do it?"

"I think it'll have to do it close up like Samantha's. I remember checking him out a couple of years ago when we were looking to see what sort of stuff we could lumber him with. He's got a nice cottage with a good sized garden which he keeps military tidy. I was only there on two occasions and he didn't leave his car out in the road. Always put it is his garage right beside the cottage."

"Could we hide behind the garage and get him as he goes into the cottage?

"Maybe but he's in a crescent and is well overlooked."

"After he garages the car does he go into the cottage by a side door or the front door" asked Alice.

"I didn't notice a side door. Always went in the front when I saw him."

"How long is the front drive? Could we get to him quickly as he's closing the garage door?"

"It's not long but as I've said it's well overlooked by the houses opposite."

"Why don't we just use the motorcycle messenger trick? I'd do it "said Tristan.

"You don't think he'd be too suspicious for that. I mean they must all have been warned to be on their guard."

"Perhaps" said Tristan "But if we do it first thing in the morning, he might be a bit off his guard then. It takes me a while to get it together after I wake up. I could even take my helmet off"

"But he'd be able to identify you then" protested Alice.

"No" replied Tristan, "You know my partner, Maurice, is a hairdresser. You wouldn't believe how different he can make me look with a bit of hair gel and some dye. Millinder won't recognize me"

CHAPTER 33

"So you are proposing that we put an undercover officer in among these FAAN people?" said Chief Constable, Phillip Torrington.

"Yes sir" replied DI Janet Morison. Bully's suggestion was to get someone undercover amongst the animal rights people and he had convinced her that he knew of the ideal candidate for the job.

"Do you have anyone in mind?" asked Torrington.

"Well sir, there is an officer who as far as we know has never been in contact with them at any time. He certainly hasn't been on duty outside the Steyn factory nor at any of the inquests. He's a constable Smith, he presently based at Brougham.

"Tolstoy Smith's boy. How well do you know him?"

Bully and DI Morison looked at each other. She was the first to speak, "Do you mean he's that Independent MP's son?" she asked.

"Didn't you know?"

"No sir. I'm surprised he's even in the force given his father's reputation for slagging us off."

"It's a puzzle to many of us Janet. He's a university entrant, Bristol if I remember correctly. I think he only got in because someone thought he'd be an embarrassment to his father. I mean, Tolstoy Smith can't say we're all bad when his own son is one of us, can he?"

"But what if he's a Trojan horse sort of thing" she paused "Sorry sir, I don't think I've put that very well."

"Don't worry Janet; I know exactly what you mean. As a matter of fact, that's what I thought when I first heard about him."

"But he's being watched?" asked Bully.

"Well, just let's say we're keeping an eye on him. That's one reason why he's out at Bourham and not at headquarters. I know he's been thoroughly investigated and it seems he's been at odds with his father since his early teens. Sort of white sheep of the family" he laughed.

"He seems very relaxed about everything, sir" said Bully, "That's the impression he given me when I'd had anything to do with him."

"Actually, that's the one thing everyone says about him. He's well respected at Bourham. Got a couple of boy's football teams going and he gives The Red Rose pub a bit of leeway about drinking up times. Not that I've told you that you understand?" Torrington said with a smile.

"So he might be just the lad for a bit of undercover work sir" said Janet.

"He could of course already be anti-animal experiments himself. There's a good chance he might be given the sort of people he was brought up with."

"We find out when we interview him "said Bully.

"Yes "said Torrington, "but even if he agrees we'll have to make sure he's suitable for undercover work. We'd be taking a hell of a chance with him. It's possible that keeping his identity as Tolstoy Smith's son could be a big plus for him with the animal liberationists. On the other hand if it all goes arse over tip you can imagine the fuss his father will make. If you're at all doubtful about his suitability drop him."

Bully looked at Janet. Both their careers would be at risk with Constable Smith. For all his joviality Phillip Torrington had a reputation of not suffering fools gladly. "I agree he'd have to be a willing volunteer sir. There's plenty of training now for undercover work, isn't there?"

"Yes Bully. With all the anti-terrorist legislation in force there's more surveillance training than ever available. Personally if you consider he's suitable I think he would be best being seconded to the Metropolitan Special Operations people for a few weeks. SO10 it used to be called although I think it's changed to some other letters now. There's that many bloody acronyms flying around it's like having to learn a foreign language every week just to keep up with them all. Any rate let me know what you make of him and if it's all hunky-dory I'll get things moving. This FAAN poisoning business could turn really nasty if we don't nip it in the bud."

After they said their goodbyes and were driving away in their car, Janet turned to Bully and said "The boss never ceases to amaze me. You'd think after working his way up through the ranks he'd be ultra cautious about involving other forces. But he's no hang-ups about using them at all. He's only interested in getting the job done."

"That's because he's got an American wife."

"Nonsense Bully."

"No maam. My family have known him for years. They say he was in danger of becoming a bit of a stick in the mud before he married her."

"Whirlwind romance wasn't it?"

"As near as dammit. Met her when he was sent to a conference in Boston. They married nine months later. "

CHAPTER 34

After Samantha had been unconscious for three weeks and the only responses from Steyn continued to be threats that they would be "hunted down if she dies" it was decided to proceed with the plan to poison Miles Millinder.

Since no one suggested any alternative Tristan had been given the job. He was thrilled feeling there was a touch of "James Bond" about the assignment as he rode his 125cc Honda around the Crescent where Millinder lived. He slowly passed the house twice to make sure there were there were no obstacles to his escape. He regretted he was not wearing a black motor-cycle helmet with a tinted visor. Somehow his white peaked helmet and goggles seemed rather tame for the task. He'd thought of buying a black leather jacket and leggings until he saw what they cost. He consoled himself that he did at least have the knee high black leather boots which he'd bought years ago as a protection against the kicks of hunt supporters when he was harassing them. He still hadn't fully made up his mind whether to go bare headed or keep his white helmet on. Just in case he did have the courage to go bareheaded his partner had restyled his hair and dyed it blonde with a cheap lotion that would quickly wash out.

When he dismounted from his bike by the cottage door he decided to keep his helmet on after all. So he felt adequately disguised as he approached the door. He had the pen with poison in his right hand beneath the clip board alongside the shoebox size parcel he held in front of him. He had only to unscrew the top before offering it to Millinder to sign for the parcel; Miranda had assured him that the slightest scratch would do the trick. But it must pierce the skin.

The large glass spy hole in the door was a shock. He'd not thought of that. When he'd regained his composure he practiced his smile a few times in front of it. He reached for the bell, then paused ...did delivery men smile? He couldn't remember. That little post girl last year had a lovely smile, the bloke that replaced her; uncouth was the kindest way to describe him. It was a miracle he could read the addresses. He...he...what the Hell was he thinking about! He was on a mission. "Keep your mind on the job" he scolded himself. Taking time to adopt a more businesslike look, he adjusted his mind into its "James Bond" model and pressed the bell.

Almost at once he heard footsteps approaching. Pressing his lips together and tilting his head slightly upwards he waited for the door to open.

"Yes?"

The voice startled him. The door stayed shut.

When he went to speak his throat was dry. "Par"...he coughed..."Parcel ...sir."

He was conscious of being watched through the spy hole. He was just about to speak again when he heard locks being undone.

The tall grey haired man blinking owlishly who opened the door seemed an easy enough target.

"Parcel sir"

"Thanks," the man said snatching the parcel and closing the door.

"Sir" Tristan yelped "Sign, you've got to sign for it." He held out the clipboard towards the retreating figure.

"Oh..." the man paused, "My glasses. I'll need my glasses, Excuse me." He closed the door.

Tristan stood bewildered on the step. He hadn't expected this. He'd already unscrewed the pen. Jesus, some of the poison was leaking unto his gauntlet. He had to summon up all his self-control to stop himself throwing the pen away. He kept telling himself that he could come to no harm as long as the poison didn't get in his bloodstream. Why was Millinder was taking such a long time returning. Instinctively he went to look at his watch then realised it was pointless as he'd no idea of the time when Millinder had closed the door. The bell? Should he ring it again? Cautiously he put his left hand out towards it then changed his mind. Patience, patience and calmness were what were needed on these jobs. James Bond never panicked. The old bugger probably couldn't find his glasses.

His arm was getting cramped holding the parcel. He went to transfer it to his other hand. He ...His thoughts were shattered by the sound of an approaching siren. He tried to tell himself it was an ambulance. But what if it was the police? He'd better scarper. It sounded more like a police one. Screwing the top back on the pen with his gauntlets on and running wasn't easy. Why had he left his bike so far past the house? As soon as he reached it he thrust the pen into a pannier.

He'd got it started just as the police car came in sight. Opening the throttle to its fullest extent he aimed the bike up on to the pavement and roared past the police car with his head turned away from it. He heard the squeal of brakes as it halted. Luckily there was no traffic approaching as he shot out of The Crescent. He daren't look back to see if it was turning to come after him.

He turned left as he came out onto the road, he could see a roundabout ahead. He wove through the morning rush hour traffic, horrified to hear the siren of the police car following him. Blindly he took the first exit on his left, just before the roundabout, reaching the bikes maximum speed as he zoomed down the hill. There was a council estate at the bottom; he'd have a better chance of getting away in the maze of streets there. He swerved so widely into the estate he almost collided with a car that was leaving.

Before him was a parade of shops, he had to use all his strength to control the skid as he turned sharply into their car park. Looking back he saw the police car coming down the hill, they must have seen him turn in here. In desperation he shot down a passageway that divided the shops into two blocks. He stopped at the end not knowing which way to turn Two lorries parked behind the shops made him realise there must be a service road here, he hurtled out into the road and turned right. Bloody idiot, the police would catch him on the steep ascent but it was too late to worry about that now. The siren was getting louder, any minute now they would catch him. James Bond always found an escape route, why couldn't…there was an alleyway just ahead on the left; he had to brake hard to prevent himself skidding past. He lifted the bike up the kerb, thanking God it was such a lightweight machine and drove down the alleyway. Again at the end he had the dilemma which way to turn. Out of the corner of his eye he saw another alleyway across the road on his right. He was just about to enter it when he saw the woman with the pram coming down it. He wheeled around in a wide u-turn but when he faced it again she was still coming towards him. Thankfully there was no sign of the police car but when he completed another u-turn she was standing at the entrance to the alleyway staring at him. "Move" he yelled as he headed straight towards her. As she dragged herself and the pushchair aside she was shouting but the noise of the police siren blocked out most of what she was saying. As he passed her she hit him with a large handbag making him wobble and hit his right hand against some wooden fencing. Somehow he kept the bike upright. Coming out into the road there was woodland opposite with an entrance to his left. His heart lifted when he saw the staggered metal barriers designed to make cyclists dismount. He got off his bike and wriggled it through unto the narrow dirt trail leading into the woods. He felt like shouting for joy but the noise died in his throat he saw the police car, its lights flashing come around the corner. They had switched the siren off. Surely they weren't allowed to do that. He almost fell as he ran alongside the bike only his quickly twisting the throttle back enabled him to jump on. At the first bend he stopped and looked back just in time to see the police car roaring away. But a policeman was running down the track towards him. Stupid fool… Then he swore as he realised that police man was there only to stop him doubling back. Opening the throttle to its maximum he roared away. Coming around another bend he saw the track forked immediately ahead. Without thinking he took the right hand fork and was thrilled to realise the trees were denser here. After a few minutes he turned the bike off the track and stopped under some trees to take his helmet off and shove it under a bush opposite a NO CAMPING, NO FIRES sign, hoping that if the police did see him soon they would think it was another motorcyclist.

While he was stopped he tried to think what to do next? He knew he was somewhere on the southern outskirts of the town. That meant this trail would come out on to a country road. He'd be easy to spot there wouldn't he? But he couldn't stay in these woods; If only he could hide the bike here but if the police found it they'd have no trouble finding him. If only he knew somebody, if…wait…he did know somebody, Tom and Mary Wilkinson lived out here. One of the posh houses about half a mile after the housing estate. Holloway Road wasn't it? Yeah? FAAN had had a party there last Christmas. Didn't know the number but there was a red reflective triangle on both gateposts; not likely to have changed them, was he?

He steered his bike along a narrow track among the trees. He was going slowly as he wanted to keep his engine revs low. He was soon sweating like a mad holidaymaker in the tropics. He was despairing of being able to keep going when he suddenly came to the edge of the wood. There was a high hawthorn fence ahead with traffic constantly passing on the other of it. What luck! He didn't have to pray for a gap to appear for there was one only ten metres to his right. He wrestled his bike through the gap and when the road was clear set off back past the housing estate. Making sure he kept exactly to the speed limit as he travelled along to Holloway Road on his left.

The two triangles were easy to spot. He drove around to the back of the house. Tom and his wife would be at work now. A garden shed was locked but there was a gap between it and a compost bin. He squeezed the bike between them threw his gauntlets after it.

When he'd gathered his thoughts he wrote a note saying he'd call back for the bike tonight and put it through their letterbox. Thank God he was never without his notebook and pencil. He'd carried them with him for years to write down the registration numbers of hunt supporters cars or details of any of their thugs when there was a fight. Getting down these details excused him from getting too heavily involved in such melees although he could fight when he had to.

He felt self conscious walking along in his knee high leather boots but what else could he do? He lingered close to a hedge at the first bus stop he came too. If only he had a newspaper to hide his face! It was almost fifteen minutes before he saw a bus approaching. It was going into the town centre. Hallelujah! He'd go to Maurice's and get all this chi- chi blond stuff washed out of his hair. Sod James Bond. The sooner his life got back to normal the better.

CHAPTER 35

Constable Smith had a face that a conman would sell his soul for. Pushing back an unruly golden forelock he said calmly to Bully "You want me to spy on these FAAN people?"

"Yes Constable Smith, have you any objections to doing so?"

Smith hesitated before he said "It's difficult to give you a straight answer."

"Why/" asked Janet Morison "Your Public School make a big thing of not being a sneak?"

"Not at all, rather the opposite as a matter of fact. At my school we were taught it was most important to tell the truth" he hesitated again "as far as possible that is?"

"And what sort of circumstances excused you from being truthful?"

"When it would be very hurtful to others"

"You mean" said Bully "Like when your wife says 'Does my bum look big in this'?"

"Exactly Sir, There was a great deal of emphasis at Springford on not hurting each other's feelings."

"Springford?" said Janet "That's the school where you didn't have to attend lessons if you didn't want to?"

"Yes, everything was voluntary, big emphasis on self-discipline Hence the emphasis on telling the truth."

"So what did you do Smith?"

"Actually, apart from Maths and later Physics, I went to most lessons. Lots of my mates thought I was real crawler. But I found that time went much quicker in lessons than it did sitting watching the clouds amble along."

"So you were always a good boy?" said Bully.

"I don't know about good. I'd say now that I've had a few years as an adult to think about it I was just terribly ambitious. I always want to be top dog."

"And are you still ambitious?"

"Yes maam, Very. To tell the truth I'd like to one day see a new kind of police, a cooperative force, not as authoritarian as we are now. But I'm realistic enough to know that's a far-off dream. Still, if I get to be chief constable one day I might be able to hasten it along."

Bully had to check himself from shaking his head. Smith's words were spoken without a hint of artifice or guile. Janet interrupted his thoughts.

"Well Smith, if you ever get that far I hope you'll spare a thought for all of us that will have helped you on your way."

""Most certainly, maam. Your pension will be much more generous when I'm in charge."

"I must remember to hang on then until you're at the top" said Bully.

Everybody laughed. Bully couldn't ever remember such innocuous laughter. Most of the station's humour depended on the how dirty the jokes were.

It was Janet who restored order. "Right, so in the meantime, Smith, while you're waiting for the all that silver to be stuck around your cap do you think you can do this undercover assignment?"

"I can't give you a straight yes or no right away. I'd like to think it over say for 48 hours. If I did it, I'd have to be absolutely sure I could carry it off."

"That's understandable. I think that we can allow you that. But what are your personal feelings about experimenting on animals for medical reasons?"

"Like many others I'm somewhat ambivalent. Most of the time I don't like the idea of furry little creatures being sacrificed. I'm not fully convinced that it is the best way to find an answer to disease. But I've spent a few years in Malawi and … well, anything that would develop a cure to wipe out even one of the horrible diseases I saw there, I'd be all for it even if it did involve doing horrible things to a few rats."

"What about foxhunting?" asked Bully.

"I'm no lover of foxes that's for sure. At school I was for a while in charge of the hens. One night a fox killed twenty of them. Sheer random slaughter. Only took one away. I've had it in for foxes, ever since."

"Ever done any hunting yourself?"

"Not in this country. I've not been at any pro-hunt demo either. So if I did take this job I'd not have any fear of anyone recognizing me."

"Well Smith, take your 48 hours to think it over. We can give you some training if you do decide to accept but really it all will depend on your adaptability. I don't think these anti-vivisectionists would go so far as to kill you if they found you out but they might give you a good kicking. So think on lad.

"Will do, maam. I'll be in touch within 48 hours I promise."

After he had left Bully and Janet looked at each other unspeaking for a minute. Janet was the first to speak "Well Bully, you thinking the same as me?"

"You mean, is he real?"

She nodded. "Yes. You know what he's called?"

Bully shook his head.

"Sunny boy. His parents in their hippy phase christened him Sun Smith"

"Jesus! He must have a thick skin to have born that cross all his life."

"Indeed. That's why I can't help feeling that in many ways he'd be ideal for the job."

"He certainly sounds like just the sort of woolly liberal that many of the animal rights people are?"

"Or used to be. These poison attacks on others are a hell of big step up in their intimidatory methods. Actually, I doubt if everyone in the group that's doing it agrees with this poisoning. It wouldn't surprise me if we might not soon be getting anonymous letters telling us who's behind it."

"I agree. That's where someone undercover might be such a big help. Might even be able to stoke up some discontent. Who knows what'll happen if they let the sunshine in?"

"That's terrible Bully. Bugger off and do some work."

CHAPTER 36

As the treadmill slowed to a halt Stephen grabbed the horizontal support bar with both hands.

"Well done Stephen" said Miranda, "Two miles in just over half an hour, that's what we want to see."

"Bloody well satisfied then are you? I'm fed up with this bloody lark."

"Don't be so impatient. You're half-way there."

"Halfway? I've got to do this for a whole bloody hour. You've got to be joking."

Miranda shook her head, "We can't risk letting you out into the big wide world if you are not fit. You know that."

"But you are going to let me go, aren't you? I've promised you I won't say anything, haven't I?"

"Yes, but…"

"What's the matter? Don't you believe me? You've got that video and the stuff you allege about Sally. Isn't that enough?"

"One would hope so, but…Miranda paused, "Let me ask you this Stephen, apart from yourself what do you love most?"

His voice slipped back into its original East End twang as he asked indignantly "Eh? Whaddah mean?"

"Put your sweat top back on and come and sit down and I'll tell you."

Stephen was having all his meals now at a little table. There was a plastic garden chair on either side of it. He sat down opposite Miranda.

"Money's very important to you Stephen."

He looked at her as if she was an imbecile. "So?"

"If I pay you £36,000 would you sign a document promising never to disclose what has happened to you here?"

He had to fight hard to keep the excitement out of his voice. Very slowly he said "Depends. £50.000 sounds a lot better."

"Don't waste my time. £36,000 is an all our nothing offer."

"Is it?" Well, I'd be a fool not to take it then wouldn't I?"

"You would "she paused, "And you'd be an even bigger fool if you ever broke your agreement."

He didn't answer. He knew it would be a waste of time swearing he'd never do such a thing. The quicker he got his hands on the money the better. He looked at her expectantly.

"Right, listen. Hold on to your questions until I've finished speaking. You can ask what you like then. This arrangement depends entirely on none of your time here ever becoming public knowledge. The moment it does the payments will stop and I promise you that you will receive another much stronger does of poison without any hope of an antidote." She paused and looked him straight in the face. The bitch was threatening him. He did his best to keep the anger out of his features. He nodded as if he was in agreement with what she was saying. He tried to keep his eyes on hers but the intensity of her expression made him look away. Sure as fuck he was going to find some way to teach her a lesson. But for now he'd be "gentle Jesus, meek and mild."

Without any softening of expression she continued "The £36,000 will be yours to keep. You'll never be asked to pay it back. But there are some conditions. First, except for the first £2000, the money will be paid in £1000 monthly instalments so that you receive £12,000 each year. (We're giving you double the first time to help you get yourself settled).Second, you can only collect the money on the first Friday of the month from one bank, the Silvertown branch of the National Australian Bank in Sydney, Australia." She held up her left hand to stop him interrupting, "You'll be paid in Australian dollars. So it will depend on the exchange rate how much you get for your English pounds. You will have to immediately post me a receipt for each monthly instalment. If I don't get one you won't get the next month's payout. Also, only you can collect the money, no one else. Not only will the bank have your photo but a friend of mine will be watching out for you on each of the Friday's. It is through this friend that I will have set up this arrangement. You can go wherever you like in the country but you cannot arrange for the money to be paid to you in any other bank or place. Is that clear?"

He nodded too quickly for her peace of mind. But what could go wrong? He could of course get back here in less than twenty-four hours but she couldn't think of any way of preventing that. All she needed was for him to be out of the way for at least a year or so. Animal experiments would have stopped by then or she would be in jail.

"Any questions?"

"What happens when the money's run out?"

"That's up to you. We'll still have the video and a lot more evidence from the various women you've defrauded. Gwen's already had three women contact her. She's checking them out. If you've any sense you'll use this money to set yourself up in some legitimate business in Aussie." (She knew he wouldn't, there was no chance of this leopard changing its spots.)

"So once I can manage an hour on that treadmill, I'll be off to Australia."

"You should be. If you agree and sign up today I'll start the whole thing rolling. The only delay would be if the National Australian Bank doesn't act fast enough. But as soon as they do, you'll be on your way £2000 to the good. The money we made from your BMW will pay your airfare, unless you want to travel business class"

"I'll think about that". (He preferred business class not just because of the extra comfort but he had could meet richer women there. On a long flight he'd have a good chance of chatting up some wealthy tart, preferably a widow.)

"You haven't got unlimited time. You'll have to make your mind up soon."

"Don't get your knickers in a twist. I'll sign. Where's the document?"

CHAPTER 37.

Peter Steyn sat at his computer studying the photographs that Marie Frampton the private investigator he'd hired to attend Desiree's inquest had taken. He wished now he'd followed her advice and hired another one of her staff to take a video of the FAAN supporters in the crowd outside. The ones doing this poisoning must surely have been amongst them.

What a good job all his senior staff were equipped with panic buttons wired to the local police station. That was "Bully's" idea and he'd got it implemented quickly. It had also been Bully" who'd told them to immediately get themselves as far away as possible from anyone they were suspicious about. Millinder had certainly done that.

If that little bastard at Millinder's door had only waited another minute he'd have been caught. It was ironic that Millender's eyes had been the perfect excuse for going indoors yet his poor eyesight prevented from identifying his caller. He ruined it as a student with all his studying. Still he'd been clever to straightaway tear open the parcel. It had been just a load FAAN leaflets.

Samantha had been unconscious for five weeks now and there was no word from her attackers about an antidote. Just weekly instructions on what intravenous feeding she should have. Neither the hospital nor his firm's research had made any progress in finding an antidote so far. Trouble was they didn't have any samples of the poison.

It would be such a relief when she was back, except for Luna of course. That bloody dog had wormed her way into all his family's affections. All the children loved the loopy hound and rushed home from school to play with her. Every day he had to remind the children that they were only looking after Luna until Sam was better but he knew there'd be tears when she had to go. His wife swore walking her twice a day was doing wonders for her figure. When the children were in bed Luna would come up and lay her head on his knees giving him reproachful looks but he wasn't giving in, she wasn't allowed up on the furniture. In Africa his family always had had dogs but they were guard –dogs, not pets. They'd lived outside but the children wouldn't allow Luna to be kept outside in a kennel. She was supposed to stay in the kitchen when alone in the house but somehow she'd learned to open the child gate he'd put up in the doorway. She was cunning enough to slip off the furniture when someone came home but the warm depressions she left behind betrayed her. He was resigned to having to get another dog when she went. He would prefer a little terrier but Esme was prattling on about how aristocratic Luna looked. They'd probably end up with a pure bred Saluki.

But he'd more important things to worry about just now. The attempt on Millender showed how serious these FAAN people were. They had to be stopped. The police agreed that these attacks on his staff were serious criminal offences but he couldn't see they were doing anything serious about it. As far as he knew they'd not had any FAAN people in for questioning and they were keeping news about Samantha out of the media. He was beginning to think that the public should know about these poison attacks. Let them see what bastards these so called animal lovers were. At the moment it was only a few of his senior staff that knew what had happened to Sam; they were the ones who had got the alarms. He'd initially agreed with the police that if everyone in the firm knew about the poison attacks it might make some think about leaving. "Bad for morale" Phillip Torrington had said. But they couldn't keep dancing forever to FAAN'S tune. They had to be stopped.

There was no way he was going to move his firm. Despite its attractions of sun and sand; his South African homeland was far too violent to consider taking his wife and children back there. No; he'd stay and fight. He'd beat these FAAN people, by Christ he would.

He'd hire Marie Frampton again and not tell the police. Whoever was manufacturing this poison surely must have a good science degree. She could find out what qualifications some of this rabble had. Some of the photos he had in front of him would undoubtedly be the ones carrying out the attacks but it was the chemist that was the key to stopping them. Even though the Internet enabled any Tom, Dick or Harriet to find out the most lethal things, the poison they were using couldn't just be picked up by mail-order.

He would get Marie to take photos of the mob outside his factory each day. Millender was certain that it was a young man that had delivered the parcel. He'd get her to concentrate on this age group. Being a University town there would probably be quite a few of these layabouts who had nothing better to do but if she concentrated on the young men who were there during the Uni. vacations somebody worthwhile might turn up.

CHAPTER 38

"Sam" Smith had never really doubted that he would accept the undercover assignment. After six weeks training he was now installed as a registered post graduate student of Caldeford University and tonight was his first attempt to get in contact with the FAAN group. He learned that FAAN often used this pub but after an hour there was no sign of them. Another pint would put him well over the drink drive limit but he'd look suspicious sitting here with an empty glass.

There had been some progress on the Dale Overton killing. Both local papers had printed photos of the distinctive Cortina and five people had reported seeing it. All were in the right area for where Overton had been killed but none had given any clear identification of the driver. Still it was something.

Now if they could only make some progress on these FAAN people, where the hell were they? He'd been told that this was one of the few pubs in town where the landlord was sympathetic to their cause. It was a quarter past ten already, they must have had a good old chinwag tonight That didn't offer him much hope of getting acquainted with them if they'd already talked themselves dry. On the other hand they might have had a bust up and someone might still be annoyed enough to give vent to their feelings. Including himself there were only about a dozen customers in the pub, five sitting at the bar, a foursome at the other end of the room and a middle aged couple one table away from him. He'd chosen to sit this distance away from them in the hope that he'd find himself in the middle of the FAAN crowd if enough of them came in.

He rose to go to the bar leaving his glass and an Amnesty International magazine open beside it so that no one would take his place. The landlady didn't hurry to serve him; she was listening intently to what a small man with slicked back black hair was saying. He'd started to read the inscriptions on the horse brasses behind the bar when out of the corner of his eye he saw the little man pointing towards him. The landlady turned and came towards him with what he thought was a genuine smile on her face.

He had always believed he had a talent for "reading faces" and his interest in this skill had been stimulated some years ago by an article entitled "The Diogenes Project" that had been in a magazine he'd read on a flight home from Africa. Diogenes was a Greek philosopher who was reported to have walked around Athens in the daytime shining a lantern in people's faces because he was "looking for an honest man." The project was an experiment by two American psychologists in the 70s that tested the ability of people to detect lies told by others. They found that only about one percent of their subjects had the ability to consistently discern who was lying and concluded they did so by their ability to read what they called "microexpressions"in the face. Some of their conclusions seemed very speculative to him but subsequently his own research and experiments with friends had, he believed, strengthened his self belief in his ability to tell when people were being genuine and when they were telling lies.

"Same again?" she said as he offered her his glass, the warmth in her voice backed up his analysis of her smile.

He shook his head "No, I'd better make it a pint of orange and lemonade, I'm driving"

"Very sensible, the police around here are very hot on drink driving."

As she drew his pint there was a commotion behind him, he turned to see a crowd coming in. Several were wearing Caldleford University scarves. When he'd registered during the University's Welcome Week for his Post Graduate Certificate Course on Child Welfare in India and had bought a scarf on impulse He'd thought of wearing it tonight but it looked so blatantly new he'd rejected the idea. Now he wished he'd done so as it would have given him a chance of being drawn into the group. He wasn't exactly an ace at this undercover work was he? The only advice that had stuck in his mind from the course was not to smile or joke. "These animal rights people don't have much of a sense of humour" had been continually emphasised throughout his six weeks training.

When he turned back from the bar he saw that the clientele of the pub had more than doubled. No wonder the landlord approved of the group. The middle aged couple were still at their table. Four of the newcomers took the table next to them so that Sam's table now separated them from the rest of the FAAN members. His glass and magazine had done what he'd hoped. Now he had to find some way of getting talking to these anti-vivisectionists.

As he sat back down at his table, he felt certain he'd seen the man sitting nearest to him before. It was the shoulder length silver hair that triggered his recognition of the naturalist Paul Hamton. He was often on the TV discussing the dangers of global warming. Sam gave him a friendly nod which was acknowledged but before Sam could speak to him one of the women beside Hamton said something that took his attention away from Sam.

Deciding his magazine might encourage someone to talk to him he held it up as he read it as if his eyesight was weak. As he tuned into the voices around the nearest table he was surprised to hear them talking about sabotaging the local hunt on Sunday.

"The bastards think they're above the law."

"I know, the hounds ripped a fox to pieces in the middle of the cricket pitch earlier this year."

"The police did nothing about it, I suppose."

"You suppose right. Useless buggers."

"See no evil, that's their motto when it comes to lawbreaking by foxhunters, isn't it?"

"I wonder how much they pay them?"

"They must…."

Sam's eavesdropping was interrupted by a female voice saying, "Excuse me, would you mind if I take a chair from your table. You're not saving them for anyone re you?"

Sam looked up at the speaker, a slim woman with chestnut hair peeking out from under a fawn costermonger's cap. Her kindly green eyes contrasted sharply with the paleness in her face. She looked to be on the edge of exhaustion.

"No. You're welcome. Here let me. You look as if you've had a busy day."

"You can say that again."

Sam checked himself from taking her literally. She really didn't seem to be in the mood for schoolboy humour. He seized the chair nearest to her and took it over to the FAAN table where he learned from their warm welcomes that she was "Alice."

He slid the chair beneath her and turned away.

"Wait, don't go. Come and sit with us if you're really on your own" said another young woman whose chestnut curls matched Alice's.

"Yes do" said a well dressed older woman smiling at him, "Someone with such good manners shouldn't' be left drinking on his own. Unless you're waiting for someone of course."

He shook his head. "No, actually this is the first time I've been in here. I'm just finding my way around." When they all looked at him expectantly he added "I'm starting a Course at Caldeford next week."

"Post graduate I presume" said the woman he took to be Alice's sister.

"Don't be so rude Connie" said Alice. Then turning to him she said, "You must forgive my sister, she's on a farm all day. Spends so much of her time talking to the animals she forgets how to talk to adults."

They all laughed and as the laughter faded Connie said "Listen to who's talking. Bosses her poor bloody nurses and patients around all day then tries to do the same to everyone else when they let her out."

Sam took advantage of the ensuing silence to move his chair over beside Alice and before sitting down offered to buy everyone a drink.

"No, no we can't let you spend your measly grant like that" said silver haired Hampton, "It's my shout. You wouldn't believe me how much I've just got paid for sitting on my arse in a comfy studio and being encouraged to ride my hobby horse full tilt."

Hampton wouldn't take no for an answer and while he was away Sam introduced himself to the others at the table; learning their names in return. The well dressed woman was Janet, a buxom middle aged woman beside her was Ursula and a young man with multiple silver rings in both ears was Tristan. By this time Hampton was back with a tray full of drinks. He'd bought Sam a half pint of bitter despite his protesting that any more alcohol would put him over the limit

When Sam protested Janet asked "Always careful to fully obey the law, are you?"

Sam answered "No, I couldn't say I was particularly law abiding."

Connie asked, "So when would you break the law, Sam?"

He paused to give the impression he was thinking deeply "Well, I've been on a few protest marches. Sometimes thing have got a bit out of hand."

"What were you protesting about Sam" asked Hamton.

"Human rights "answered Sam "Mostly, I'm sad to say, against African dictators and our Ministry of Defence arming them with weapons to kill their own people."

"What about animals' rights?" asked Ursula.

"I've been out with hunt saboteurs a few times when I was at Bristol. Hunting was a big thing in the West Country before the Act came in."

"Still is" said Tristan.

"Really, I though only drag hunts are legal now?"

"Supposed to be but many so called drags are just excuses to let their hounds wrinkle out foxes and kill them. There's one this Sunday. You're welcome to come if you want" said Tristan"

Sam nodded, "I'd enjoy that. Be good to get involved again."

"What have you been doing that's stopped you until now?" asked Connie.

Before he could answer Alice said "You really must forgive my sister Sam, she's a nosey cow."

"No, just natural female curiosity." said Connie.

Before she could answer, he added "I've been stuck behind a desk for some months working for Oxfam. I caught Malaria in Zimbabwe some years ago and got a particularly bad bout last year. They brought me back to a desk job here to give me a break and time to recover. (He was on safe ground here for in his student gap year he had caught the disease in Africa and had slight recurrences occasionally.) I hope to go back abroad when this diploma course finishes next year."

They were all congratulatory about the work of Oxfam in Africa and fortunately did not question him closely about his supposed recent work there. It was Alice who asked "What do you think of medical experiments on animals?"

He took his time answering. "I've not made up my mind one way or the other about that. Seeing the terrible effects of Aids in Africa I am inclined to think that anything that leads to a cure must be worthwhile. But I'm no entirely happy about experiment on primates"

Tristan said "Do you know they euthanize primates when they're finished with them?"

"No. I didn't know that."

"What about rats and mice?" asked Ursula.

"Well, to be honest I don't feel so bad about them. I mean they experiment on fruit flies as well, don't they."

As he expected everyone started to speak at once but Hamton's voice was the one he heard most clearly.

"You don't think that all life is sacred then Sam"

Sam again took his time answering. "No. I don't. I've splattered hundreds of mosquitoes without compunction."

That silenced them. It was Alice who spoke first, "I'm afraid I've done the same abroad. I hate the little buggers."

Tristan and Janet looked at her as if she'd just admitted assassinating the Queen. He was surprised when it was Carrie who spoke in her defence. "I've got to admit I've killed an insect or two when I'm feeding the pigs but I don't think that means I can't protest about vivisectionists experimenting on animals."

Sam nodded in agreement, "I think you're right. Killing insects that can do you harm doesn't make you a hypocrite when you object to primates or smaller mammals being experimented on. After all, it was a female mosquito that infected me with malaria."

Before he could add that it hadn't turned him against woman Connie said "That's right, blame the women again."

141

CHAPTER 39.

Miranda handed Steve his flight tickets

"That's the second boarding call; you'd better get going now. You'll need your passport."

"I've flown before, thanks." He pulled the ticket from its folder and studied it. "Over £1300" he paused before adding "and that's only one way. Bloody dear, isn't it?"

"You're the one who wanted business class."

He pulled the rest of the stuff out of the envelope. "Here what's this? A cheque for £650. You said I was getting £2000."

She brought another envelope out of her bag. "There's the balance of the second £1000. There's over £300 in notes here."

"What are you playing at? Why can't I have the money in cash now?"

"Too big a temptation Steve. You've never known how to keep hold of money." He started to protest but she checked him, "It'll be three weeks before you can draw your first £1000, having the money split like this will help make sure you don't blow it all in the first week The bank will cash your cheque. They've got your photo."

"But I'll get my monthly [payments all in one lump sum won't I?"

"Yes, you should have a better idea of your expenses after three weeks but how you spend your money will be up to you if you want to live like a lord for one week and starve for the next three, so be it."

He hated this stuck-up bitch treating him like a child but he kept his mouth shut because there was nothing he could do about it now. In Aussie things would be different, there were bound to be lonely middle aged women there that he could find and exploit. The only thing that worried him was what if she had friends of hers spying on him there and he didn't know who they were. Was that why he had to stay in Sydney so they could keep an eye on him?"

Her voice cut into his thoughts. "Don't look so worried Steve. Just think if all goes to plan one day you might one day be famous as the first person who proved our poison injections weren't toxic."

"Thanks a million. Suppose I come back here?"

"If you want all your money you'll have to stay the 3 years. The bank has instruction to pay only you in person and never more than £1000 per month. After 3 years as long as you keep your mouth shut where you live is of no interest to us."

He was trying to think of a smart answer when the final call for his flight was broadcast.

"Bye Steve" She turned and walked away. He stared after her. He'd expected her to stay and make sure he got on the plane. She was treating him like dirt. One day he'd make her pay, by Christ he would.

Miranda made her way to the short stay car park. It was just after four o'clock. She thought of phoning her younger brother in Australia but with the twenty three hours time difference he would probably be in some conference or other. He had been such a disappointment to her father and her. A brilliant mathematician they had expected him to go into pure research but from Cambridge he had gone straight in the world of finance. She used to call him "Bible Boy" and chant "Matthew, Mark, Luke and John" at him because his names were Matthew Marcos but since he'd become so immersed in the financial world she'd renamed him "Money Marc." Grudgingly she had to admit he must be good at what he did for he was some sort of district manager over all the Standard Australian Bank's branches in Sydney. He'd not made any fuss about making the financial arrangements for Steve. She'd told him Steve had information that would put some of her friends in FAAN in jail and he had to be paid off and got out of the way. All he'd said was "I suppose I'll have to provide some sort of refuge for you one of these days with your madcap schemes."

As she drove out of the car park she saw the Quantas plane taking off. She knew Steve wouldn't miss his flight. She wasn't going to waste any time thinking about him anymore, she had something much more important to do tonight.

A week ago they'd sent the antidote for Samantha to Steyn. The firm had made no move to cut-back on its activities but she'd expected that. Samantha had been almost seven weeks in a coma and Miranda had decided that was long enough for a first attack, Through Alice she knew that yesterday Samantha had opened her eyes and started her recovery. Now that she knew both the poison and the antidote worked Miranda had decide it was time to make a more serious attack on the Steyn Staff.

For the last three weeks FAAN members had been watching Derek Jobson. Using a different team each night had not only lessened the chances of detection but had enabled them to build up a comprehensive picture of his movements.

She drove home to pick up her equipment for the attack. It had been agreed that he was most vulnerable when he parked his car in The Retreat car park. As a committee member he had a reserved parking spot. It was well lit being near the back entrance to the club but because it was the first in a line of parking spots it was also close to a mass of rhododendrons on the boundary of the factory adjoining the car park. The high wire fence protecting the factory meant that it wasn't easy for anyone to get from the car park into the factory grounds.

She had a light meal and went over in detail her plan of attack. There didn't seem any reason why it should fail. After a good soak in the bath (She felt entitled to this indulgence to get rid of all traces of Steve from her.) she picked up all she would need and set off. Tristan was watching the road where Jopson lived and he would phone her when Jopson left his house.

She drove towards The Retreat and parked a few hundred yards away. When Tristan's call came she made her way to The Retreat. It took only six minutes to get from her car to the factory fence. She'd timed it last Friday night. There was a gap low in the wire at the opposite end of the fence of The Retreat's car park. She hoped that it hadn't been repaired but just in case she'd brought a pair of wire cutters with her. When she got close she saw she wouldn't need them, the gap was still there. She was wearing her black running top and jogging trousers under her mackintosh with its large poacher's pockets. She'd have preferred not to be wearing the mackintosh but she needed its voluminous pockets to hide the blow pipe and darts as well as the wire cutters.

It was the native Indian children who had taught her how to make and use blow pipes. She'd two twenty inch children's pipes she'd brought home as a souvenirs. She had also brought home some darts; they had to be a tight fit to be effective as a weapon. She had been practicing for months in her back garden and in the woods and reckoned now she was able to hit a six inch diameter target every time from up to ten feet away. She reckoned on being closer than that to her target tonight. It was a warm pleasant summer evening so there was little chance of Jepson's face or body being overprotected with clothes. If he was wearing an open necked shirt, the back of his neck would be her target.

As she expected his parking spot was empty. It would be ten minutes before he arrived. On the three previous occasions she'd watched him he'd been alone in the car. She presumed he dropped his wife off at the Club's entrance. She took off the mackintosh spread it beneath her and settled down well back from the fence. She wasn't risking getting caught in the car's headlights as he drove in.

She didn't have long to wait. Jepson as always was punctual and alone. As he reversed the car into its parking space she loaded the blowpipe and rested it on the wire where she'd marked it last week. When Jopson got out and paused to lock the car she blew the dart at him. It hit his neck; he swung around quickly started towards the fence but only managed a couple of steps before he started to stumble. Instead of falling he kept on coming, his arms raised towards her. She jumped back fearful that the poison had failed. He couldn't possibly reach her, he couldn't climb…her couldn't…he began to slide down the fence. She stayed where she was even after he hit the ground, it might be a trick. He was a trained soldier after all. How long she stood motionless she didn't know. It was not until she'd convinced herself that he was completely motionless that she moved towards him. He had twisted away from her but the dart in his neck was within reach.

She cut the wire and used the cutters to retrieve the dart. Although it took several seconds of anxious manoeuvring to get hold of it; this was a doddle compared to what she's expected she'd have to do. When she'd safely stowed it away she walked back to her car and took out the cheap mobile phone and the cassette recorder from the glove compartment. She phoned Peter Steyn's home number and when he answered played him the pre-recorded message telling him where to find Jopson. The attacks on Samantha and Millender had been kept under wraps but now it was time for the world to know what power FAAN had. When the message was finished she ignored Steyn's questions and shut off the recorder and phone,

As she drove home she couldn't believe how well everything was going. With her rational; mind she had no belief in any supernatural powers but things were working out so well that she almost wished there was some being or power that she could thank.

CHAPTER 40

"You think your family are being included in this threat?" Janet Morison asked.

"I'm certain they are. I don't see any other way you can read this" Peter Steyn replied. He was sitting in her office with Bully and "Sam" Smith.

Bully looked down again at the typewritten copy of the note that had been pinned to Derek Jepson's body. It certainly didn't leave any room for doubt.

TO THE STEYN KILLERS.

Y0U HAVE DELIBERATELY CHOSEN TO IGNORE THE WARNING WE SENT YOU IN THE CASE OF SAMANTHA KETTERIDGE.
HOWEVER WE DID NOT EXPECT YOU TO ACT IN ANY OTHER WAY. SAMANTHA WAS CHOSEN TO LET YOU SEE WHAT WE CAN DO. WE HAD ALWAYS PLANNED TO REVIVE HER AFTER SIX WEEKS, SO DO NOT THINK THAT YOUR INTRANSIGENCE HAS IN ANY WAY WEAKENED OUR RESOLVE.
WE HAVE CHOSEN TO ATTACK DEREK JOBSON WHO IS THE HEAD OF YOUR SECURITY. IF HE IS NOT SAFE FROM OUR ATTACKS THEN NOBODY CONNECTED TO YOU IS SAFE.
WE ARE GIVING YOU EIGHT WEEKS TO WIND DOWN YOUR EVIL ANIMAL EXPERIMENTS. JOPSON'S LIFE WILL BE IN GREAT DANGER IF YOU DELAY ANY LONGER THAN EIGHT WEEKS.
WE WANT A PUBLIC ANNOUNCEMENT OF YOUR SHUTTING DOWN YOUR TORTURE CHAMBERS WITHIN THIS EIGHT WEEK PERIOD OTHERWISE WE WILL POISON OTHERS OF YOUR STAFF.
            THERE WILL BE NO ANTIDOTE FOR JOPSON OR ANY OTHERS IF YOU DO NOT HEED THIS WARNING.
FRIENDS OF FAAN

.Steyn spoke as Bully finished reading "Someone is going to die if these attacks are not stopped."

"Your PA Samantha Ketteridge, is recovering; isn't she?" Janet replied.

"So far, yes but we don't yet know what the long term effects are going to be" he replied "being unconscious for six weeks takes its toll. She's still in a very weak state"

"And they gave you the antidote even though you didn't give them the slightest indication that you'd stop your research?" asked Janet.

"Exactly. All along I thought they'd get scared that if they kept her in a coma too long her life would be in danger."

"You really believe that these FRIENDS OF FAAN people would go so far as to kill Jepson?" asked Sam, "None of those I've met over the past six weeks seem to me be as fanatical as that."

Steyn didn't hesitate to answer, "This "friends" stuff is just nonsense. It's still the same FAAN nutcases. They're fanatics alright. Just look at the terrible stuff they've already done. If they're willing to ruin someone's life by accusing them of crimes like paedophilia it not such a big step to be willing to let them die, is it? And you know we can't stop our research. It would be immoral to give in to blackmail."

"Especially when they can blame you for a death because of your not complying with their demands" said Bully. "They can always say they have offered you the antidote, can't they?"

"Exactly" said Peter, "That's how their minds work. Everything is our fault because of our experiments. This poison they're using, it completely relaxes all the body's muscular system, so much so that prolonged exposure to such a state must result in death. Also if they attack someone whose immune system may already have been weakened by say influenza, the results may be fatal after only a couple of weeks. I've discussed this with Professor Collins at the hospital and he agrees that it's possible."

"Has he any ideas on the origin of this poison" asked Bully.

"He says it is probably based on one of the poisons the Amazonian Indians use. The trauma it induces is similar to what is known about the effects of such a poison on the animals these Indian tribes hunt. But exactly which one it is very difficult to establish. All there is to go on is the effects of the poison in the victim's blood stream."

"So you've no idea as to what this poison is?" said Janet.

"Not FOR SURE. The best guess seems to be Curare. I was hoping that we could get some clues from the antidote but the accompanying note from FAAN insisted we must use all that was in the syringe. When I suggested to Collins that we keep some back he wouldn't hear of it. Said we couldn't risk Samantha's life"

"Is any Amazonian poisons imported into this country Peter?" asked Janet.

"Yes. Several types. I've made enquiries. Research Laboratories and Medical schools have it, especially those doing ethnobotony research into the medicinal use plants. Collins says he's asked some of them for advice but nothing has so far come of it. Do not think that because victims are unconscious they do not experience pain. Some of these poison can be extremely painful, others can do irreparable damage to organs like the liver. We really have to stop these people before they kill someone".

"So you're of the opinion that we should be treating these attacks as attempted murder?" said Janet.

"Most certainly you should."

"We are already treating Dale Overton's death as a murder investigation. If the chief agrees that these threats are potentially murderous it will certainly heighten our investigation."

"I'm sure Phillip Torrington will agree. He's a very level headed bloke." He stopped and looked at his watch, "I afraid I'll have to go now. I've got a previously arranged meeting I can't miss. What do you think we should do about Jopson, should what's happened to him be leaked to the newspapers and Television even though FAAN wants us to keep quiet as we did with Samantha? If we do it will let them know we're definitely not giving in and that they're wasting their time? I've certainly no objection to letting the world know."

"Let us think a bit more about that, Peter. Another day or two won't make much difference. I'll be in touch after I've talked to the chief. We'll keep it quiet just for now."

Peter said his goodbyes and left.

As soon as the door closed Sam said "He's ready for a fight, isn't he?"

"Well, he's sure as Hell not going to comply with their demands" said Janet.

"I'm afraid this makes your work all the more urgent Sam" said Bully, "Some of these FAAN people are nurses aren't they? Do you think they might be the source of this poisoning?"

"Whoever it is certainly must have considerable medical knowledge to be able to work out the dosages that are safe as well as being able to manufacture the stuff. As it happens the FAAN member I'm getting to know, Alice McKinister is a nursing sister at The Central. She's never given any hint that she knows about any poisoning taking place."

"There's a younger sister Patricia whose a veterinary nurse, isn't there?" said Bully.

"Yes" replied Sam, "Nice girl and there's the oldest sister, Connie. She stays a home on the farm. I think she's a nurse too but gave it up when her mother died."

"What about that one with all the rings in his ears, Tristan Wills Hope." asked Janet.

"Now he is interesting" said Sam" He rides a little motor bike just like the bloke did who tried to deliver that parcel to Miles Millender. That's what made me take a special interest in him. I've managed to have a few drinks with him. He's a perpetual student. Stays at Uni. because of his Student Union activities"

"What about this South American Indian connection? Do you know if any of this FAAN group been there recently?" said Bully.

"Not for sure but a Miranda is as brown as a nut." replied Sam "I'll concentrate on her from now on. The only other one I know who's spent any time abroad is Alice McKinster but that was in India with VSO and it was a few years ago. There are the University students of course; some of them may have worked in Brazil"

"If the chief agrees we're dealing with a potential murder I may be able to get into the university records of each student to see if there's any South American connections" said Janet.

"I think we ought to publicise these attacks. Get Steyn and our Press people to liaise to get these attacks publicised." said Bully.

"I agree" said Janet, "I think if we let the public know what FAAN are up to it will turn more and more people against them, I'm going to suggest it to Phillip."

No one raised any objection

CHAPTER 41

When the news about Jopson being poisoned became public; the newspapers and television stations seized on the story like lions on a Wildebeest. Mary Jopson had been warned by Steyn and the police about how she would be hounded by the media when the news of what had happened to her husband was revealed but she'd still agreed to go ahead with it. Her house and front garden were besieged by reporters until she sold exclusive rights to the BRITISH BANNER. They put her into a luxury London hotel and paid her a fee in the thousands of pounds.

Every animal rights group throughout Britain was affected by the BANNER'S lurid stories; WAR HERO POISONED BY MINDLESS ANIMAL LOVERS was one of the newspaper's milder headlines. The poisoning of Sam Ketteridge had also been made public; Stenyn arranged for someone at the hospital to leak her story but he also made sure she and Luna were well hidden away from the press. Her recovery through FAAN's supplying an antidote wasn't what he wanted the public to know. Nothing that presented FAAN in a good light was good news.

All FAAN members were depicted as mindless fanatics and the opposing demonstrators outside the Steyn factory more than trebled their numbers. Some FAAN demonstrators were followed home and their houses attacked. It was especially difficult for those in the group who knew nothing about Miranda's scheme. Their protests in public and in private were either ignored or totally disbelieved. Even the pub where they met on Tuesday evenings told them they were no longer welcome.

Many were now drinking in Caldeford University's Student Union Bar. But Sam had managed to lure Alice to the local drama group's performance of An Inspector Calls and they were now sitting in the theatre bar discussing the play.

"What do you think of Priestley's theory about splitting time in two?" he asked.

"If only it were possible. We'd all be wiser if we were granted a second chance" Alice replied.

"Yes. I suppose these Friends of FAAN who poisoned that woman and this Jepson regret it now? It's raised so much opposition to the anti-vivisectionist cause hasn't it?"

Alice took a long drink of her cider before she answered "Well, it's not exactly poisoning, is it? Although THE BANNER mocks it, they can't deny that there was an antidote and that it worked for that Samantha Ketteridge."

"So you think that's what will happen with Jopson."

"Got to. Stenyn can't let Jepson come to any harm, can he?"

"No; everyone will blame him if Jepson dies."

"They must do."   She spoke with such assurance that he felt sure she must know more about this poisoning that those who professed ignorance of the whole scheme. If she was involved he'd be sorry for he was becoming very fond of her. Deciding not to pursue the matter of Jepson's possible death any further just now he asked, "Have you seen what one the letters in today's Guardian is arguing that it's all a set-up by the vivisectionist companies to discredit those opposed to them?"

"Yes" she replied "We've always been a Guardian family. When we were all at home father always used to like to read out bits at the breakfast table. Now that Patricia and I live away he phones us if he thinks there's something we mustn't miss."

"And that's what he thinks?"

She nodded "Great believer in conspiracy theories is my dad."

"What about you?

"I don't know. Personally I wouldn't put anything past such horrible people."

"Yet it's hard to believe that either animal experimenters or those opposed to them would experiment on humans."

"What about those who get paid for volunteering to be guinea pigs?"

"I'd forgotten them."

"It shows that these companies are willing to experiment on humans doesn't it? So what's so different about what these Friends of FAAN are doing apart from the volunteering?"

"So you agree with these poisonings then?"

Alice looked him straight in the face and said "Yes, if I'm put on the spot I'd have to say I do. I can't bring myself to blame those who sympathise with us going to such extremes."

"But some of those who have been most ferocious in their condemnation have been other animal welfare groups. The RSPCA called it 'totally immoral' didn't they?"

"They don't count .They're a lily livered lot. More concerned with the 'Royal' than with the 'Animals' in my opinion."

Sam was careful to keep his voice light as he said with a smile "Oh. Quite a little extremist aren't you?"

"Yes, that's exactly it. These "Friends" actions may be extreme but what else is there left to do?   For years we're tried ever other way, both legal and illegal. I'll admit that. There's got to be some way of stopping these hideous experiments."

When Sam didn't answer immediately, Alice continued, "We're right, aren't we? No matter how much you dislike it, it's the only way that's going to get results."

"Well, you're very persuasive but I can't see how you can possibly be right? After all, if these companies like Steyn refuse to close down, what are you going to do next, kill someone?"

"I don't think it will ever come to that. But I must admit that sometimes I've thought that if killing someone was the only sure way of stopping the torture and mistreatment of animals I wouldn't object. But I'm not so naive to believe that would ever happen. Someone's death would be fatal to our cause. We're already being charged with being no different from the people at these animal laboratories."

"So really you've got to stop these extremists "Friends" haven't you?"

"Only if someone's life is really threatened. From what I know there's a perfectly safe antidote available. We know from Sam Ketteridge's case that it works. So it's Steyn's intransience that's putting Jepson's life in danger."

"Maybe" said Sam, "But I don't think you'll ever get the Great British Public to see it like that"

CHAPTER 42

It was the admiration in the young WPC's voice that made Bully look closely at the visitor she introduced. "Miss Mary Bruce to see you Sir." The slight young woman with the page boy hairstyle who came towards him moved with such suppleness that he knew he should know her from somewhere. Although Rugby was the only sport he was really interested in; he recognized her as her was shaking her hand. She was one of Britain's premier track athletes and lived locally. Everybody knew about the trip that knocked her out of the last Olympic 10,000metes semi-final when she was leading with only 300 meters to go.

"The Mary Bruce, our Olympic athlete?" he asked as he shook her hand. "Pleased to meet you. I hope you've fully recovered from that terrible Achilles injury."

She showed a film star's set of perfect white teeth as she answered. "Thankfully, yes."

"That's good to hear. I suppose you must get fed up people asking about it?"

She shook her head, "Not at all. It's good for the sport that people are interested."

"So what can we do for you Miss Bruce?"

"Well, I hope I'm not wasting your time but I've come about Dale Overton. You may not know that he was a highly respected athletics sprint coach. In my early years I was a 200 meter runner and he was a great help to me when I began."

"I didn't know that Miss Bruce. We here knew him mostly as a political activist."

"He was certainly that alright. He always used to tell us at the National School Championships 'Now remember why you're there. To beat the shit out of these Public School Pansies.' Our parents didn't like it but we kids thought it was wonderful."

Bully laughed with her, "That sounds like him alright."

"It's terrible that he was killed in such a way."

Bully waited expecting her to continue but when she remained silent he asked "So do you have any knowledge of why he was killed?"

"No. I can't think why, all I've been told was that he was deliberately targeted, is that right?"

Bully nodded," That's what we think. It was no accidental hit and run."

"That's terrible. Look , I may be wasting your time but when there has been nothing in the papers since about the car or the driver being found I felt I just had to tell you what little I think I may know about him.."

"Take your time. It's amazing how important some little detail turns out to be in cases like his,"

"Well, I do a lot of my distance training around the county's roads. As it happens I only live about four miles away from that place where cars are often dumped. There's a bit of concrete hard standing at the edge of the road there. But then I suppose you know that already. "

Not wishing to interrupt her Bully just nodded.

"Anyway, a week before Dale was killed I was out running on Sunday morning and there was a car parked in this very spot with two men in it. As I passed one of them called out "Lovely legs darling. He definitely had an East End accent. I ignored him as I always do. That morning I was running two five mile loops and when I passed the spot again the men were still there. They were standing outside the car smoking and looking around. This time I got a wolf-whistle me but five minutes later a car drew up alongside me and one of the men who'd been standing around wound down the window and said "Give you a lift darling" I ignored him but the car kept alongside me with the man making more and more suggestive remarks. I was a getting worried because it's a bit isolated along there so the first gap that I saw in the hedge I leapt through it and ran back and away from the car. Thankfully that was the last I saw of them. Now, they may have had nothing at all to do with Dale's death but I keep thinking it was an odd time to be parked there on a Sunday. It's possible they were looking for somewhere to dump the hit and run car isn't it?"

Bully thought it was a bit tenuous but on the other hand she could be on to something. "Did you get a good look at the man who spoke to you?" he asked.

"Yes, he was probably in his late twenties and very good looking with his curly blonde hair. But when he was harassing me from the car there was a twinge of Irish in his speech it was the change that made me remember him."

Bully was so impressed with what she had just told him that he wanted to hug her. "Now that is interesting. It just so happens that someone we have interviewed in connection with this crime likes to put on a stage Irish accent when it suits him."

Mary smiled "Stage Irish? That's just it. That's exactly how he spoke. A bit too Irish to be really Irish, if you know what I mean."

"Exactly. What you've told me may prove very helpful. Anything else you can remember?"

"The car number plate was XJ 51 OLE"

"You're sure of that?"

Oh Yes. I've been memorising car number plates for years. When you're a woman running out on the roads on your own you'd be surprised how many drivers try to pick you up. I've got a little mnemonic that I've used for years to help me remember number plates."

"Wonderful. Would you be willing to look at a line up to see if you can identify this bloke in the car?"

"No sweat. I'll do whatever I can to find the bastard who knocked down Dale."

"You may have just made that possible. We're very grateful."

After discussing when she would be free and adding a few more wishes for a continued full recovery from her Achilles injury Bully bade her farewell.

When he fed the number she had given him into the police computer data base he was not very hopeful of a positive result thinking that any friends of Danny O'Hallerhan were not likely to be the kind who road taxed and insured their vehicles. So he was surprised when almost immediately he got an address in Canning Town with the owner named as one Maurice Silks. He immediately phoned DI Loomis at East Ham police station. When he answered his phone Bully asked "Derek, have you had any dealings with a Maurice Silks?"

"That little toe rag. He tags along after your mate O'Hallerhan. Got something on the pair of them, have you?"

Bully told him about Mary Bruce and what she had seen and heard. When he had finished Loomis said "Now that is interesting. It doesn't prove anything of course but it might give us enough to rattle the pair of them. Silks is a few sandwiches short of a picnic, likes to hang around villains that he considers more exciting than himself. You give me a day and time your Mary Bruce is available and I'll see if I can pick up Silks and O'Hallerhan early that morning. It will do them no harm to sweat in separate cells here until she arrives".

Bully said he'd fix a day as soon as possible and as he replaced he receiver he reflected how often it was that solutions suddenly appeared for cases that had appeared to be going nowhere. After Constable Smith had reported his conversation with Alice McKinster, it was agreed that her radicalism was sufficient to make her a suspect for membership of "Friends of FAAN." A surveillance team had been mobilised to shadow her for a few weeks. There was also a warrant being sought to tap into her phone. The thinking was she didn't have to have been to the Amazon to know about Indian poisons. You could find almost anything you needed on the Internet if you knew where to look and she certainly had the medical knowledge. He was not a believer in premonitions even though his mother insisted she often had them but this morning he couldn't stop himself feeling that both these cases were drawing to a close.

It was therefore in a cheerful frame of mind that he went to listen to "The Cowboys" sing Beethoven's Mass in C and Christ on the Mount of Olives. It was the first concert that Hélène was singing with them and he'd heard the all the alto parts many times over in the past weeks. It would be a relief to hear the whole thing at last.

Helene had been rehearsing with the choir all afternoon so they met in a nearby pub over an hour before the concert was due to start. He ordered two roast beef sandwiches for himself as Helene said she was too nervous to eat anything. However when they brought the sandwiches on separate plates surrounded with loads of salad and crisps she somehow managed to make considerable inroads into these side dishes.

It was as they were leaving the pub that he caught sight of someone that made him seize Helene's arm and force her to stop and in front of several prints of London Costermongers.

"Why are we…"she started to protest but he stopped her.

"Look at these prints for a second then turn briefly to your left as we leave. There are a couple of women sitting at the last table under that beam that has the plaque that says 'Duck or Grouse' I know the red haired one but the well tanned black haired woman, she must be in the choir for she's wearing a white blouse and black skirt just like you.; tell me who she is when we get outside."

Helene did as he asked and when outside she said "That's Miranda Woolston. Nice woman. Not very chatty but friendly enough when you speak to her. Why? Fancy her, do you?"

He shook his head, "As if! It's the red head I'm particularly interested in but I want to know everything about whoever she meets."

"This about the Friends of FAAN poisoning?"

"Yes, how did you know?"

"The red head was at Desiree's funeral. It's not easy to forget her with a mop of hair like that"

Before he could answer their way was blocked by two stout women dawdling along in front of them. One turned to let them pass.

"Clarence. It's Clarence, Betty. I told you we'd see him here."

"No it was I who told you. Bound to be here when that lovely wife of his has joined us."

To try to stop them yelling out his name at what seemed to him the top of their voices he said quickly "Lovely to see you Aunt Betty and Aunt Mary. Looking forward to performing this Mass in C? Some tricky bits in it I've been told." Helene gave him a swift surreptitious dig in the ribs as his Aunt Betty replied, "Yes, but nowadays we both just mouth them, don't we Mary?"

"Indeed we do. No sense in us straining our voices when we've got such talented singers like your Helene to help us" Mary replied.

"That's what I'm always telling her" said Bully

"What, that your aunts are past it? A couple of old crows that should have been shot years ago?" said Betty.

"No, of course not, aunties. I mean that's she's got such a lovely voice." He got another dig in the ribs for this.

"Clarence has become very interested in our choir lately" said Helene, "He was asking me about Miranda Woolston, you often talk to her don't you?"

"Wilberforce Woolston's daughter? She was a spirited little thing wasn't she Mary?"

Bully remembered that both of them had taught for years in the town's grammar school.

"Yes, especially where animals were concerned. She got lots of the girls involved in the antivivisection movement I remember."

"But she seems to have quietened down a lot now. I was reminding her about it only last rehearsal of what a firebrand she used to be. She sort of laughed it off. Quite surprised me. I told you, didn't I, Betty."

"Another case of age inducing tolerance is what I said."

"Just as well. I was always afraid she'd do something extreme. While my brighter girls were becoming excited about Woman's liberation she kept criticising them for not caring enough about animal's liberation. I think that going to University must have taught her to be more tolerant."

"And later working in the jungle with her father. He was a great botanist, you know. Seeing the poverty of the natives may have deflected her to their cause rather than animal rights."

Their conversation was interrupted by the surge of singers and audience heading to the auditorium. They let themselves be carried along with the crowd. Bully smiled as Helene whispered "The police are surplus to requirements when there are Bullerton's around."

"Too right kid" he whispered back.

When he'd settled down in the audience he kept a close eye on the doorway and was surprised to see the innocent faced Sam accompany Alice into the Hall. They passed him close enough for Sam to make eye contact but he gave not the slightest hint of recognition.

For the next couple of hours he sat in a state of bliss, induced not only by the beauty of the singing but also by or what he had just learned from his aunts

On the following Thursday as he travelled up to London with "Union Jack" Paislee and Mary Bruce, Bully soon realised it had been a waste of time his researching Mary Bruce's athletic career on his computer the previous evening. She was much more interested in extolling Dale Overton's contribution to amateur athletics than talking about herself. "What I especially liked about him as a coach" she said, "Was that he just wasn't interested in those who showed they had the potential to become top performers. He gave his time and advice to all the girls in our group. Many coaches like to latch on to runners who have the potential to be international's so that they can bathe in their reflected glory but Dale wasn't like that."

It was Union who monopolised the conversation when the present state of British athletics was discussed. Bully was amazed to learn that Mary knew Union's teenage daughter Elizabeth because she was the top ranked 18year old Javelin thrower in the country. But Union seemed to know as much about the track runners as he did the field performers like his daughter. So while they chatted away about suitable diets and hundreds of seconds and millimetres gained or lost he was able to reflect on all that had been learned about Miranda Woolston in the past few days.

The surveillance had just one report of Alice meeting a woman whose description fitted that of Miranda. They had met lunchtime in a busy city centre pub. There was no mention of anything being handed over between them. They had left the pub separately and a good photo had been taken of Miranda outside but she had quickly gone into Debenhams and given the policewoman who was following her the slip. The policewoman was adamant she hadn't been spotted so it was agreed when Bully and Janet discussed this with the Chief that Miranda was either extremely paranoid or more likely that she had something to hide.

The Chief and Janet were as usual mockingly respectful of the power of the "Bullerton Mafia" when Bully told them how he had learned of Miranda's name and history. Subsequent enquiries about her had been most revealing. While at University that she had been arrested and fined three times for "disorderly conduct" on Animal Rights demonstrations. But for the past sixteen years there was no record of her being arrested in connection with the Animal Rights movement in this country. "Presumably" Janet said "because she was abroad for most of that time." It was decided to find out where and when she had been abroad and if she had any police record there. Another surveillance team was to be set up to follow her.

Derek Jepson had now been in a coma for just over eight weeks and newspapers both local and national were becoming more and more insistent that his attackers be found. The view that the big chemical companies and animal research organizations were behind these poisonings in an effort to discredit the Animal Rights Movement was gaining wider acceptance and the companies were pressuring the authorities for more determined action to bring this matter to a close. Letters in the local press from members of FAAN claiming that the organization couldn't possibly have any involvement with such poisonings were reproduced in several national papers adding to the theory of a vivisectionist conspiracy. Some of these letter writers were interviewed on TV and were very convincing in their arguments that no matter how extreme FAAN had been in its defamation of chemical companies employees they would never go so far as to poison them. They were joined by other Animal Rights activists around the nation in their condemnation. A TV poll showed at only 15% of the public supported such extreme measures.

Bully's thoughts were interrupted by their arrival at East Ham police station. They were soon seated with D.S. Loomis who wasted no time in questioning Mary on her Sunday morning experience. When she'd finished he nodded and said "We've had these tykes here for over two hours and we've gathered a few bods in for ID parades. Have a cup of tea while we set them up; I'll call you when we're ready."

Loomis, Bully and Union went behind the one way mirror to watch Mary being lead along the line by a uniformed officer for Maurice Silks. She went all along the line, then back again. She then asked if they could turn left. When this was done she walked the line again then went briskly back and touched him. When she was lead out to the line with O'Hallerhan in it she was far more direct and certain, turning around before she reached the end of the line and indicating O'Hallerhan who had stood in the middle of the of five. Bully was pleased to see the smirk leave the man's face when she touched him. Despite being warned in advance not to speak O'Hallerhan immediately yelled "I'm being set up here lads. Wait for me outside when this farce is over and give me your names and addresses like the good men I know you are. My brief will want them."

When Mary came back to Bully and Union she was shaking her head. "That man's an idiot "she said "I hadn't the slightest doubt it was him but I was doubly sure when I heard him speak."

"You did well Miss Bruce" said Loomis, "You picked the two we suspect, can't do better than that." Mary blushed as if she'd just been presented with another trophy. Union raised no objection when asked if he wouldn't mind staying with her while Silks and O'Halleran were questioned.

As soon a Loomis and Bully went into the interview room Silks stood up saying "I ain't done nothing Mr.Loomis. What am I being kept here for? I've got lots to do."

"Sit down Silks," replied Loomis, "This is no tuppenhencehapenny breaking and entering you're in here for today. Now, do you want a solicitor or should we just have a little chat first before we get all involved with the law, eh?"

The speed of Silks answer surprised Bully," Naw, don't want no solicitor. Thieving buggers the lot of them"

"Right then. Just let me get this recording stuff set up and then I'll tell you just what deep shit you're in."

Silks kept standing while Loomis set up and tested the equipment. As soon as he was satisfied and had identified everyone in the room he turned to Silks and said "Right, I'll tell you straight now, this is a murder charge."

Silks went several shades sallower than his normal unhealthy pallor. He had to grasp the edge of the table to manoeuvre himself back into his chair. "Murder? Naw, you've having me on. You know I ain't never done nothing like that. Bit of thieving maybe, that's all. This is a windup isn't it?"

Loomis shook his head. "You should know I wouldn't joke about a thing like murder, Silky. No this is real serious. You are going to be charged at least with accessory to murder. You're kids are going to be well grown up before you share a fish supper with them again."

Silks shook his head from side to side. "No good doing that" said Loomis, "Your mate O'Callaghan has dropped you right in it this time. You should never have driven him down to Calderford to commit the crime."

Silks continued to shake his head, "No. No. You got that wrong. We never hit nobody."

Loomis glanced at Bully, his eyes dancing with amusement. "What was that you said Silky?"

"We never hit…" his words trailed off as if he had suddenly realised what he'd said.

"What do you mean, 'you never hit nobody. Who are you talking about?"

Silks took his time replying "That bloke in that place you mentioned, Castle something. He was knocked down wasn't he? It wasn't us Mr.Loomis. Swear on my daughters lives it wasn't."

"Castleford is quite a while from here. I take it you don't read the local paper?"

"I do. I can read you know. Have read The Stratford Times for years."

"Sorry Silky. Wasn't casting aspersions on your reading. I meant the local Castleford paper. The Castleford and District Recorder."

Silks looked at him suspiciously before replying "No. We don't get that."

"So had did you know about somebody being knocked down there then?"

"It...It...was on the Telly."

"Oh yes. What did it say then?"

"Said somebody was knocked down didn't it?"

"Who? "

"Dunno. Wasn't paying much attention."

Yet you remembered it?"

"Well, I got a good memory for some things. I know all the winners of the FA Cup right back from the start, I do. Go on; ask me, any year, any year you like."

"No just now. You'll have plenty of time to test your football knowledge on your cell mates when you're banged up for accessory to murder."

Silks shook his head violently, "No, you can't get me for that. I ain't done nothing like that, never."

Loomis sat staring at him for a couple of minutes. Then leaning confidently forward said confidently "Look Silky, I know you wouldn't willingly get mixed up in anything like a murder. But unfortunately, O'Hallerhan would and has. He's dropped you right in it as I said. You're in real big trouble. Your only hope of getting a lighter sentence is to tell us all that happened, that will help you, take years off your sentence, won't it Mr.Bullerton?"

"Yes. Cut years off it will."

"Naw. No way. I ain't done nothing."

"Look, that young lady picked you out, didn't she? She's identified you as one of the two blokes waiting at the spot where the car that killed that man was burnt out. She'll testify to that in court and the judge will believe her. Why did you get involved in a thing like this for? As you say it's not your style."

"Look Mr. Loomis. I don't know nothing. All I heard was that some bloke got knocked down and had his legs broken. Some sort of punishment like."

"Is that what you've been told? Well somebody's lied to you. The bloke your mate O'Hallerhan ran over was dead before he reached the hospital.

You're in serious trouble here Silky. Best to tell us all you know about it. What were you doing down that country road on the fourth of June this year?"

Silky stared at the table top as if there was some hidden pattern hidden in the blue Formica that would solve all his problems. When he did look up he shook his head saying, "I really don't know nothing like I said."

"Are you denying that you were parked in that layby on the date I said?"

"Dunno. It's months ago innit. I mean sometimes Danny and me go for a drive around a couple of pubs in the country. I think we might have got lost once and stopped on a pull-in like. Can't remember where it was. As I said it was ages ago."

"You do your pub crawling early Sunday morning do you? Pull the other one."

"Maybe we was just driving around. Danny and me are mates."

"What sort of mates gets you involved in a murder charge? Are you going to do time just because your mate's killed somebody? You've got more sense than that Silky."

When Silks didn't answer Loomis suddenly said "How much did he give you? O'Halleran must have been well paid for this killing. What did he give you?"

"Nufink. I'm saying nufink. I ain't a telltale." He folded his arms and looked at them defiantly.

"It's up to you. If you want to go down with your mate on a murder charge, that's your outlook. We'll let you think about it for a while."

Loomis formally terminated the interview for the record and he and Bully left the room. Outside he said "He's pulled this silent trick before. We've not got enough to charge him.

Let's see what Danny boy tells us."

But O'Hallerhan's interview proved as barren as Silks. All that he would admit was that they sometimes went out in the country Sunday mornings for a drive around. Eventually both had to be released.

CHAPTER 44.

"We've got to stop this poisoning."

"Yes Alice, I agree" said Tristan, "It's causing us nothing but grief"

They both looked at Miranda but she shook her head. "No, we can't stop now. We've come too far. "

"It's absurd to say we can't stop" retorted Alice. "We can't get anywhere unless we have the public behind us. All we have to do is send the antidote to the hospital. You must surely see how we're losing public support."

"Is that really so, Alice? What about those who think this is a stunt by the chemical companies to blacken our name? That's not doing us any harm."

"That's ridiculous, Miranda. Don't you see that when it all comes out that we really are the ones who poisoned Jepson the people you are talking about will never trust us again. You've got to face facts. Your idea hasn't worked out the way you planned. The sooner we pack it in the better."

"No Tris. It's too soon to give up. Jepson's still alive after all these weeks so that proves we're not endangering his life. He and Samantha are proof we can incapacitate Steyn's staff without killing them. Instead of drawing back I think we should attack them even more. I don't think anyone will want to work for them if they know they're likely to be poisoned. Surely you can see that?"

Alice and Tristan spoke over each other in their eagerness to disagree. Blushing, Tristan indicated for Alice to speak. She was as forthright as he'd ever heard her. "No Miranda, we can't carry on with this. It's gone too far. As Tris says it's causing us nothing but grief. People whom I've known for years who have been sympathetic to our cause have been coming up to me and asking me to say that it's not us who are doing the poisoning. They are shocked when I say that it may be a breakaway group among us who have taken such drastic action. I can't keep on letting them assume that I'm not involved. They are good people but enough is enough. We've got to stop now."

"Yes" added Tristan "Look at our own members at the meetings. Most of them don't believe we'd do such a thing. As Alice says, now's the time to stop."

Miranda shook her head again, "No. That's just what we mustn't do. This poisoning works. I've got proof it does."

"Proof?" asked Tristan, "How can you have proof?"

Miranda hesitated before answering. "From my experiences in the Amazon. Loggers who were attacked by the natives weren't in a hurry to continue to cut down trees in that area. They soon took their operations further afield."

"That's not what I understand happened" said Alice.

"No" added Tristan "Surely the loggers just came in with soldiers and killed the natives."

"They had to find them first and some of them lost their own lives while looking."

Alice and Tristan looked at each other. "You're saying that this poisoning worked only because people were killed? Is that what you're expecting to happen here?"

"No. No. That's not what I mean at all. All I'm telling you is that if people believe the threat of death is real enough they'll give in."

"No they won't. Not in this country they won't. If Jepson dies it'll finish us altogether. Why are you exposing us to such a risk?"

"Because I know what I'm doing. I've been working on the strength and toxicity of this poison for years. I know it's not fatal."

"I don't see how you can be so certain. When the internal organs become so weak the body must be susceptible to all sorts of illnesses."

"That's what the medical students at uni. are saying" interjected Tristan. "They're amongst the ones most opposed to what you're doing"

"What else do you expect? Many of them will end up working for companies like Steyn."

When neither of them responded Miranda continued "Look, this is getting us nowhere. Why don't we agree to let things continue as they are for another couple of weeks and review the position then? I really will think seriously about what you've said. Honest. Now how about a drink? Tea or coffee?"

"O.K. But you'd better come up with more convincing reasons than you have so far for keeping this poisoning going Miranda. I'll have coffee please."

Tristan suddenly stood up saying "Thanks but I can't stop any longer. There's a Union meeting tomorrow night and I haven't finished the agenda for it. I'll see myself out." He picked up his briefcase and hurried out of the room.

When they heard the front door close Miranda said to Alice "Do you think Tris. is O.K.? He's very impetuous isn't he? What if he goes and blabs who we are to the papers or something?"

165

"Oh I don't think he'd do that. He's well used with debates and arguments around him."

"I suppose so. He's been sec. of that union for years. God knows when he's going to graduate."

"When some other trade union post becomes available. He's going to make a career in politics. Be a bit of alright if he's prime minister one day."

"Dream on girl. Now let me get that coffee. It's Bath Oliver's again I'm afraid. I've no sweet biscuits at all in the house. I can butter them if you find them too dry."

"Don't you dare. My clothes are straining on me as it is. I'll take them as they come."

When Miranda came back with the tray of coffee and Bath Oliver's she said as she set them down "I know I said we'd stop talking about what's happening with Jepson and all but I can't help wondering about Phillip. I feel awful saying this but I can't get it out of my mind. You don't think he would betray us do you? "

"No. I can put your mind at rest regarding that. Phillip and I had a long talk the other night. He didn't exactly say 'I told you so' but he left me in no doubt that was what he meant. He's very upset at how all this is reflecting so badly on our movement. But there's no chance of him revealing our involvement. He hates the police and all that they stand for. No. We're safe with him no matter how misguided he thinks we are."

"I never really thought otherwise. I think I'm getting a bit neurotic about this whole thing. Let's change the subject altogether. How are you getting along with this bloke I keep seeing you with, Sam's his name, isn't it?"

"Actually, very well. I do like him. Unfortunately he is one of the ones who have argued most persuasively against what we are doing. He's got a real gift of stating his case logically without sounding dogmatic and overbearing."

"I really am being left on my own aren't I Alice."

"I'm afraid you are. Talking about being on your own Sam and I are going to a music festival on the Isle of Wright next weekend and we'll probably travel on down to Cornwell for a few days afterwards."

"Lucky girl. Actually you're awakening the wanderlust in me I haven't had a holiday for four years. I think a few days away would help clear my head."

"I'm sure it would do you good. Four years is a long while without a break. Any idea where'd you'd go?"

"Have you heard of the Munroes?"

"Mountains in the Highlands aren't they."

"Yes, they're all peaks over 3000 ft. There are 284 of them. Daddy and I set out to climb them all years ago. We had as they say "bagged 228" of them before he became too ill to continue. I've always intended to complete the lot for him. You can do between 10 or 12 of them in a week. I might have a bash at some of them while you're away."

"Don't for Christ's sake fall down any of them. Then where would we be with the poisoning?"

"Oh there's not many of them that are really dangerous. Anyway you and Tris know where everything is."

"I suppose so. That really would bring our campaign to an end if anything happened to you."

"Don't worry. I've too much invested in this campaign to take unnecessary risks. I've planned all this for years you know. I was sure it would work where all else failed. I've got to give it a bit longer. I just can't give it up now."

"Well, a couple more weeks won't do us much more harm but I really think that's as long as we can keep this up."

"We'll see. Now to really change the subject. You know that concert of ours you came to?"

"The Beethoven Mass in C and that Mount of Olives thing?"

"Yes, well we've had a C D made. Like to hear a bit of it again?"

"Yes, can you hear yourself?"

"Good God no. But everyone says it's good."

"Then play on McDuff."

They listened for the next half hour to the various parts of the CD then Alice made her farewells.

When she'd gone Miranda continued to listen to the music but it failed to lift her spirits. All she had worked and planned for years was failing around her. She had to find some way of making her threats to Steyn effective. Perhaps an attack on Peter Steyn's family was what was needed. With that thought giving her scant comfort she turned out the lights and made her way up to bed.

Some fifteen minutes after the lights were extinguished Tristan switched the cellar light on. He had opened and closed the front door before making his way down to hide in the cellar. He went along to the end of the last wine rack and undid the two catches that allowed a section of ten bottles to swing back. The fridge behind them containing the poison wasn't locked. Evidently it was thought that the wine rack was sufficient protection Miranda's father had used it for years to protect new varieties of orchids that he developed.

There were eighteen phials of antidote as well as the jar of poison in the fridge. He took the rolls of cotton wool and the protective envelopes out of his briefcase. He had thought it all out. He knew Miranda wouldn't give up her poisoning campaign. She'd no idea of the damage she was doing to the cause. He'd heard students previously favourable to the movement now bitterly attacking it; calling the movement fascist blackmailers. Miranda lived too much in a cocoon of her own making, only hearing and seeing what she wanted. It was time to stop and it was up to him to do it. He packed the antidote carefully. He'd decided beforehand to take it all. He would leave the poison. It was too dangerous to play around with; it was of no use anyway without the antidote. Miranda could of course make more antidote but everything would be over and done with by then.

He was going to give the antidote to Steyn. With the resources at their disposal they would surely be able to analyse it and make more of their own. No one would be in any danger in future. He would have to trust them to let the world know that FAAN had given them the secret of the antidote. That would surely help to rehabilitate it in the eyes of the public.

The long summer break at the University started next week. After he'd delivered the antidote he was going up to his parents in Birmingham for ten days. Then he was flying down to Heathrow to meet his partner and they were off to India for another ten days. He'd have to face the wrath of Miranda when he got back but public opinion would be behind him. There was nothing she could do about it. He was sure Alice would support him. Look how strongly she'd sided with him tonight. Phillip would also back him. Phillip's voice carried a lot of weight in the movement. And if the worst came to the worst and they threw him out of FAAN he could easily start up a parallel organization of his own. Everyone said he had good administrative and organizational skills. He'd nothing to worry about. It would all work out in his favour.

With the phials securely packed in his briefcase he swung the wine rack back in place and made his way silently up stairs and pushed against the door. It seemed to have gone rather stiff but when he pushed harder but it still didn't move. It couldn't have locked itself shut, it just couldn't. The steps were so narrow he found it difficult to get a good base for a firm shove. He was just manoeuvring to launch himself at the door when he heard Miranda say "Don't waste your time battering against the door. It's firmly locked. I'm calling the police.

CHAPTER 45

Bully nodded for the warder to leave and sat down opposite Frank Mills. "How long is it till you get out now Frank?" he asked.

"Couple of weeks if you don't cock things up."

"We wouldn't want to do that especially apart from one incident you've been a model prisoner."

"So what are you here for then?"

"Just a little bit of information. You know Danny O'Hallerhan, don't you?"

"Can't say that I do. On the telly is he?"

"Don't get funny Frank. You know who the Gomez brothers' drivers are."

"Can't say that I do. Never paid them much attention"

"You'd have noticed this one. Always plenty to say for himself. Did a three stretch about five years ago for some smash and grab."

"Naw...not...wait a minute. Bit of a loudmouth is he?"

"You could say that."

"Can't really say I know him. Maybe passed a few words when he dropped any of the Gomez's off."

"Well, he's in the frame or the Overton killing."

"How so? Driving the car was he?"

We've got a witness that identifies him being at the spot where the car was burnt out."

"That's not the same as driving it though."

"No, but he's sure to be fingered soon. You see, he stole a very distinctive car. A green and white Cortina. Not many of them around Frank. We've got the word out."

"Well when you get someone who's seen him knocking down Overton let me know."

"Why. Want to reward him?"

"Don't go putting words into my mouth. Just curious, that's all."

"We'll do our best to satisfy your curiosity. But I think you made a bad choice there Frank. He's not the type who can keep his mouth shut for long. You should see the gear he's bought."

"Fuck off. He's nothing to do with me."

"You'd better hope he says the same when we nick him for Overton's death."

"I tell you I know nothing about him."

"Well, somebody paid him well to kill Overton and you've more motive than most."

Mills shook his head. "I'm going to ask for a solicitor if you keep on quizzing me about Overton."

Bully pushed his chair back and stood up saying "I've a feeling you'll have to exercise that right sooner than you imagine Frank. Dale Overton was a very popular bloke. We're getting a lot of co-operation from the public."

"Best of luck Mr. Bullerton. Then you can leave me in peace."

"We'll see Frank. We'll see. Goodbye for now"

"Up yours."

Although the governor was in the prison today, Bully made his way along to Bill Feaherstone's office and was welcomed in. When he was seated Bill asked," Well, how did you find our Frank today?"

"A bit edgy. He's uptight about his parole hearing."

"He certainly is. Although he's mostly kept his nose clean in here Bully I think it has been a considerable strain. He's got quite a temper simmering under the surface there."

"That's the way I read him Bill. Someone going to pay for all his restrain in here. But it's not just him I've come about. How well do you know one of your choir members, Miranda Woolston?"

"Really Bully! Coming into my office and accusing me of lusting after our Amazonian beauty. As if I would do such a thing!"

"Of course not. A respectable married man like you. So you do know her then?"

"Not as well as I and most of the other men in the choir would like to. Afraid she keeps herself very much to herself. She's one of these animal rights people isn't she?"

"Very much so. Between ourselves she could be part of this FAAN group that's involved in the poisoning of Steyn employees."

"Really? I wouldn't have thought her that extreme. The only time I recall her being a bit bolshie is a couple of years ago when your aunts put on a pig roast to raise funds for the choir. You'd have thought we were going to roast a human rather than a pig the fuss she kicked up. But come to think of it she's been a bit more subdued and reticent about her vegetarian and animal rights views recently. It's only a small breakaway group of these FAAN people who are involved in this poisoning, isn't it?"

"Seems like it but we've got very little to go on."

"You don't just suspect her because she spent time in the Amazonian jungle with her father, do you?"

"Well, it does seem as it is the same type of poison that the natives in the Amazon jungle use to catch their prey. Bit of a coincidence, isn't it?"

"Yes…but…well; I suppose working here nothing should surprise me. I take it you've nothing more concrete to go on."

Bully shook his head "Not yet. But if you see her stuffing a blow pipe into her handbag you'll let me know, won't you?"

Bill laughed, "Ever the optimist Bully."

"That's what keeps me going. Anyway, mustn't take up too much of your time Bill but I'd appreciate it if you'd let me know when Frank gets his parole."

"Will do Bully. I'll phone you myself."

"Thanks. See you at your next concert if not before."

"Hang on while I get my coat. I'll accompany you to the gate. I've been sitting on my arse far too long."

CHAPTER 46

Tristan banged on the cellar door shouting "No. No police Miranda. It's me, Tristan."

"Tristan? What are you doing in the cellar?"

"Let me out and I'll tell you."

"You alone?"

"Yes. Yes. Honestly"

Much to his relief he heard the door being unlocked. Sheepishly he stumbled forward. Miranda stood facing him in rather low cut mauve nightdress but his eyes were drawn more to the stout walking stick in her right hand instead of her figure.

"What were you doing in the cellar Tris?"

When he didn't speak she said "You were after the antidotes, weren't you?"

He nodded.

She didn't put down the stick as she said "You were wasting your time. Every time that fridge door opens a red light flashes in my bedroom. You were extremely stupid to think that after all the years I've been working on this scheme I wouldn't have taken precautions. Now return what you've taken."

He opened his brief case and took out the envelopes with the cotton wrapped phials in them. With exceeding care he pulled the cotton wool wrapped phials out one by one."

"My God, you've taken them all. How stupid can you get?"

The derision in her voice spurred him into replying. "There's nothing stupid at all about taking the lot. I wanted to make sure you wouldn't immediately attack somebody else. I assume it takes some time to manufacture this antidote."

She looked at him as if he was some creature from outer space. "Why?"

"Because I can't let any more damage be done to FAAN. Your scheme hasn't worked Miranda. Everybody's turning against us; calling us hypocrites, willing to experiment on humans while protesting against experiments on animals. Alice and I tried to get you to change your mind tonight but you wouldn't I …."

"You're saying that Alice is party to what you're doing? I don't…"

"No. No. Alice knows nothing about this. This is all off my own bat." Not knowing what else to say he looked down at the floor.

172

When he made eye contact again Miranda was still staring at him. He went to speak but she beat him to it. "That's what you really believe is it? You want to give up and let evil bastards like Steyn win?"

"No. You know I'll never do that." Seeing she was going to speak again he hurried to interrupt her. "Look. Before you say anything more you've got to admit we've been making progress over the years. Slowly but surely we have been winning public support. Look how foxhunting has been made illegal. Now, by this poisoning madness you're in danger of losing us all the goodwill that we've built up over the years. I decided I couldn't let that happen. I just couldn't."

"Tristan, you're wrong. These chemical companies aren't like the foxhunters. With them there's million and millions of pounds involved. They've got the money to buy the prostitutes of the press to keep the public sweet. We'll never be able to match them financially. It's got to be something that lets people see what happens to the animals they experiment on. There's all this fuss about one man, Jepson, yet thousands of animals are having the same thing done to them every hour of every day. You can see that and I can see it and I'm convinced it won't be long before thousands more people come to see it. We've got more people than ever before talking about our cause, it…"

Again he interrupted her "But not favourably. Look at these opinion polls. Only less than 20 % back us."

"That's only in respect of what we're doing to Jepson. The public are not being asked if they're in favour all this animal experimentation are they? ".

"No. But it's still doing us no favours to have Jepson's poisoning laid at our door. I think it's time to revive him, I really do."

"And then what? They'll just carry on with their vile experiments won't they?"

"Not necessarily. And to ask you your own question. If they don't agree to stop? Then what? Are we going to let him die?"

When she looked away he realised she'd thought about it. He found himself shouting "You wouldn't go that far. You couldn't. You just couldn't."

"Not even if Steyn was blamed for his death? The public would know…"

"Miranda, you're out of your mind. The only people who'd get blamed for his death would be us. Don't you read the papers? Who's getting blamed now? We are. We'd be branded as murders; Phillip would never keep quiet if we went that far. He wouldn't let FAAN be destroyed just because we three went to such lengths. You know he wouldn't."

"Perhaps." Before he could speak again she continued, "Anyway, we don't need to concern ourselves about that. We're not going to let Jepson die."

He was so relieved he was speechless. When he did find the words he asked, "So you'll send one of these antidotes to Steyn?"

"Perhaps. I'm thinking about it."

"Miranda you've got to get some antidote to him."

"I don't have to do anything. As a matter of fact I don't think you can be trusted to be a member of FAAN any longer. You…"

"Who the Hell do you think you are? FAAN is democratically organized. That's one of the first things we decided when we set it up. No hierarchy. One member, one vote. All of…"

"True, but our little group was something different. It had to be and I don't think Alice will want you to stay a member any more than I do once I've told her how you were going to betray us."

"You can't…"

"Don't waste your breath. I can. This is my house and I don't want you anywhere near it in future. Actually you'd better go now."

Without a word, he got up, seized his briefcase and hurried out. As he opened the front door he called out, "You'll be sorry" but closed the door softly. When he was certain that he was far enough away from the house not to be seen he reached up his jacket sleeve and retrieved the phial. For many years he'd supplemented his funds as a children's entertainer. It had been easy to palm one of the phials as they were being put back in their envelopes. No way was he going to allow Miranda destroy FAAN.

174

CHAPTER 47

Miranda went back to bed after Tris left but she couldn't sleep. Tris's accusations rankled even though she was convinced they were unjustified. She knew she was right no matter how much people misunderstood her. Direct action was the only strategy that achieved anything. Hadn't she proved that years ago in the Amazon?

She could still see the sneering face of the fat surveyor as he waved the forged logging permits under her nose. Once she'd learned he was in the area she'd hunted him down. She'd got everything she needed to deal with him. It was unusual for such a senior official to come this far into the jungle; the company must be anxious to start their depredations immediately. She knew him from her protest visit to the firm's offices in the provincial capital.

"The elders know logging is not allowed in this area" Miranda protested.

The surveyor gestured towards the back of his Land Rover, "They'll agree to anything once they get their hands on what's in there"

He had no need say what he was carrying, Miranda knew what it would be, crates of cheap whiskey and lots of multicoloured trinkets .Miranda knew she had no chance of dissuading the tribal elders from accepting his gifts. Her being a woman was in itself sufficient grounds for them to ignore her. She hurried away and got into her own jeep and drove off.

There was only one track that the surveyor and his driver could take from the village back to the highway. She had not expected any other outcome so she had come prepared. As she drove along she studied the foliage alongside the track. It was over forty minutes before she saw the tree she wanted. It had a trunk about two and a half feet across and was leaning some 60 degrees over the track. She halted the jeep well past it and got the chain saw out. When she got back to the tree she couldn't believe that everything could be so perfect.

She stripped bare to the waist, leaving only her bra on. and getting a large silk scarf out of a side locker and wrapped it around her neck. Although she used the petrol driven chain saw regularly to cut fuel for cooking, it seemed unusually heavy today. It was twenty minutes before a high pitched creak warned her to move out of the way. For one horrible moment she thought the tree would snag on the dense foliage opposite but with what she choose to interpret as a dying sigh the tree collapsed across the track completely blocking it. She went to her vehicle to revive herself with draughts of glucose and water from the four litre plastic container she always carried with her.

175

She reckoned it would be at least another couple of hours before the surveyor's Land Rover reached here but decided it would be best to get everything ready now. She drove her Jeep another half mile further on and hid it facing the track; making sure there were no obstacles to hinder a fast exit. Now in the safety of her bedroom she could smile at all the effort she'd taken to mark the trees with her machete so she could find the Jeep quickly again. She'd even left the keys in the ignition to be sure of a quick getaway.

Her estimate of the time when the Land Rover would appear proved remarkably accurate. When only the native Indian driver got out and the surveyor stayed in the vehicle she'd been afraid all her work had been in vain because she was hidden on the opposite side of the track from where he was sitting but eventually he alighted and came around to the front of the Land Rover to inspect the fallen tree. He was only some 12 feet away from her and an easy target for her poisoned dart. He swatted his neck in annoyance when it hit him and pulled it out. When nothing happened immediately she had feared the poison wasn't working but before he'd finished swearing he collapsed. She had painted her body to scare the driver but the sight of the dart plus her primeval screams did the job before she needed to reveal herself. He ran to the Land Rover and reversed back down the track but in his panic he stalled and careered it off the track into the jungle. Screaming loudly she zig zaged from bush to bush to make him think he was being attacked by a band of Indian hunters. He jumped out of the vehicle fled back down the track. She was relieved because she'd no wish to harm him. Better he survived and spread alarm about how dangerous the natives were. Even if he didn't, the failure of the surveyor to return would make the company think twice before sending any more employees into the area. Since all their documentation was false she didn't think they would be anxious to reveal the presence of their employees nor would the authorities send soldiers along to see what had happened to them and that indeed proved to be the case.

The only major task left for her was the disposing of the Land Rover and the surveyor. Getting rid of the vehicle grieved her more than disposing of the man for it was a brand new model and would have been a great improvement on her ten year old Jeep. But too many questions would be asked if she came back to her own camp with such a vehicle. It was dark when she'd finished cutting up the fallen tree and dragging the logs away to make room to drive past. She would have preferred to have left the surveyor lying where he fell but was afraid the corpse would attract predators. She didn't want any trace of the surveyor to be found. So she drove the Land

Rover back to the tree and dragged the body across the back seats, Even now after all these years she was amazed how casually she had dealt with everything.

She had never thought she'd ever become a killer. But she told herself she'd had no choice. She'd been driven to it. It still didn't trouble her conscience that she'd killed him. The man's arrogance had robbed him of all humanity in her eyes and she knew that too many natives had been robbed of their land without any recompense for her to feel any sorrow for those who exploited them.

She camped there for the night and next morning made her way in half mile stages to the river, driving each of the vehicles in turn. It took her some six hours to reach it. She was tempted to take some of the tools from the Land Rover but decided against it. The worst thing was getting the surveyor behind the steering wheel but eventually she managed it.   There was a rope bridge across the abyss and she thought about driving into the middle of the bridge and then cutting the ropes at one end. But she knew the natives depended on the bridge forget easy access to wider hunting grounds and the transport of their goods and decided against it. Anyway there was a wide tract of flat land alongside the bridge. When she'd got the Land Rover facing the abyss she left the engine running and the handbrake off and dropped a heavy log across the surveyor's right leg. It took several attempts before she could engage the gearlever with the rope she'd attached but she finally managed to get it into first gear and it moved hearse like forward to disappear over the edge and tumble into the rapidly flowing river below.

In the following years there was no mention of the fate of the surveyor or his driver. What happened to him she never knew. She thought she might have nightmares about what she had done but she slept undisturbed.

Now was she prepared to let Jopson die? She'd come this far, so why stop now. These vivisectionists must be stopped. Would an unexpected death do it?

177

CHAPTER 48

Peter Steyn was breathing heavily as he looked down at the jiffy bag on the cabinet. It had taken all his self-control to stop himself snatching it up off the hall table and throwing outside it. He was relieved that Esme was at her mother's with the children. Mrs. Heston the daily must have brought the Jiffy bag in with the rest of the post. She was an efficient and cheerful cleaner and had been fully briefed about the dangers the family faced from FAAN. But she was a born optimist. The only thing that ever worried her was if the town's football team was going to survive in the First Division. "We've been there twenty-two years so why shouldn't we stay there for the next twenty- two." was her mantra.

Gingerly he turned the package over. On the back was the legend "OPEN CAREFULLY." He slit the top of the bag all the time telling himself that it wouldn't be a bomb because FAAN worked with poison not explosives. There was a small card attached to the package inside. Spreading it out on the workbench he read;

To Dr. P. Steyn.
Accompanying this note is a phial of
antidote that will restore your employee
Derek Jopson to full health.
We are sending this as a gesture of
goodwill and in the hope it will help
you decide to suspend your infamous
experiments.
Do not misinterpret this gesture as a sign
of weakness. We have an abundant supply
of poison and will not hesitate to use it again
Next time maybe
ON YOUR OWN FAMILY.

Peter found himself shaking with fear and rage. Those bastard FAAN people. How dare they threaten his family? If they touched any of his family he'd make them pay, by Christ he would. He stood imagining several scenarios where he extracted revenge on FAAN members. When he had exhausted his imagination he took the phial out of its jacket of cotton wool and went into the lounge. Putting the phial on the coffee table he took two pens out of his breast pocket and put one each side of the phial to prevent it

178

rolling off. He went to his drinks cabinet and poured himself a generous Scotch. Sitting down beside the coffee table he, studied the phial lying there. There was 50ml of liquid there. If that was what FAAN estimate was needed for Jobson to recover then he would need at least 200ml to provide cover for his family.

Then there were his employees, there was no guarantee that FANN wouldn't still attack them or even their families. It was impossible to trust fanatics. Once you have the Truth you can do no wrong. That was their philosophy. No way was he going to use this stuff on Jopson until he'd analysed it and was able to manufacture it himself. If he worked on it exclusively it shouldn't take long. It might be difficult identifying all its constituents but he was sure he could do so. Amazonian Indian poisons had been thoroughly analysed over the years. The Internet would let him get what he wanted quickly. He'd contacts at the Institute of Tropical Diseases. He'd find out what they knew. Another week or so shouldn't make any difference to Jopson; he'd survived seven weeks already. Why the Hell hadn't he thought of finding out the antidote before? He supposed it was because he'd assumed that FAAN would provide it before there was any danger to the victim's life. But this threat to his family was too much. He'd put everything on the back burner and work exclusively on increasing his supply of this antidote.

CHAPTER 49

Bully stared at his desk calendar. Four days until Mill's parole hearing. If.... his thoughts were interrupted by the phone. He recognized DI Loomis's voice immediately, "Bully you haven't sent any of your turnip tops down here to sort out our Danny boy, have you? "

"No Fred. As if we'd do such a thing. Been in a ruck has he?"

"So it seems. You know we've been making him report here every day at noon. We've done it just to annoy him, hoping he'd lose his rag and do something stupid. But, he hasn't been in these last couple of days and when we went round to his house his father says he's in hospital. Apparently he was in a fight late Wednesday night"

"And Frank Mills is still in prison. Perfect alibi what?"

"Indeed. Just as he was when Overton was killed. Terrible to think of her Majesty's Prison Service providing cover for the bastard."

"Well, we have him for another few days. If we can get the prison authorities to do an extra thorough strip search of his cell we might find his mobile phone. That's the only way he could have got in touch with whoever's roughed up Danny boy."

"Unless he's had some of the Gomez's brothers henchmen visit in the last week."

"I don't think he would risk anything so obvious but I'll have them check that."

"Best of luck Bully."

"And you Fred."

Bully put the phone down, waited a minute then picking it up asked for an outside line and phoned Caldeford Prison. While he waited he prayed that the governor Marion McKenzie would be away on one of her courses, she'd want everything in writing and in duplicate before taking action, Frank and his phone would be long gone by then. He felt a warm glow of satisfaction when he was told she was indeed absent and was put through to Bill Featherstone

"Hallo Bully, what can I do for you?"

Bully told him exactly what he wanted and why it was so urgent.

"No problem Bully, we'll take that cell apart right away. Let you know immediately if we find anything."

"Thanks Bill. Good hunting."

He put the phone down and sat back. When Fred had told him what had happened to Danny he had thought he'd feel a pang of guilt but his conscience remained untroubled. "I must be getting a callous bastard in my old age" he thought. From the earliest days of his police training he'd been warned against policemen taking the law into their own hands. Many a career had been ruined because officers were disappointed that the law failed to convict criminals they were convinced were guilty and deciding to punish them by their own methods. He never thought the day would come when he would ignore such advice. But Danny Boy's arrogance had got under his skin. Dale Overton was a decent if misguided man. It was no use him deceiving himself, he'd deliberately wound Mills up. He prayed Danny had only been roughed up and not killed. He didn't know what he'd do if the Irish blaggard was dead.

As if in answer to his prayers the phone rang. It was D I Loomis again, "Bully, I've just had a word with the hospital. Both Danny's legs are broken and he has multiple fractures in his right arm. He has to be fed intravenously because his jaw is broken. Can't say I feel sorry for him. We'll pick him up when the hospital discharges him. I don't suppose we'll get anything out of him to implicate Mills but you never know."

"That's the spirit. Hit the bastard when he's down."

"You took the words right out of my mouth.   Thought with a broken jaw and arm I don't know how we're going to communicate with him."

"We've got the time, he's not going anywhere. But what about Silks? Maybe he'll panic when he sees Danny."

"You could be right there. He's bound to go to the hospital to see Danny. It will either scare him into petrified silence or loosen his lips in panic."

"We can but hope it's the latter. If there's anything you want me to do, let me know and I'll be with you pdq."

"Will do Bully. Goodbye now"

"Bye Fred."

Bully put the phone down and tried to think if there was anything more he could do now to loosen Danny O'Hallerhan's tongue but nothing came. It was annoying to think that Mills had been too clever for the police but it certainly seemed like it. Their only hope now was if Mill's mobile revealed anything incriminating.

Looking at the clock he saw it was just after three thirty.   Over four hours until dinner and God knows what Vegetarian concoction that would be. He could have something here in the canteen but someone from the path. lab might see him and squeal to Helene. There was a new café open just opposite the Precinct; it had been advertising "All Day Breakfasts" all this past week. No harm in giving it a try.

CHAPTER 50

As Peter Steyn worked on the antidote, he couldn't stop thinking suppose Derek Jopson died?

Already FAAN had lost a great deal of support because it had poisoned him. The protestors outside his gates were declining in numbers and there were increasing numbers of supporters gathering to oppose them outside his gates. But Derek Jopson was a loyal employee and he couldn't risk his life. Yet the though persisted. If he could once and for all get rid of these fanatics from outside his premises and stop their vile attacks on the homes and cars of his staff it would be a great victory would it not?

Whether he intended to let Jopson die or not became of no consequence when word came to him that Jopson had died of paralysis in hospital. His muscles operating his diaphragm and lungs stopped functioning. Although the hospital brought the full measure of its emergency procedures into operation he couldn't be revived.

Peter Steyn rushed to the hospital with the phial that Tristan has sent him but when he learned that Derek had been dead for over 12 hours decided it was expedient to keep quiet about the antidote he had. But he could not rid himself of the guilt he felt for not revealing its availability earlier. His guilt rather than shaming him into silence made him all the more ardent in his condemnation of the protestors. Not only did he speak at length about "the murderers who have abandoned all decency." but through the BRITISH BANNER he offered a £10,000 reward to anyone who "can reveal even one name of those who perpetrated this heinous crime." The BANNER immediately doubled this reward and also opened a "HERO FUND" for Derek's family.

This rewards offer turned into a farce because anyone that knew any FAAN member immediately suggested him or her. As the weeks past and no one was given the reward, it unlocked a greater flood of hatred against them... The crowd outside the Steyn plant opposing them more than doubled. So many bottles and stones were thrown and the police were so slow to intervene that it became so unsafe for the FAAN members there it was decided to temporarily postpone the protest.

The Pro-Hunting group established a web site asking the public to identify FAAN members homes and they were targeted daily. As soon as one mess was cleaned up another was dumped; often quite openly and without any attempt at disguise on the part of the perpetrators.

This site also gave many personal details of their lives and places of employment. Their children were picked on in school and taunted as "murders" and "poisoners"

The police established a murder inquiry and Tristan was arrested. He was perplexed by Jopson's death but did not want to reveal his part in supplying the antidote. Instead he insisted that the "Friends of FAAN" had assured him that they had supplied the antidote to Steryn weeks ago. The police demanded that he give them the names of these "friends" who had given him this assurance but of course he couldn't do so. They kept him in custody for three days but eventually had to let him free.

Peter Steyn had expected that the police would question him about the antidote and had after much self examination had decided to deny all knowledge of it. He reasoned that the worse he could make things for FAAN the better everything would be in the long run.

Alice and Miranda found all this increasingly difficult to bear. Alice especially was under constant pressure from Sam Smith to convince her that the so called "Friends of FAAN" were going to cause the complete disintegration of the organization.

She repeated his arguments in detail to Miranda adding "It certainly hasn't worked out the way you hoped has it?"

"But we never planned that someone should die" she answered.

"No, but now Jepson has, what can we do about it? Even if we gave ourselves up I don't see that it would erase the hostility that his death has created".

Miranda had to agree with her. Everything had gone horribly wrong. "The thing is Alice; I just don't know what we can do now. There doesn't".......The ringing of the doorbell interrupted her....

"I'd better see who that is. Excuse me"

When she opened the door, Tristan was standing there. Before she could speak he said "Miranda, I know I'm not welcome but I've got to tell you. I stole a phial of your antidote that day you found me in the cellar and delivered it to Steyn. You haven't altered it in any way have you? I mean it worked OK for Samantha, didn't' it?"

"When? When did you do it?"

"The day after I took it from here. I delivered it personally. So I know he got it."

"How did you get it?"

"I palmed it when you weren't looking. Didn't' put all the phials back"

"Jesus! You'd better come in, I want Alice to hear this."

She led him into the kitchen where Alice was sitting close to the Aga. When he repeated his news she immediately said "So why didn't Steyn give it to Jepson then?"

He shook his head "I don't know. He definitely had the antidote for weeks before Jepson's death. It doesn't make any sense."

"No" said Miranda, "Unless he has been trying to manufacture more of the antidote himself. Then he'd have got us stymied, wouldn't he?"

"Yes or else he decided to deliberately let Jepson die in order to turn everybody against us."

"Do you think he would be so wicked Alice?"

"I dunno. We've said often enough that he and his like are diabolically wicked, haven't we?"

"True. We argue that experimenting on animals must desensitise those who do it to the sacredness of life"

"Yes" said Tristan, "But Jepson wasn't just anybody. He'd been with him for years."

"And, although I hate to admit it, he's got a good reputation as an employer" added Alice.

"Nevertheless, if he got the antidote when you say he did, he must have deliberately withheld it from Jepson."

"But why?"

It was Miranda who broke the silence that followed. "Tris, sit down. I know I said you weren't welcome here anymore but we've got to try and work this out. What exactly did you say to him when you delivered the antidote? Did you threaten him further?"

Tristan thought for a moment. "Well, I told him not to think that we were giving up our campaign. I think I said that sending him the antidote for Jepson was just an act of mercy on our part."

"Hmm. But did you make any specific threats? Did you threaten his family for instance?"

Tristan did not want to admit that he had indeed said that next time Steyn's own family could be a target. "I can't remember exactly what I wrote but I did say something along the lines of that in future no one including his own family would be exempt from being one of our targets"

"Sweet Jesus. That's probably what made him decide to try to manufacture more of the antidote for himself."

"Oh I don' know Alice. I mean I didn't' especially single them out. I only said no one would be exempt. I did say none of his employees would be safe in future but that's no different from what we've a ways said, is it?"

184

"Maybe not. But something made him decide to try and manufacture his own this time."

"You can't be sure of that Miranda. There could be lots of things that account for his acting differently this time. Some of his scientific friend could have assured him they could manufacture more antidote from what I sent him."

They continued talking but the only decision they came to was that it must be made public that Steyn had had the antidote in his possession two weeks before Jepson died.

Alice had to leave because she had a date with Sam. The fact that he had not crowed triumphally because he had been right in predicting what would happen if FAAN continued their poisoning campaign had made her greatly increase her trust in him but not so far as to tell him that she was one of the "Friends" that sent out the poisons.

The complexities of the play they attended; a student production of Piarndello's Six Characters in Search of an Author, helped to take her mind off the Steyn problem but in the bar afterwards she could not rid her mind off it.

"Ten pence for your thoughts Ally" Sam said jovially.

"Ten pence?"

"Well, we've got to allow for inflation and besides you seem to have some very heavy thoughts weighing down on your mind."

She nodded "You're right there. Earlier tonight I was told something on good authority that I just can't understand."

"Can I help?"

"I don't think so but I'll tell you anyway. You know this bloke Jepson who has died of this FAAN poisoning? Well, his employer Peter Steyn was given an antidote for the poison at least five weeks before he died."

Sam didn't answer immediately. When he did he said slowly "Perhaps the antidote didn't work."

"No. It was the same as the one that cured Samantha Ketteridge. So there is no reason why it shouldn't work with Jepson, is there?"

"H'mm. That is strange. I'm no scientist but the Ketteridge woman's poisoning was some months ago wasn't it? I don't suppose that the antidote could have deteriorated in that time? Some of these elements used in these potions can be very unstable. Don't have much of a shelf life. I know some of the drugs that we got in Africa were useless because they were so out of date."

185

Alice leaned over and kissed him. "Sam Smith, you're a bloody genius. I feel a fool not thinking of that. We're always extremely strict on checking expiry dates of the drugs we use in the hospital. Mind you, it would be unusual for something to have such a short working life but it does happen."

She wanted to tell Miranda immediately but waited a full ten minutes before she excused herself to go to the toilet and phone her on her mobile. Miranda although she admitted that most native poison was freshly made on the day of hunting expedition didn't give much credence to the idea. "Be careful how much you tell him, he might want to find out who you're getting your information from" she warned.

Her words made Alice think. It was strange that Sam had never questioned her about that.

CHAPTER 51

"You think this Alice is reliable Sam?"

"Yes, Sarge. As a matter of fact I think she's more deeply involved than she's willing to admit"

"Is there any chance she might be one of these "Friends of FAAN"?

Sam was slow to respond but when he did he kept full eye contact with Bully. "I think there is a strong possibility that she is. I have no direct proof but nearly always when I'm with any of the FAAN people, either individually or as a group, the question about who these "Friends" are arises but never with Alice; she's hardly ever mentioned them in all the time I've known her."

"That's not exactly proof but it is strange nevertheless."

"And she was excessively upset at Jepson's death. All the FAAN people were of course but I felt she took it to heart much more than any of the others I've talked to. I was with her when she first learned about it and I couldn't cheer her up afterwards."

"Your humour didn't meet her approval then?"

"I wasn't telling her jokes. Just trying to get her into a more positive frame of mind."

"And you usually succeed do you?"

"Oh yes sir. Calls me her little ray of sunshine, she does"

"Does she indeed? Well, if you usually succeed then I grant you it's another strike against her. And I just thought of another one, her being a nursing sister gives her the medical knowledge to know what doses of poison to administer."

"True, I've had exactly the same thought."

"It's just a pity Sam that all her experience abroad has been in Africa. She's never been to South America"

"Yes, but her best mate has. You know that beautifully tanned girl, Miranda she's spent years there working with her father."

"He was a renowned orchid hunter wasn't he? Actually, I've enquired from the Royal Botanical Society exactly where he worked and several of the areas where he was working for years are locations where the natives hunt with curare."

"You're ahead of me there boss. Do you think we ought to have her in for questioning?"

"I think we ought to have both of them in. We can't let them see you of course but there's no reason why you shouldn't watch them in the observation room."

187

"If we're miked up I might be able to suggest some questions you ought to ask her"

Bully not for the first time was amazed at the perfectly natural way Sam was willing to give his superiors advice. His own education had made him very respectful of his superiors. He resolved that if he and Helene ever had any children they would go to Springford, Sam's school

"Always glad of your help" he said, intending to be ironic but it was wasted on Sam so he told him to write up his suspicions about Alice and they'd bring her in for questioning.

While that was being arranged Bully studied the surveillance reports on Alice and Miranda. There was nothing sensational in either of them apart from the fact that they met together at least once a week. Most of these meetings took place at Miranda's house. It was decided that Miranda should be brought in for questioning.

CHAPTER 52

"We appreciate very much your coming in to see us Miss Woolston." Said DI Janet Morison.

"No need to thank me" replied Miranda "If I hadn't come in you'd probably have arrested me."

"Why do you think that?" asked Bully.

"Ever since Derek Jopson died anyone who is a member of FAAN is under suspicion of being a murderer."

"That's somewhat overstating your case Miss Woolston" said Janet "But you must admit that those who supplied the poison that killed him must be members of FAAN".

"They says they are Friends of FAAN, that doesn't make them members"

"Well, it would be remarkable if they are not, but we can argue that point later. At the moment we'd like to ask you how much you know about this poison curare?" asked Bully.

"Since I'm sure you've researched my background thoroughly, you'll know I've spent a number of years in the Amazon jungle so I am of course acquainted with it."

"You've seen it in use?"

"Many times."

"Have you ever used it yourself?"

"The Indian children used to like me to try to knock down animals with their little blow pipes but I was hopeless at it. Never hit a thing."

"I don't suppose it's as easy as it looks" said Janet "but surely you have done some research on curare. You are a qualified ethnologist, aren't you?"

"Yes and I do know of the use of curare in anaesthesiology and as an antidote for tetanus and its anti-anxiety effects but I've not done any work with it since I was a student. I'm afraid most of my work has been concerned with the coca plant."

"Does that include work on cocaine?" asked Bully

"Of course."

"But you've not done any recent research on curare?"

"No. Actually I think it is a mistake to talk about curare as if it was just one simple substance. There can be over thirty different plants used to make up the mixture. There can be many different varieties."

"Do you think that is why Derek Jobson died? Because it wasn't possible to get an antidote for the curare that he was poisoned with?"

189

"Possibly. Most antidotes for curare are based on inhibitors such as the physostigmines. But as I've said I've not had a lot to do with it in recent years."

"So you've no samples of curare at home?" asked Janet.

"None whatsoever."

"Miss Woolston, what do you think of an anti-animal experimental group experimenting on a human? Somewhat inconsistent is it not?"

"Many people would say so."

"But what's your opinion? Do you agree with it?"

"Well, chemical companies pay people to allow themselves to be experimented on don't they?"

"So you don't see anything wrong with it."

"I didn't say that. I'm merely pointing out that it is often done by these vile companies .Nobody seems to object to that."

"But surely by no stretch of the imagination can you call Derek Jobson with a willing volunteer>"

"I'm not saying he was. Just pointing out that people as well as animals are experimented on by these companies."

"Miss Woolston, are you sorry Mr.Jobson died."

"Of course. Just as I'm sorry for the thousands of animals whose lives are lost in these experiments every year. It's a complete waste of a life. .Perhaps now the whole evil practice will be stopped now."

"I think that is rather a vain hope now that Mr.Jopson's died. It's surely much more likely that many people will turn against organizations like FAAN." said Bully.

Miranda shrugged her shoulders.

"You find that hard to accept?"

"I think it's too early to say. There is a lot of hostility to us at the moment but when people have had more time to think about us they may not be so antagonistic."

"I don't think even you can be so optimistic" said Janet loudly.

"Don't you? Well there's not much point in continuing this conversation then is there" said Miranda rising.

"As you wish Miss Woolston but I must tell you we will want to speak to you again on this matter." said Janet.

Miranda shrugged her shoulders and left.

Bully turned to Janet and asked "Why did you let her go so easily?"

"Because I want to get a search warrant for her house. I'm sure she's involved in these FRIENDS activities and I want to surprise her."

Bully nodded "I agree she must be."

"And" said Sunny Smith, who had just come into the room "She was lying to you."

They both looked at him in silence.

"I don't expect you know about the latest technique for detecting liars but I've been studying it for years. It's based on something called NRL. Neuro Linguistic Programming. It depends on detecting what they call microexpressions on the person's face.

"Is that" asked Janet" where right-handed persons look up and to the left when they are lying and to the right when they are remembering facts?"

"Yes, where did you learn that?"

"Read it in a Woman's magazine in the dentists."

"Yes, well that is a very simplistic example of a liar's behaviour but it is generally true nevertheless. But there is no one specific behaviour of the face that says "I'm lying." Instead, you must learn to look for the clues to deception and put them together with many other facts to form an objective analysis. This analysis is often difficult to do in real time because the behaviours are difficult to see and occur in rapid sequence.

"And we are not skilled enough to detect them "said Janet

"Afraid not maam" said Sunny.

"So give us an example where Miranda lied" asked Bully.

"Well, when you asked her if she'd done any recent work on curare she gave you a very elaborate answer, telling you all about its complex nature and how there can be many different varieties. There was no need for that; a simple 'yes' or 'no' would have sufficed."

"So you're convinced she lied to us."

"Definitely maam."

"Your eyes moved to the left as you answered that" said Bully "Of course. I'm a proper little George Washington Sarge."They all laughed until Janet cut them short. "Right let's get that search warrant. We've no time to waste

CHAPTER 53

As Bully was entering his office the phone rang.

It was Bill Featherstone, "Bully, Mills had a mobile all along."

"You've found it?"

"No. The bastard was too smart for us. He had several of his mates keeping it for him. So it was never in his cell for long. Gave it back to one of them as soon as he'd finished his calls."

"Damm. How did you find that out?"

"It was all around the prison the day after he left. The stupid buggers were so pleased at having got one over on us that they couldn't keep their mouths shut.

"Found the phone now have you?"

"No. The word is Mills smashed it before he left."

"Not much we can do about it now, is there?"

"No. Even if he was still with us it would be a job to search all his mates' cells. He had a lot of influence around his wing."

"H'mm. What about his accomplice outside, Danny boy? Is there any there any chance there would be a record of Mill's calls on his phone?"

"Jeezus Bully, you're not just an ugly face. I don't see why not. They can trace exactly where people are and what they've said via their mobiles can't they?"

"True. Our SSD bods should be able to retrieve what messages were sent, especially if they are texts."

"Terrific. I'll let you get the ball rolling Bully. Good hunting."

Bully put the phone down and immediately dialled East Ham police station and asked for D I Loomis. When he came on the line he told him the good news about the mobile phone.

"That's marvellous Bully. O'Hallerhan's still in Hospital. Bit slow getting back on his feet poor soul. I'll send someone down to get his phone straight away. We had a similar case two years ago. Wife's lover beat her husband to death with a baseball bat. Tried to make out it was a burglar. Our SSD boys got everything from her mobile. Even got her making arrangements with her boyfriend for her to be at Bingo while he killed her old man. Open and shut case it was. As long as O'Hallerhan hasn't changed his SIM card we've got them."

"Let's hope not."

"Right Bully, I'll get on with it."

CHAPTER 54

It was seven o'clock in the morning when two police cars drew up outside Miranda's home. Two police men and two policewomen were in one and DI Janet Morison and Bully and Union Jack were in the other. At the front door Union rang the bell while the four uniformed police went around the back. Union had to ring the bell twice more before there was a sound of someone approaching.

"Who's there?"

"Police, open up, we have a search warrant."

"I was at the police station yesterday afternoon. Why do you want to speak to me again?"

Janet Morison called out, "We know you were there Miss Woolston. It was DS Bullerton and I who interviewed you. We need to speak to you again. Open up."

When there was no reply Bully hoped that the uniformed police wouldn't have to use the battering ram they had with them. Just as Janet was about to give the order to do so there was the sound of a bolt being withdrawn. The door opened only wide enough for Miranda's arm to come through.

"Let me see the search warrant."

When Janet handed it to her, the door immediately closed again.

She turned to Bully and said "Tell the uniforms around the back to be ready to break in if we give them the word."

Bully conveyed the message to the sergeant who was leading the group and received an affirmative reply which he had to immediately cancel for Miranda opened the door wide and handed Janet back the search warrant. She evidently had been up some while for she was fully dressed.

"You'll have to forgive me, but as a woman living on her own I have to be careful to whom I open the door."

"Very sensible of you Miss Woolston" said Janet as she stepped into the hall.

"Do come through" said Miranda with more than a hint of sarcasm as she turned away. "Make sure you close the door won't you." She led them through to the large back room where she'd first brought Stephen.

"I suppose you're going to search all the rooms. When Janet nodded she added "I hope you're not going to be long. I've a busy day ahead"

"We'll be as quick as we can" said Janet, "Actually we've brought some extra help to speed things up. They're outside your back door. Would you be so good as to let them in?"

Miranda glared at her and shouldered her way past Janet to the kitchen. She unlocked the back door and turned away without a word. Bully who had followed her had stopped by the kitchen door asked her as she approached "What's in there?" nodding his left.

"That's the conservatory where my father kept his orchids. I would prefer you to search it first so I can lock it up quickly again. It's got to be kept at a high temperature and I don't want you wandering in and out of it"

"Right, two of you search the garden, the rest in here" he said rather loudly.

When they were all inside, Miranda closed the door rather theatrically. "Take care that you do not touch any of the plants" she said "and if you feel you absolutely must root around inside any of the tanks I would prefer it if you'd let me do it."

Bully nodded and said, "We'll be careful. O.K. everybody; you know what you're looking for. Get going."

While he and Janet checked the drawers of the cabinets Union and the others peered into the tanks. Almost immediately, one of the police women gave a slight scream and jumped back from the tank she was peering in, "Sorry" she gasped "I don't like frogs. My brothers used to torment me with them when we were kids."

"But these are so beautiful" said Union, "Look at the vivid blue of this one Sylvia."

"No thanks" she replied.

The other policewoman came over to Janet and said "Can I have a word Maam" and walked away to the far corner of the room where she whispered at length to the DI. When they'd finished Janet turned to Miranda and asked "These blue and yellow frogs are they poison dart frogs?"

"Yes"

"And is it true that the Amazon natives get the poison off their backs and put on the darts that they use to paralyse their prey?"

"Yes."

"So could these frogs here have been the source of the poison that was used on Jopson?"

"No."

"Why not?"

"Because they've been here in captivity for several years and they lose their toxicity after they've been kept in captivity for only a short time."

"That true of all species "asked Bully.

"Yes."

"Why is that" said Janet.

"To put it simply, Dart frogs also do not synthesize their poisons, but sequester the chemicals from arthropod prey, such as ants, centipedes and mites. Because of this, and the fact that they are not fed such food, captive-bred animals do not have significant levels of toxins. You can stroke one if you like; you'll not come to any harm"

"No thanks" replied Janet, "I believe you."

"Nevertheless" asked Bully, "These frogs would have been venomous when first in captivity,"

"For a short while yes."

"How short?"

"I don't know. They are…were…my fathers. He brought them here. I've never tried to find out how long they retain their venomous state."

"But if their poison was harvested off them at the beginning there is no reason to think it would lose its toxicity is there?"

"As I've said I don't know."

Before Bully could reply, Janet said "This is a murder investigation Miss Woolston, and someone who supports your group must know and we are determined to find them."

"That's what you're paid to do isn't it?"

CHAPTER 55

"I think I like this one best Maurice."

"Hmm. It's not bad wig Mirada. Fits you well but a bit on the dull side don't you think."

"But that's what I want; anonymity. The less people notice me the better."

"Wear a tighter bra then dear, one of those sports ones It's your tits that people notice first about you."

"Thanks a bunch Maurice and here's me thinking it was my beautiful face."

"It's not bad but your nose is a bit on the big side. Bit of a ski slope you've got there don't you think?"

Amanda was so shocked that all she could do for a second was look regretfully at all her raven locks scattered around her. When she found her voice she asked "Do you talk to all your customers like this?"

"Of course not dear. I'm a wonderful liar. Most women walkout of here thinking they're Helen of Troy. But I can't lie to my friends."

"What? Both of them, Tristan and me?"

"Really Mandy; what a thing to say. I get hundreds of Christmas cards. Costs me a fortune reciprocating to them all."

"Well, you'll get one less this year if you don't stop insulting me."

"I thought you were disappearing off the face of the earth. You won't be hard to find if you tell everyone where you are with your cards.   Even the wooden tops can read postmarks you know."

"Gee, thanks Maurice, I'd never have thought of that. Actually, I don't intend to send any to the cops, not even that nice Bully. What I'll do is send a lot in one parcel to a friend who will post them on for me."

"That's better. You are now thinking like a fugitive. But you're certain the cops are onto you?"

"Yes, if not now they will be in a few days. I thought I was being clever hiding my blow pipes among the other garden bamboos, you know, a la 'The Purloined

Letter,' so I'd better scoot while I've got the chance."

"Life's so much easier in books isn't it?"

"Sadly yes now how much do I owe you for this and the haircut?"

"These wigs I usually charge £500 for, as I've said they're real human hair but since you're such a good friend you can have it for £450, and with the hair styling let's say £550. That alright with you?"

"Yes. There is just one other thing." She reached into her handbag and took out a wad of notes. "There' £5000 there, will you keep it for me?"

"My God, that's some tip."

"It's not a tip you Wally. I'm afraid the police will stop my withdrawals when the find out I've scarpered. So I'm taking out as much as I can each

day and distributing it around my friends so I can get my hands on funds as I need them. You can keep any interest that accrues; I just want the £5000 to be available as I need it."

Maurice looked at her in amazement. When he spoke his voice was an octave or two higher than usual.

"Miranda, this is one of the biggest compliments I've ever been paid. Of course I'd be honoured to help you and I wouldn't dream of snaffling any interest. I take it

You're doing the same with Tristan?"

"Yes."

"What happens if they catch you? What do we do with the money then?"

"Keep quiet about it. I'll plead for Legal Aid first. I'm not helping the State prosecute me."

"But they could put you away for years."

"Don't be too sure of that. Tristan can testify that Peter Steyn received the antidote at least a month before Jepson died. I'm sure we could build a good case against him."

"Good luck to you then. Now let me see you put this wig on correctly, don't want you having it all arse over tip

CHAPTER 56

"Bully, it looks like as if Miranda Woolston has done a bunk. This is the third time we've been around to arrest her and she's not been home"

"Perhaps she's taken a few days holiday"

"I hope to God you're right. We'll look right fools if we've let her slip through our fingers."

"I'll get on to Sunshine and see if Miranda has left any instructions to that girlfriend of his to look after her house. You know feed the frogs etc."

"If she hasn't we'd better get a general alert out. I suppose we should have taken her in when we found that bamboo blowpipe. "

Bully had privately wondered why Janet hadn't done so but he wasn't going to tell her that.

"It's always easy to be wise after the event. I assumed if we found traces of poison on the pipe we'd intensify our surveillance of her to see if we could identify her accomplices. She couldn't have managed to do all this 'Friends of FAAN' business

all on her own."

"That's what I thought. I never expected her to do a runner so quickly. We'll see what Sunny boy finds out; his girlfriend seems to have been Miranda's closest friend. "

When Sunny Boy Smith was told of Miranda's absence he arranged to meet Alice that night.

They went to a Cleedon pub that was running an "Open Mike" Comedy night which was a great success. In his car taking Alice home he said during a lull in their r conversation "Bye the way, is Amanda in any trouble with the police? I saw two rather severe policewomen coming out of her gate this afternoon?"

"No, I don't think so. A least no more than any of us have. They've been round us all lately trying to find out if any of us locals are mixed up with these' Friends of FAAN.'"

"They didn't seem very happy not finding her at home."

"They wouldn't. She's gone off to see some friends in Ireland for a few days."

"Back soon then?"

"She didn't say exactly. She went Friday so I suppose she'll back in the next couple of days. I'm calling in her house every couple of day to collect her post and feed her frogs."

When he reported this later that night he caused no little consternation at the station. D.I. Morison had left orders to be told immediately there was any news of Miranda but she was none too pleased to woken by the duty sergeant at one o'clock in the morning to be told she was in Ireland. She thought of phoning Bully but decided against it, reasoning little could be done at this time of night. If Amanda had gone Friday and it was now Tuesday morning it was unlikely she would be hanging about in Ireland. She would surely have moved on within twenty-four hours at the most. Time enough to start enquiries in the morning. But was it? She didn't get back to sleep until her husband who was being kept awake by all her doubts and questions took her in his arms and made love to her. It was the one infallible "nightcap" that had never let them down.

In the morning while Janet, Bully and Sunny Boy were discussing what course of action to take, their quarry was happily packing up her camping gear. She

was in the Highlands of Scotland , a couple of miles outside the village of Achnasheen and about to commence her climb of a Munro called Moruisg. It was the   last Highland Walk she and her father had taken. They were an hour into the climb when the heart attack had disabled him. Fortunately it was a broad grassy (if rather boggy) ascent and the rescue team found it easy to reach them. Now she was again on its grassy banks starting it over again so that she could say she had finished it all in one go, it was a mild Highland morning, the other distant "Munroes" looking a mild grey and khaki instead of the dark navy blue that they often wore. The slope was soon steep; she had to concentrate on every step she took. But she still had time to think.

It was Phillip Thompson's words that preoccupied her. He was the one who'd been proved right but she was still convinced she could have succeeded if they'd all united behind her. It was very rare for her to be in the wrong. She'd never intended Jepson to die. That was Steyn's fault. Everyone said he was such a good employer yet he let one of his most trusted employee's die. There was no way she could have foreseen that.
 It wasn't like that surveyor in the jungle. She'd no regrets over his death. No one who saw the ravages that the diseases introduced by the logging companies inflicted on the native communities could have any feelings for such men.

Her whole plan had been to spread fear and panic among Steyn's workers. It had been a big mistake not to publicise the poisoning right from the start. It all might have turned out differently if she'd done that.

Still she had to consider what she could do now.

 Even if Tristan was believed Steyn could easily invent some lie that would get him off the hook. Probably say he was analysing the antidote so he could manufacture it himself and wipe out any threat from FAAN. She couldn't go back to Caldeford, she was finished there. The question was where she could be of most use to the cause now?

The peace and tranquillity of her surroundings contrasted sharply with her inner turmoil. She had to force herself to concentrate on the beauty around her. She wanted to phone Alice and find out what was happening in Caldeford but decided she'd not do so until she'd "bagged" this Munroe.

CHAPTER 57

On Thursday morning she had successfully "bagged " the Munro of Moruisg and its companion Sgurr nan Ceannalchean and had a goodnight's rest after the long climb. The two were not particularly beautiful or exciting Munroes, more long steep climbs with flat extensive summit plateaus. But the views of the surrounding deep glens and the remote mountains to the north and west from the summit were heart lifting. Her step was light as she strode along the road into Achnasheen where she'd left her car.

On her way to the car park she saw the shop boasting it was a mini-supermarket;

She hurried in and stocked up on bread and foodstuffs. She had always thought that that one of the most wonderful things about the Highlands was the different types of bread; all of it a nice handy size. She bought a soda farl, a small wheaten loaf and a pack of potato bread plus three packets of batteries for her torch and lantern.

One of the reasons she had come up here was the rarity of surveillance cameras so she received s nasty shock when as she was leaving the shop she saw her own face looking at her from a newspaper rack. Her first thought was to go back in the shop and buy a copy of the paper but then she thought it might make the shopkeeper suspicious so she continued on her way out. She didn't see another newsagent in the village and as she now looked nothing like the newspaper photo she soon recovered her composure. She loaded her shopping in the car and sat in the driving seat eating a Mars bar as she wondered what to do. She had expected something like this to happen but it had been a shock nevertheless. It meant she would have to take extreme care if she went near Caldeford again. The McKinster's had said she could stay on their farm if she needed and that's what she would do. She'd get Alice to fetch what she wanted from the house for her.

The house would have to be sold as quickly as possible. Alice could do that. Half was to go to her bank manager brother in Australia who was keeping a discreet eye on Stephen for her. The question was should she carry on with her work to ban animal experimentation or return to the jungle to help the natives? She would have to choose one or the other. She longed with all her heart to stop the cruel exploitation of laboratory animals but the natives needed all the help they could get plus the jungle offered her greater refuge. She would be no use to either from a prison cell.

Of more immediate concern was what to do with her car? Was there a trace out on it? It was essential to have some form of transport. Having the tent enabled her to avoid hotels and guest houses.

She decided she'd make her way down south using minor roads to the McKinster farm. She'd be safe there for a while and she'd have the benefit of their advice.

She phoned Alice on her mobile before she set off. Fortunately Alice was able to talk at length and she agreed that it was a good idea to come back to the farm where they could plan in relative security what to do. They arranged to talk again at eleven that night. If she used the motorways she could have got to the farm by then but it would be much safer on the back roads. But there was no need to hurry.

CHAPTER 58

"Do you think she's gone further abroad than Ireland?" asked Janet.

"I wouldn't think so" said Bully, "She has so much stuff here. The house and all that."

"I agree" said Sam, "Although she's got Alice looking after the house."

"We'll have this Alice in for questioning. Find out what Miranda has told her. What do you say Sam?"

"I think that would be best" he answered, "If I start quizzing her she might become suspicious."

"We've not found any more of this curare poison on her property, all we've got is the traces that were on the bamboo." said Bully; "she must have it well hidden."

"It can't be too far away, she's got to be able to get hold of it quickly hasn't she?"

"I think we'll arrange a much more thorough search of the house. Get a specialist team in. There could be all sorts of hidden cavities in an old house like that."

"You could be on to something there" said Sam, "Alice once told me that Miranda's father was paranoid about his orchids. Always afraid someone would steal one of the new varieties he was cultivating. So it would be natural for him to have a couple of hidey holes in his house, wouldn't it?"

Alice was met at the end of her hospital shift that afternoon and agreed to follow the police in her car to the station. Janet and Bully interviewed her.

"Thank you for coming in Miss McKinster" said Janet "We won't keep you long. We just want to know if you have any idea of Miranda Woolston's whereabouts."

Alice shook her head. "She did mention she fancied going to Ireland for a few days but it wasn't definite. All that happened was she texted me saying she would be away for a few days and would I keep an eye on the house and the animals for her."

"You didn't see her then before she left?" asked Bully.

Alice again shook her head.

"So how do you get in the house?" asked Janet.

"I know where she hides a key in the garden. I've looked after the house before."

"Even when her father was alive?"

"Yes. He was in the early stages of Altzimer's this time last year. She didn't leave him very often but when she did she always arranged proper medical care but didn't feel she could ask them to check on the heating and the animals as well."

"You a good friend of hers then?"

"Yes, for many years."

"Did you know she was one of these Friends of FAAN?"asked Bully.

Alice shook her head emphatically. "They weren't altogether popular with us you know. Many of us were totally opposed to what they were doing."

"Were you opposed to this poisoning?"

Alice didn't answer immediately. "At first I had mixed feelings about it. I could see that if the threats worked it would greatly help our cause. But

I'm a nurse. I could never approve of endangering anyone's life." She paused then added "Miranda never hid the fact that she approved of what they were doing."

"Did you not suspect that she might be a part of these Friends/" asked Janet.

"Actually, I often did. We argued quite a bit about it. Miranda was a very strong willed girl. "

"Were there any other members of your group that you thought might be members?" asked Bully.

Alice stared at him "You don't really expect me to answer that do you?"

"You have a civic duty to do so "Janet said very formally.

Alice's eyes opened wide in amazement. "Bollocks to that. You know what E.M.Foster said about choosing between betraying his country and betraying his friends"

She stood up; "Now I've had a very tiring day. If you've no more questions I'd like to get home."

"Just one more, you're certain Miss Woolston didn't say when she'd be back?"

"Just a few days. That's all the text said"

Janet looked at Bully but he shook his head.

"Very well. That's all for now. But we may need to question you further Thank you for your help."

After she left, Sam came back into the room.

"What did you think of that Mr. Lie detector?" asked Janet.

"I don't think she's as innocent as she makes out. Look how often our surveillance shows us she's been meeting Miranda these past months. I've no proof but I've long had a feeling that she's one of the Friends. I think it would pay us to watch her even more closely."

"You don't believe what she says about being a
nurse rules her out of being one of the' Friends 'then?" asked Bully.

"Not really. But I'm sure none of the' Friends 'ever intended anyone to die from this curare poisoning." Sam paused then added "I also think that they're being truthful when they say that they gave Steyn the antidote at least 5 weeks before Jepson died. Alice was adamant he'd had it at least that much earlier."

"So if we arrest Miranda, she'll blame Steyn for Jepson's death?"

"Yes maam. She's sure to."

"That'll make for an interesting trial then" said Bully.

CHAPTER 59

When Miranda phoned Alice from The Little Chef she learned all that had happened at the police station. When Alice added "I think you'd better tell me what you want from your house now so I can get it tonight." it made Miranda realise just how much danger she was in.

"Right, Alice. I'll need some time to work out exactly what I want. Then you can get everything at once. Give me another couple of hours while I make a list. After what you've said, I think it's going to be too dangerous for me to go anywhere near the house. I'm only about two hours away from your place. If your dad leaves the barn open I'll drive straight in."

Miranda ordered another coffee and started to make her list. It was difficult because her mind kept returning to the question of where she should go to live.

She had been on many trips to protests in France and Germany about animal cruelty. She had friends she could stay within those countries that would save her from having to stay in hotels with their passport checks. If she decided to go back to the Amazon it wouldn't be difficult to get to South America from there. She must make sure Alice brought back her address book. On a coach trip she could easily tell the courier after the first day there was a family emergency and she had to fly home immediately.

When she reached the farm the barn door was wide open. She got her stuff from the car and put it down by the barn door.

The voice made her jump. "Leave that Miranda. Get yourself in by the fire. I'll see to your car and bags." Dave McKinster was a small but exceptionally powerful man as many a pro-hunt supporters had discovered to their cost. She was glad she could feel him restraining himself as he hugged her. She got an equally warm welcome from the rest of the family and it was well after two o'clock in the morning before she got to bed. Alice came up with her and Miranda was amazed at the amount of stuff that was in the suitcase on the bed.

"My God Alice, You'd have had a job convincing the police you weren't a burglar if they'd caught you with this stuff."

Alice laughed. "Actually, I took Patsy along with me. I thought it would be best to fetch as much as possible. We went just after nine in the morning. Thought the wooden tops would think that would be too early for a burglary."

CHAPTER 60

"You finished your surveillance at midnight constable?" asked Bully. He wasn't usually so formal with his staff but constable Wickremasinghe was new to the station and he wasn't sure how to correctly pronounce her name.

"Yes sir. It wasn't easy."

"It never is, especially when you're on your own. It's when she finishes her shift at the hospital, sometimes she just seems to disappear. She leaves the hospital car park at a hell of a speed. I've just have to gamble that my car's facing the right way. Otherwise
it's a job to catch her."

"You've done very well.

"Thank you sir."

"You say she was at her father's farm when you left. She'd not been to her own flat down by the canal here in town."

"No. She went straight to her father's. All the McKinsters were at the farm yesterday evening. Maybe it was one of their birthdays or something."

"A Birthday? You could be right. We'll look that up. Fortunately we've got a lot of information on the whole family because they've been involved in protesting for so long. Barney Truss your mate on the early surveillance reported she and her youngest sister Patricia went around to Miranda's nine o'clock yesterday morning. Came out with what he says were two well loaded suitcases. So it looks as if they are going to help Miranda do a bunk very soon. I'm going to ask DI Morison if we should get you some more help. Don't think for one moment it's any reflection on your work. You're doing an excellent job. Barney will have a companion as well. It's just that I think they're going to speed Miranda be on her way very soon. If they meet up to hand over the suitcases there will need to be another officer there to be able to follow each one when they split up."

"Thank you sir. I think you're right. I've got the impression something's like that will happen soon. Do we arrest Miranda as soon as she's seen?"

"As soon as you have back up. Phone for it immediately. It's not a one person job. "

"I see sir."

"Right. I'd better let you get along then. Keep up the good work. Where do you meet Barney when you swap over?"

"On the days she works we've met in the hospital car park at 4 o'clock"

"Right then off you go."

A few minutes after constable Wickremasinghe left "Sam" Smith knocked and entered. "Morning Sir I see Wicksy's enjoying herself trailing Alice."

"How do you know that?"

"I had a chat with her in the canteen. I have to confess I was dying to know how she was getting on. I mean to say, I was surprised when she was given that job. She's not the most unobtrusive constable we've got is she?"

"Practising your chief constable's role already Constable Smith?"

"No sir. I'm not criticizing. It's just with her being so black I thought Alice is bound to notice her sooner or later."

Bully laughed "Don't worry Sam. I got a right tongue lashing from Helene as well when I told her the same thing. If this force gets any more politically correct I'll be out on my ear."

"Oh I don't think you need worry about that. I don't think Wicksy is too sensitive.

She's the one who told us to call her "Wicksey". Says how surname is too much of a mouthful for us poor uneducated plods."

"Really? She's got a point there. I can't get my tongue round it. I just call her constable. Now what do you want to see me for?"

"Actually, it's about Wicksy. She told me about all the McKinsters being at the farm last night. I got to thinking what with Alice and Patsy lugging those two suitcases out of Miranda's house they might be meeting up with her very soon."

"You've been reading my mind. We need to watch that farm. You're supposedly on vacation from your uni. studies. You could start the ball rolling."

"O.K. boss. Will I be on my own?"

"At the moment yes."

"Then I suppose I'd better work the evening shift. If Miranda's going to appear she's more likely to turn up when it's dark, don't you think?"

"If she's thinks she's being watched she will. I think something like from six until two in the morning would be a good start. But that farm's fairly isolated, you're going to have to find somewhere you won't be noticed."

"I've been there a couple of times with Alice. The lane off Hadworth road is the only way in and out. I'll find a spot that overlooks the lane."

"You know her car."

"Yes. It's amazing how often crooks take so much trouble to disguise themselves and don't think to change their cars."

"Thank heaven they do."

Sam spent his first night watching from a large Rhododendron bush on a sharp bend of the farm track about a quarter of a mile from the house. When he'd realised that would be his best vantage point he left his car at home and cycled back to the bush. He hid his bike around the back of the bush and used a couple of groundsheets to rig up a bivouac to protect him from the worst of the weather. He blessed Old Sailor "C.Sides" his Springhill Outdoor Activities Master who had taught him the quick release knots he used to secure them to the interior of the bush. He spent an unsuccessful but not a too uncomfortable eight hours watching the house. The next three nights were equally unrewarding; the only non-family member to visit was Tom Mackintosh the conductor of The Cowgirls. Alice had visited on only one of these occasions but just after 8o'clock on the fifth night Alice's car came speeding down the lane to the house as if she'd learned there was bad news at home.

Sam was tempted to leave his hideout and creep down to the farmhouse but he was so inappropriately dressed for a social visit that he decided against it. There was no further activity for another couple of hours. Then the door of the big barn opposite the

House slid back and Miranda's 2CV came out. It stopped in the yard and was surrounded by the McKinster family. They were all waving goodbye and giving things to the driver. When it came alongside him he couldn't see the driver's face as she was crouching over the steering wheel but he'd seen Miranda many times in that fawn coat. He sent the pre-arranged signal for her flight on his mobile phone decided to leave his bivouac as it was; grabbed his bike and cycled diagonally across the field behind him in the hope of seeing which way she turned at the end of the lane, but there was no sign of her when the end of the lane came in view.

He relayed his lack of knowledge to HQ and was reassured to be told that police cars were approaching from both directions. He cycled back to his hide and pulled down his groundsheets, stuffed them in his rucksack and pedalled off again across the field.

Before he reached the gate he was told that the police cars had reached each other without any sign of Miranda. Checking that there was still no one coming after him, he stopped at the gate and got out his O.S.Map. If Miranda had turned Left there were two roads off the main road she could have taken , one going due north the other south east. If she'd gone Right there were no roads off before she'd have met a police car so she must have turned to the

Left. Studying the map he saw that it would be possible to reach Stanstead airport using the road to the north from the south easterly road it was possible to come out unto the Caldeford by pass from where she could either head for London or the port of Harwich. He'd no idea of the times of either flights or sailings but he when relayed his thoughts to Caldeford HQ he was told rather smugly they were way ahead of him. One car had gone north the other south East and both the airport and the port police had been told to be on the lookout for Mirada and her car. There didn't seem much else he could do but make his way back to headquarters.

He had been cycling for ten minutes when he got a puncture. A large oak provided some shelter from the rain showers but little refuge from a cold crosswind. He was not in the mellowest of moods when he reached headquarters. He put his bike in one of the racks around the back and ran up the steps into the station. He went straight to Bully's room, knocked and opened the door. Bully looked up from his desk and said "Make yourself scarce Sam. They've got Miranda. She'll be here any minute."

CHAPTER 61

DCI Janet Morison made no attempt to hide the anger in her voice as she asked "So Miss McKinster, why are you impersonating Miranda Woolston?"

"I'm not."

"Come off it. You're wearing her coat and driving her car. Do you think we're stupid?"

"Miranda told me I could use anything of hers that I wanted.

"When did she do that?"

"A few days ago."

"You'll have to be a bit more precise than that Miss McKinster."

"I think it was last Saturday morning."

"And where did she tell you this?"

"I was in my flat. She phoned me and said she was going to be away for much longer than she'd first thought and as that meant I'd be lumbered looking after her house for quite a long time I could use anything of hers that I wanted. She specially asked me to use "Dolly", that's her car. Said it would seize up if it wasn't kept in use."

"But you've already got a car of your own" interjected Bully.

"Yes, but she didn't mean that I was to exclusively drive Dolly. I could easily switch between the two as I wished"

"And where were you going in her car when you were stopped by our patrol?"

"To meet some friends in Peterborough."

"A bit late at night to do that wouldn't you say?"

"Not if you're an animal liberationist it isn't. People like you who are in the pocket of the big chemical companies harass us so much we are forced to do most of our work at odd hours."

"You mean sneakily and underhand?"

"If you want to call it that, that's your problem." Alice looked down at the table and stayed silent.

Bully broke the silence by asking "You say you were going to Peterborough. That's a journey of over 100 miles. Surely your Peugeot 206 was a much more suitable car for a journey of that distance?"

"Perhaps. But I've not driven a 2CV before. I thought a long journey was a good chance to help me get familiar with it more quickly."

"And that's the whole reason for your journey tonight?" asked Janet.

"Yes"

"You realise that your actions could just as easily be interpreted as attempting to help a fugitive escape justice?"

"Really? I never thought of that."

"Not even when you're wearing her coat?"

"I've always loved that coat. And it looked as if it might rain. If I broke down due to being unfamiliar with the car I wanted something that would keep me warm and dry. I never thought anyone would mistake me for Miranda."

"You're not that naive and I don't for one moment believe that any jury will believe that you are."

Alice shook her head and said "We'll just have to see, won't we?"

"Indeed we will" said Janet. She turned to the constable standing by the door. "Take Miss McKinster back to the cells officer"

"Do I need to phone my solicitor?"

"You can if you wish but if I were you I'd wait until you knew exactly what we're charging you with."

"I thought you said helping a fugitive escape justice."

"That's for starters. There are other charges to consider."

"Such as?"

"We'll let you know as soon as we can."

Alice shrugged her shoulders and turned and walked to the door.

When she had gone Bully said to Janet "What else are you thinking of charging her with?"

"Being a member of Friends of FAAN. You remember how sure Sam is of that."

"Yes. But it won't be easy."

"Perhaps not, but even if we don't, sitting on her arse a couple of days in a cell will serve her right for buggering us about."

CHAPTER 62

Tom McKinster said quietly "We're at least three miles away from the farm now. You're safe to sit up Miranda."

"Thanks Tom. It's a good job Patsy was such an observant girl?"

"Yes she's a quiet little thing but she doesn't miss much."

"Well, none of the rest of us saw that bloke in the bush, did we? I'm sorry to cause you all this trouble"

"Trouble? This is nothing compared with some of the scrapes I've been in."Nevertheless, the police are sure to make trouble for you and Alice later on."

"What can they do? Alice has got her story off pat. You're entitled to give her whatever you wish. And that bloke's buggered off now. So he can't say he ever saw you in this car."

"That's true."

"Right. Now you've got that overnight sleeper to Edinburgh to look forward to."

"Yes. It seems an awful waste of money but as you say it keeps me out of public view."

"Yes. But it's the Rosyth to Zebrugge ferry that's a bit of a worry."

"Oh I don't think so. I'll find out tomorrow if they look at our passports and if they do I'll get one of those little ones they have for day trips and I don't look much like that police photo they've got of me in the papers."

"And this friend you've got in Germany, he really can get you a fake passport."

"So he says. I've no reason to disbelieve him."

"So, all should be well."

"Yes. Then all there is to be done is to complete the sale of the house."

"Your brother doesn't object to Alice handling that."

"No he trusts my judgement and I know Alice will make a good job of it."

TWELVE MONTHS LATER.

"Twenty years for both Mills and O'Hallerhan. That's what you call a result Bully."

"I'll say Union. It certainly wiped the smile off O'Halleran's face. Mind you it will be a miracle is he does anywhere near twenty years if he's in the same prison as Mills"

"True. Mills blames him for leaving the texts on his mobile."

"But we all think they're gone forever when we wipe them. I never knew they could be recovered, did you Union? "

"I had read something. But then an upright man like me doesn't have to worry about what's stored in my phone."

"You must sleep well at night then Union."

"I would if it wasn't for that Miranda. I suppose I just don't like to think of her getting away with it. I keep wondering where she could have got to. She just can't have vanished of the face of the earth."

"But the great pity is we never prosecuted the other members of FAAN."

"The CPS said there wasn't enough evidence."

"But we know that Alice and that twit Tristan Wills Jones were helping her."

"We do but we can't prove it. Never mind we'll get them for something someday. Just as I'm sure we'll nab Miranda."

"Yes. She's bound to turn up someday"

"Mind you there's plenty hope she never gets caught. Between us; I think my wife Helene is one of them."

"So are both my daughters"

"I think she's probably gone to the Amazon."

"You could be right. If so she'll have to come out of it sometime. Not a healthy place to live, is it?"

"Depends what you get used to. The natives seem to do alright."

"Yes, but they're born to it."

So they are. But cheer up Union. We don't get many major triumphs. Let's not spoil this one by talking about the one that got away. Another pint?"

www.ingramcontent.com/pod-product-compliance
Lightning Source LLC
Chambersburg PA
CBHW020656030726
47498CB00002B/538